W9-CKE-108

"MOVES AT A HEADLONG CLIP . . . GOLD REVEALS ONCE AGAIN HIS BEAUTIFULLY SATIRICAL EYE AND EAR."

—*Publishers Weekly*

Herbert Gold

FROM THE HIGHLY ACCLAIMED AUTHOR OF *A GIRL OF FORTY*, THE CHRONICLER OF TODAY'S SAN FRANCISCO . . . AND THE FOIBLES OF OUR TIME . . .

DREAMING

"SAN FRANCISCO IS AS MUCH A CHARACTER IN HERBERT GOLD'S NEW NOVEL *DREAMING* AS ANY OF THE OTHER CHARACTERS . . . A GOOD STORY . . . EXAMINING SOME INTERESTING EIGHTIES PEOPLE WITH SOME RATHER LARGE WARTS."

—*Los Angeles Times*

"EXPLOITS A SOURCE OF DRAMA WHICH WAS APPRECIATED BY THE NINETEENTH-CENTURY NOVELISTS LIKE BALZAC . . . THIS IS MONEY—WHICH HERBERT GOLD CALLS 'THE OTHER FORM OF SEX.' "

—*Newsday*

"GOLD KNOWS THE SAN FRANCISCO SCENE AS BELLOW KNOWS CHICAGO."

—Budd Schulberg

DREAMING

Herbert Gold

A DELL BOOK

Published by
Dell Publishing
a division of
Bantam Doubleday Dell Publishing Group, Inc.
666 Fifth Avenue
New York, New York 10103

ISBN: 0-440-20430-5

Reprinted by arrangement with Donald I. Fine, Inc.

Printed in the United States of America

Published simultaneously in Canada

September 1989

10 9 8 7 6 5 4 3 2 1

OPM

To Mel and Patricia

1

Hutch had heard a rumor that the meek might someday inherit the earth. Therefore he knew he'd really have to hustle to get his first.

His appointments for today were pleasant ones. He liked to stack the late afternoon appointments in good order on the terrace at Enrico's, his cappuccino-and-fresh-grapefruit-juice office; maybe a grilled rex sole followed if one of his meetings stretched into an early dinner, just watching the traffic on Broadway in North Beach.

First his brother, Dan, poor fellow.

Then Suki Read, who was the right kind of tired blond.

Before Dan arrived, Hutch strolled in smiling and nodding to waiters, shaking hands with a buddy or two, feeling the need of the fresh grapefruit juice, his handkerchief flowing from his breast pocket. His mouth was a little dry. He was a man who had just enjoyed an invigorating chat with his bankers.

Hutch Montberg dressed like someone with a license to make money. But he only had the license to dress like that. Ray Aratunian, one of his bankers, sat inside near the piano. Hutch took his table outside, slightly hidden from Ray by the statue of Cupid. He couldn't help overhearing a group at the next table, though he preferred to keep entirely off the subject of business for a while. "Look at the demographics south of Market. Let's prioritize. What you're putting in ain't worth the return." "This time I'm going with my gut." "Second mortgage, man, that's a shitload of gut."

Oh, turn that stuff off now. "Large, no ice, the usual," Hutch said to the waiter.

"Darling," said Kenny, the waiter, "how come you never give *me* my usual?"

Sometimes Hutch liked kidding around with Kenny, but today he had lots on his mind. It happens when you're on earth, yet not meek, and Ray Aratunian is sitting near the piano.

Hutch had done a little shopping on the way. He liked to buy six-packs of toothbrushes, neat little jobs, each with a different color, and he always carried one in his jacket pocket. The handle leverage on mini-toothbrushes was less efficient for scrubbing the gums, but they didn't break up the line in his pocket. Then, if he found himself overnight at some friendly woman's place, he could leave it behind, both as a symbol of his willingness to come back and as a reminder to her, Hutch Was Here. He associated colors with persons— Linda was yellow, Sharon was pink, that architect on the Kearny steps was blue. If he stayed with Suki tonight, it would be pink, just like Sharon.

Eventually they gave up waiting and used the brush for polishing shoes. That architect—probably this was the reason he forgot her name—told him with a charming smile she had used it behind her heel on caked dog-do one rainy day. She was an intellectual, like his brother Dan—life wasn't a festival.

From day to day Hutch's hairline changed so slightly a person could never notice it; at least not the persons with whom he left toothbrushes. The line of his gum did not retreat. Hutch was not riding *with* the flow; he was riding it. When he ran up a walk or stairs, trotting with youthful eagerness in case the lady was watching for him, he always cast a glance at the fog-speckled flying San Francisco sky. Just checking. The sky was still there, still the limit. Later, in the morning, he strolled slowly and proudly out toward his white BMW, master of his day, not in a hurry, the relaxed stroll expressing regret at leaving the lady because, in fact, he was eager to get away. With two fingers he lifted the ticket from beneath his wiper and stuck it in his pocket without looking to see what the fine would be. In case she was watching.

Then, before the day's work and telephone calls, because each day in San Francisco must be a festival, he went for his run on the Marina green, or out under the Golden Gate Bridge, or sometimes in Golden Gate Park. It was important to take care of both the body and the soul, the arteries and the meaning of life. No matter how disappointing this or that young woman might be, a good run never disappointed. When a person's father died prematurely of heart disease and a person's kid brother has a really saggy look to him, it's always fun to make sure the cholesterol gets pushed through.

Hutch also took good care of his pelt. He went to a barber in the Columbus Towers, an artist at his trade, who snipped away at the blondish, now graying hair, and used the proper lotions and razor cuts, and then blew the whole thing dry so as to finesse the line of retreat on the forehead. Losing his hair was not a great idea for a man with Hutch's concept. His doctor described the little retreat at the forehead as "virile bald-ness." Hutch liked the term. But what about that pol-ished look where the hair used to be? Was that virile gleam? It reminded Hutch of the wear on an old horse when the bridle or saddle has rubbed against aging pelt. Boyish was his aim, and it was a struggle.

After the grapefruit juice, Hutch retreated to the Gents to scrub his teeth and gums with the toothbrush planned for Suki's big evening, slipping around near the bar so he wouldn't have to continue any discussion with Ray Aratunian. Ray saw him, lifted one hand in the beginning of a wave, lowered it, respected his desire for privacy after a hard day's work explaining why a short-term loan schedule needed to be ex-tended. He explained one thing and Ray explained the opposite. Short-term loan schedules were not part of the festival.

By the time he finished in the Gent's, Dan was al-ready sitting at Hutch's table. His cab was parked in the taxi zone where he could watch it. Hutch liked to treat Dan to a little break at Enrico's at least once a week or so, and liked to have pink gums, teeth without tartar for these difficult occasions between two fellows who took seriously the problem of having a brother. Even in San Francisco, where everything is still possi-ble, a person can't be entirely free.

Hutch believed Dan's problem (he had several of them) was partly that he was jealous of Hutch, and he was one of those California seekers, and so they had to go through these Basic Brother discussions. Hutch was patient with him. He even believed he could learn from Dan; it was possible. They would sit on the ter-race at Enrico's in the sweet afternoon of North Beach, smelling the coffee and the spicy smells of women, or perhaps of Kenny, the waiter, and Dan would be saying: "We should be more like each other."

"We got reasons to be different."

"We both had the same mother," Dan said.

"No."

"No?"

"You had a mother who loved you."

"Didn't you, Hutch?"

He grinned and winked. "I had a mother who liked you better. But now I got a lot of tired blonds who like me."

All Dan had was a wife and a daughter. "I haven't got any tired blonds," he said, and the two brothers were both laughing with good family feeling and understanding.

So it didn't always end badly. Hutch knew that his own ease after a day of running in the morning, getting Ray Aratunian to agree to one more postponement, buying a new set of toothbrushes, waiting for cheerful and cooperative Suki, gave him the inner peace to deal with a fucked-up brother. Oh, he wasn't so bad. He was a good husband and devoted father and the nicest dummy in the world.

Hutch hoped his favorite brother could take a little joke. "That degree in the liberal arts from San Francisco State really turns out a bunch of reliable cabbies, doesn't it?"

"Yeah, I should have been studying Downtown Gridlock when I was doing James Joyce—"

See, Dan didn't mind. He knew his brother cared, was only kidding a little for his own benefit, maybe push him into growing up.

"—but at least I got something to talk about with all the creative writers at Yellow, we get each other on the radio. 'The snow still falling all over Ireland? Roger and over.' 'This time Molly says No.'"

"Huh?" said Hutch. "Is there a crack here I'm not getting?"

Dan stood up. A man with a sticker badge, Hello I'm . . . , was peering into his cab. Dan had a fare and they had accomplished what they usually accomplished during these meetings. Hutch covered the check with his hand and Dan shrugged his thanks. They were keeping the fires going, as brothers should.

From his chair, his legs extended, stretching, needing another run although he had already run this morning, Hutch grinned and waved. He had wanted to say, I respect your life agenda, but maybe he could save it for another time, when Dan would reply, And what do you mean by that?

Borrring. On that occasion Hutch would again pay the check. Always pay small checks was his rule.

And now, pretty soon, he could expect Suki Read to come along, greeting him with her startled giggle and her spicy smells. She was over forty, on the slickety-slide, but lively, with a little extra fraying on her face when she thought nobody was looking at her. There had been a period of sadness in Suki's life after her son died. An only son must be a pretty heavy deal for a woman. Hutch liked the idea of helping her, especially since she was so good at helping him in ways that made him smile to himself, not impatiently, letting the pleasure build up, enjoying the early evening, enjoying the waiting.

Suki was so good at it. A little sadness gives an extra dimension to a blowjob.

A Chinese gentleman climbed into his Toyota parked in the taxi zone where Dan had been. As he drove off, Hutch moved his lips, reading the two bumper stickers: I FOUND JESUS along with I'D RATHER BE SKIING. Impressive how fast, during the life of one model change, the F.O.B. Hongkongers became thoroughbred Americans. They were really buying up North Beach property.

Next thing he knew, the Chinese would start driving BMWs and Hutch would have to rethink his entire life.

2

Suki excused herself. She slipped away, running her fingers along his flanks, letting him feel the tickle, the nails, something for him to remember her by while she took care of a few things in the bathroom. Like Hutch, she was fastidious. Like Hutch, she was sure to keep her mind on business. Perhaps even more than Hutch, she wanted to give pleasure.

He lay there alone, stretching, flexing, not impatient, listening to the off-and-on squeak of faucets—fastidious nice Suki—and used the time to reclaim his privacy among the neat turned-back sheet and quilt. Alone like this and waiting to sink into the mystery, Hutch admired how he could open and close his legs at will. Others could do it, so could a crab, but these were *his* legs. He had control. His legs could grasp things, and did.

He liked to smile and reveal his confidence about his need for the best in pleasure, good food and good loving, good money for keeping his health perfect, his arteries, for keeping his hair—and then he smiled again. Suki was standing by the bed looking down at him. She didn't speak. Still standing, letting him enjoy the pink glow, the fresh scrubbing, a few damp droplets visible, she put her finger to her lips. Not to talk. It was gratitude already, and a kind of understanding.

Gently she peeled back a fold of the sheet which had fallen over his thigh. Still standing—shh, don't move, he understood her—she gazed down. She skimmed her fingernails lightly again among the hairs on his thigh. Her smile was almost a little girl's smile, opening her present from a nice uncle.

Shh! Don't move! They both watched his erection, throbbing upward like a winch.

Oh! she said silently. Today was her day to admire.

There was a lassitude in Hutch's arms, but he lifted them just a little to ask her to come on in toward him. Still with that sweet smile, with a glance of regret, she consented. She lowered herself, just very slowly, upon him.

"Don't move," she said. "Wait. Just be with me."

"I won't move. Let's wait. We'll be together."

Hutch smiled up at her, his head on the pillow, Suki smiled down at him, her hair glowing in the halflight of reflections off San Francisco sky glow and metal in the room, digital numbers and lights on clock, radio, answering machine. The man who a moment ago had felt the power of his runner's legs, the flexing and speed trained into them, now let himself slip and slide into mere gentleness. He felt something the crab's legs couldn't feel, kindliness and gratitude and the presence of another who wished him well.

After a while a hoarse voice spoke from his mouth. "Let's not smile anymore," and she nodded, let her eyes close, her head fall, her hair tumbling. In his legs the power broke through the lassitude and he could hear Suki gasping, praising, giving him control, more power after holding back, more and more, until both of them lay there with their mouths fixed together to breathe from each other.

The good part went on and on. There was that scrunchy, squiggly, squirrelly squeezing together when everything has gone just right. By God! Hutch thought. What he said to Dan turned out to be right. There was nothing for a fit self-employed entrepreneur to complain of here on earth and in San Francisco. And look here how his festival also applied to his partner, Suki in this case.

The silent squeezing together was right and so, now, was the little regretful moving apart. Propped up on one elbow, Suki was shaking her head over him again, and then she lay back down. Hutch looked over the becalmed expanse of milkiness tumbled among sheets and pillows, her tucks and hillocks a little slippery after love. It was like a runner's sweat, sweet when fresh. Gently he touched her chin and wrinkled up his eyes. He was hinting that she could look, too. He wanted her to witness his gratitude, his goodwill, his pleasure. He wanted her to witness the pleasure she had given him.

They had given each other. She was grateful. She smiled back, then blinked shut again. Not sleeping, only subsiding. They had been good to each other.

He had a premonition, but maybe it could wait. He rested in the moment. It postponed all the realities: the light on his answering machine which meant he should play his tape for calls; the buzz in his body which meant he should take a pee one of these minutes; the flickering digital signals, minutes and seconds on his clock, which meant that the day's rounds and necessities were not ended by a sharing of sweetness and longing.

It wouldn't wait. The privacy crept back. She seemed so absent he half-expected a little snore. She was out of it. He could just courteously leave her there to get her beauty sleep; neither Suki nor Sharon nor Linda nor any of them knew about, needed to be concerned with his privacy.

If she ever asked, he would assure her that he remembered and was grateful. But Suki was a bright person with her own problems and too smart to ask. You can't name the sort of thing they had just gone through if you don't name it love and neither Hutch nor Suki wanted to call it that.

There was nothing. And then there was something. And then the nothing again, just a crab's articulated legs, claws tangled with another's. But a crab doesn't feel, within its slow wavings, this gratitude and sweetness despite the familiar privacy.

Hutch called it privacy, what he sometimes felt, because he wasn't the sort of person who felt lonely.

Suki wasn't watching him, but he glanced at her with a moment of pure thanks. No need for him to tell her.

Suki had been through some griefs. She was smarter than the Lindas and Sharons. But even thinking like that—*smarter*—meant that the wonder was over, the connection was gone, the privacy was back, and the hard work of the world was still out there, waiting to be done.

Let her sleep. Better that than conversation.

Hutch had good reasons to keep moving and unworrying.

Dressing and knotting his tie, then changing his mind, folding the tie and slipping it into his pocket, peeking at his teeth, unbuttoning the top two—no, top three—buttons of his shirt, he turned and glanced back at the sleeping stranger in the bed. She looked like no one or anyone. He stared at the mirror and he looked like no one or anyone, too. Was this the price?

Was this the emptiness after festival? When people are bored, is this what they feel?

This, Hutch decided, is what wasting time is.

He shrugged and turned away from both the woman in the bed and the man in the mirror. He knew what he was doing. Some things are better not to look at too closely. A person who did that turned into a Dan.

When Suki left, she would pull the sheets tight, straighten the quilt, and maybe leave her card on the pillow with a one-word note. Something like: Kiss or Thanks or Soon. Or nothing at all.

One of the things Hutch did not do best, and he knew and accepted this flaw in his character, was to work the phone. He was better at smiles, touches, stretching the legs, showing the suntan, suggesting another grapefruit juice, a little cold pasta salad, paying the small checks. Working the phone was cold, it had no fun in it. Nevertheless, in the life of every entrepreneur, there comes a time when he has to do what he doesn't do best.

Since Ray Aratunian was asking for more than explanations, this was one of those times. Hutch explained about how he was looking for new investors. The interest due on Hutch's big score, the redeveloped land down near Pier 22, was piling up. Trouble was, the flow-through on the income didn't come near to covering the payments on the first mortgage, the second, the little bank loans, plus the bigger one from Vecchio Investments which was secured just on Hutch's good name, good word. There was a little downward blip in the market on valuable land with small buildings that needed to be torn down and developed upward. So the total due kept increasing and Ray Aratunian, who didn't seem to mind the phone, kept calling on behalf of Vecchio and saying they wanted to be sure he met all the payments.

"Sure," said Hutch.

"But you're not doing it," Ray said. "You're just saying sure, super, you'll come in with the check, the checks, and you're not."

Hutch knew that. Ray didn't have to tell him.

"So maybe you'd like to come in," Ray suggested.

"Well, actually, I'm busy with this very deal right now," Hutch said. "I was just talking with some possible investors."

Ray gave a little groan or sigh; hard to tell on the telephone. It was almost as if he knew how much Hutch hated to have to sit by the phone in his little office on Broadway above Enrico's, hassling with Ray Aratunian while Suki finished up her beauty sleep; at least he could have been telephoning from his own place, feeling better among his things. But of course Ray couldn't know that. When Hutch felt worried about someone, he felt the someone knew more than he could possibly know—that was the kind of entrepreneurial edge they had. This thought was not clear. Suki had temporarily fuzzed Hutch's clarity. "Exponential," Ray was saying.

"Pardon?"

"It's growing. What you owe keeps pace, Hutch."

"What is this?" Hutch asked. "I told you I'm working on it."

"What this is," said Ray, "it's America. I'm glad you're working on it, Hutch."

When he hung up, Hutch saw his face in the little mirror on the desk. There was that purplish paleness underneath the tan. First Suki driving him out of his own apartment, now this, it was tiresome. But he wouldn't let a nice day be spoiled. He waited till his breathing was easier, the color came back, and then he opened the Rolodex.

Hutch worked the phone, going down his file of Enrico's pals, running pals, good folks he liked to play with. "I have an investment," he said, and they interrupted, "This isn't a good time, but let's have lunch real soon," and he said, "I'm eating light these days, keeping lean," and they said, "Good move, stay off the wine myself at lunch. . . . Fully invested these days, Hutch."

He paused between calls. Telephoning was always a bad way to set about this matter. But when a person was in a hurry, it covered a lot of ground and then he could meet them for a long slow lunch filled with friendly jostlings and heading toward fuller explanations.

"Hey, buddy! I got something better than junk bonds, something with people you know, a project right here in San Francisco—" "I like paper, Hutch. I kind of like my junk bonds from Drexel Burnham. I don't like projects right here in San Francisco I got to worry about they move the headquarters out to Marin or Napa."

"Freddy, Hutch here. Could we take a meeting on a sweet little deal I found . . . ?" "Later, Hutch, kind of full up just this point in time."

Couldn't get through to Gerson.

Al Wilsey didn't return calls, either.

Hutch didn't let it get him down. When you let things get you down, you lose the touch. Instead, he called Ray Aratunian to give him a progress report: "Talking very seriously to some new investors, reliable people, personal friends of mine I helped out in the past, now they want to return the favor—"

Ray answered sweetly, "Sure, Hutch. No need to lather me first, just come in and give me the shave."

In general, there were many things Hutch would have preferred to be doing with his time—running, visiting his niece Trish or his brother Dan, hanging out with the Enrico's terrace people, even having a nice chat with Suki Read if she were the sort of person who liked nice chatting. But an entrepreneur had to do the entrepreneurial things and so Hutch had done them for today. Now he was going to meet his favorite Russian writer, what's-his-name, they told him the name when they called from New York.

Not many people in San Francisco get chosen to entertain a star of Moscow journalism, a real luminary.

Hutch splashed a little water here and there, freshened up, put negative thoughts behind him, and strolled down toward the Enrico's terrace and what could only be a very special event in a life filled with good things.

3

"Only three?" Hutch asked. "No sweat, buddy."

The laughing Soviet journalist, composing his personal travelogue of life in America, needed three big things for his visit in San Francisco, plus maybe a couple of little things. He needed to meet an Italian mafioso. He needed to eat good Hunan food in a restaurant where Chinese street gangs came to dine and kill each other. And he needed (the really big thing) to get laid by a Jewish whore on silk sheets in a room with a ceiling mirror.

"The big things we take care of right away," Hutch said, his dark eyes excited by the imminence of festival. "The little things—well, let's hope we don't get too tired."

"You are champ!" Avigdor cried in his high-pitched voice, the light off the bar flashing in his gold-rimmed glasses.

Hutch Montberg loved playing host to visiting celebrities. He would do his best for his new pal Avigdor, because any friend of important East Coast network personalities was a friend of his. And Babawa had sent word that she had met Avigdor in Moscow, where he had graduated from the All-Soviet State Institute for Journalism. And the sent word of Babawa, via someone who worked in her office, was good enough for Hutch.

"You promise help?" Avigdor asked.

"For my friends, everything."

"I am your friend?" He was an insecure little gold-rimmed bugger. Much suffering, destruction, the Hitlerite hordes, long winters, world suspicion of the revolution of the workers and the peasants had created this pot-bellied eagerly smiling person, flashing gold teeth and gold spectacles, who deserved some traditional American hospitality. Willingly Hutch took up the burden of assuring him that detente was a special memory in the hearts of the people. "I am truly good friend, Kotch?"

"The best! I endorse that bond."

Avigdor wished to countersign the blood oath with a little scotch. He waved his arms at the barmaid pushing by with her tray, her bills between her fingers. "Is no need for hatred and prejudice, two great powers of white peoples. Our enemy is China and someday, who knows, Africa."

"Whatever's right, Vig. Foreign policy's not my strong suit." Hutch treated the Russian to a keen smile from his healthy, whitish, sun-dried lips. "Domestic matters is what I do best. Hey, you give me a little leeway on the ceiling mirror—make it optional?"

The visiting journalist loved clapping his new best friend around the shoulders. He almost pinched Hutch's cheeks, although U.S.A. males were cold and unfeeling. This didn't seem to be true in progressive, fun-loving circles in San Francisco. Avigdor looked forward to the silk sheets, and counted on Hutch to tell

him if the woman was really a dedicated Zionist. In
fact, upon further thought, he did reach up and pinch
Hutch's cheeks. They fell to laughing like school
chums in the first stages of a reunion. Sure, the ceiling
mirror could be optional, and Avigdor tugged greedily
with two fingers at the San Francisco tycoon's lean,
healthy, tanned cheek.

Personally, Hutch preferred to get his exercise from
money, running, and sex, but if the Soviet celebrity
liked isometric pinching of face on a busy night at the
Washington Square Bar and Restaurant, well, whatever was right. What Hutch deeply preferred about
living on earth, at this western end of the continent, at
this open end of the twentieth century, was not too
much for a capable man to ask. The film of his life led
toward pleasure, riches, success; it was already tend-
ing in that direction. Being graceful and easy about
helping the operation along took a lot of time. Sometimes there weren't enough hours in the day (for his
wrist, he had left digital behind and gone to a chic
Italian analog timepiece purchased from a traditional
Nigerian jeweler with a small but elegant shop in a
briefcase on the Marina green, where Hutch liked to
do his morning run).

Hutch's kid brother, Dan, on the other hand, failed
to give his attention to essential matters, being distracted by wife, child, problems he brought on himself. Dan was a living object lesson. He came to mind
just now because Hutch spotted him at a corner table,
having dinner with Gloria. Wouldn't you just know,
this being a small town and all, Dan would turn up on
precisely the evening when Hutch could do so nicely
without him. Soon Hutch would pretend to notice
them, go into the hey-what-the routine, and introduce
his robust gold-spectacled visiting star.

Hutch disliked namedroppers and vulgar social
climbers. There wasn't enough time for such things.

Still, chatting casually with the great and the near-great of our modern era had to be a definite plus for a few fun-loving entrepreneurs. Hutch didn't know everybody world-wide, of course, but he was personally acquainted with most of the Washington Square and Enrico's terrace elite of San Francisco.

About the time he noticed his brother, Hutch also spotted Larry Klotz, the screenwriter, charter member of the Enrico's terrace lunch bunch, waiting for his table with a new future wife. This was a perfect time to lay the groundwork for solving Hutch's daytime problem with Ray Aratunian. Hey Larry, who's this young lovely, meet my friend Avigdor—this sort of thing shouted over the clatter and roar at the bar. And then, leaning close, leaving Avigdor to make Soviet charm with the young lovely: "Tomorrow, listen Larry, can we make an appointment to talk about an investment opportunity?"

"Probably not, Hutch. I'm working."

"Listen, the tax laws for real estate are still in our favor. I don't want you to slave over a hot typewriter all your life—"

"I've gone to cool word processor."

"This is only for my good friends, Larry. I'm putting together a pool—"

Larry repeated precisely: "Not. I'm not investing, Hutch."

Hutch shrugged. It was like copping a feel at a party. Ten times out of twenty she'll slap your face, nine times she'll turn and walk away, but one time maybe she'll say, You're cute. So he would just keep trying. Someone else, a couple of others, were sure to come through. And he hoped, later, when Larry looked deep into the young lovely's eyes, he could see her alimony lawyer looking back at him.

Whatever Larry thought about him, Avigdor loved him. Too bad he didn't have a little investment capital stashed away, but he was fun anyway; could still be of use.

Avigdor had come to San Francisco to write a travel book entitled *Alone on Bourgeois Highways*, and Hutch was something of a lonely bourgeois on life's highway himself. A Jewish party girl was exactly the sort of challenge, coming from a dear friend, to which he liked to rise. "No sweat, ne worry pas, I take care of it," he promised. By this time they were arms-around-the-shoulder buddies. Hutch's cheeks were pink, one pinched worse than the other.

Hutch had the connections.

Avigdor enjoyed his researches at the Washington Square Bar and Restaurant, and before that, Enrico's Café, and before that, MacArthur Park, "the heart and ribs of San Francisco." A little like Henry Kissinger, they were reviving detente on the scale of person-to-person.

Hutch took pleasure in hearing about Avigdor's simple, typical, down-home life of a Soviet professional. Avigdor showed Hutch his American Express Gold Card and a Polaroid of his Mercedes sedan outside his modest brick-and-log dacha in Peredelkino, "honored artist and gonzo journalism village." He also had a Toyota for his "urban capital pad" in Moscow, a red-haired English wife whom he didn't have to beat anymore (she had finally learned to behave), and access to the most central circles of literature and advanced cinema art of the Union of Soviet Socialist Republics. Some slanderers said he was corrupt, but what difference did that make? Yes, a big difference: gave him a hearty laugh.

When an article appeared in the New York *Times*, entitled "Would You Buy a Manuscript from This Man?" he wrote to deny everything. He was an accredited reporter for Novosti, independent official Soviet news agency, and he printed special stationery,

headed in red type, KGB FOREIGN DISINFORMA-
TION SECTION. Now he was preparing the story for
his series, "California Dream, Fertility or Rot? An Ob-
jective Report." Then he would polish it up for his
book.

"You who are famous for worldly sophistication,
dear cultured colleague," said Avigdor to Hutch with
his ingratiating wide-lipped smile, "someday in my
own great nation I also shall offer deluxe hospitality."

"Whatever's right," said Hutch.

"Private icon collection, superb one, also original
Trotsky papers I show you in Moscow."

"That's what I'll want to do in Moscow," said Hutch.
"If there's anything I love, it's a tasteful icon."

"You are millionaire, wish to buy?"

Hutch shrugged. "Let me explain about America. In
America most people are millionaires, most of the
ones you'd meet, anyway. I'm sure you understand a
hell of a lot about our country, more'n I know about
Russia for sure, but the inflation just fucks up your
statistics. Millionaire is no big deal these days. Are we
talking net worth? Are we talking income per year?
Are we talking before or after taxes? See what I
mean?"

"Yess," said the Russian, with an expression that said
No.

"Okay, so you're not sure. That means you got something to learn, pal. And I'm here to teach, since you're
a friend of Barbara Walters and all."

"Babawa," said Avigdor happily, returning to solid
ground.

"Let's call and tell her we're hanging out together,
just thinking about her, hey? You got her private number, Vig?"

Vig turned his pockets inside out. They were empty
of Barbara's private number.

"Okay, but there's another thing. What's so good

about Russian icons, should I really get into them, are they collectibles?"

Sam Dietsch, one of the owners of the bar, noticed that their glasses were empty and sent refills on the house, raising his own glass from his station in the crowd alongside the piano. They were having a serious cross-cultural conversation and Sam wouldn't interrupt. Hutch made a mental note. Maybe later he could talk to Sam about the quick-turnover investment opportunity that was pressing down on Hutch. Goddamn Ray Aratunian was doing a lot of pressing. *This is only for my friends,* Hutch would tell Sam.

The drinkers shoved and bumped, the waiters hurried past with their trays and their moneyed fingers, and Avigdor liked many aspects of American folkways. "Communism in Russia," he confided, "is like . . . Let me tell you story. Is like you hold birch branch, *beryozha,* to stone rock and wait to take root."

"Pardon?" said Hutch. "I'm a practical fellow, Viggy, but I'm sure what you said is pure poetry."

Avigdor sighed. "Most comprehensive response, down to the earth—"

"Mainly because," said Hutch, "I don't know what the fuck you're talking about."

They embraced again. They had reached the point in a friendship, on a smoky evening in San Francisco, when two friends who had not yet found two women were spending a lot of time appreciating each other's emotional depth by throwing arms around each other's shoulders in a manly fashion.

Avigdor loved birch trees. He loved nightingales. These were special Russian tastes. He had a whole stand of white *beryozha* on his little estate in Peredelkino (here's another snapshot). But the Washington Square Bar and Restaurant in North Beach was A-okay, too. And the imminent Zionist girl, silk sheets, club sandwich, would console him for white-birch-tree-and-nightingale homesickness up to his kazoo.

Friendship and philosophy were moving fast amid clatter of silver, late eating, that last drink shipped over by Sam Dietsch, a barmaid who shook her head and curtseyed when they offered her a tip. Everyone has both a major aim in life and a minor one. Some have more—the cultural elite. Avigdor and Hutch shared several major ones which, for convenience's sake, they could lump together in one of Hutch's words: the *bessst*. To eat the best food, drive the best automobiles, stop in the best hotels, go to bed with the best women. The minor aims, not worth explaining to those who don't understand, included pleasant interludes such as travel to the major destinations, acquaintance with tropical paradises off the beaten track of your ordinary tourist.

This time they didn't fling arms around each other in sensitive agreement. Too much of a good thing raises unnecessary questions.

Avigdor had another request, minor in comparison with his heartfelt need for Cordelia's house of good repute. *"Dzhinzy,"* he said.

"Sir?"

"I must to take home *dzhinzy*, for home use."

"Gin?" asked Hutch.

"No, *nyet*-no," Avigdor cried, hitting Hutch perilously near his crotch by way of interpretive emphasis. *"Blu* dzhinzy. Video-kazety, scotch-visky, A-okay. Blu-dzhinzy for dacha on vik-end, your Teddy-Kennedy, your Mike-Wallace, dear close mutualny friend Babawa. From your fine Jewish tailor Levis I already have, but always ask myself—supply! In great motherland twenty millions lost by Hitlerite aggression, Leningrad famine, Stalingrad, hence our Soviet blu-dzhinzy technology not yet state of the art. Mental institutes must answer Star Wars aggression. Jewish tailor Levis hold secret." He paused with a parenthetical face-saving thought. "Yet speaking frankly, as between dear friends, your space program is full of shit."

"It's not my fault," said Hutch. "That was a great tragedy."

"I mean no blame," said Avigdor. "All Soviet Union send heartfelt reproach. Teacher, Japanese American, poor little Jewish girl, all for benefit of spy satellites. I mean no blame."

Hutch said nothing. Since the visiting Soviet scholar meant no blame, he would ride with the flow. He was only the expert on living well in San Francisco; Cape Canaveral wasn't part of his deal. "So you want to pick up some threads?" he asked. "Non es problema. Let me tell you the kind of system we run in this country. I know a place you can buy 501 button jeans at midnight and you don't even have to show a special card. It's open to the public."

Avigdor breathed heavily. His thick short nose couldn't always reach enough air. He was allergic to something in these bourgeois climes, much as he liked the atmosphere—smoke, chocolate, perfume, veal, clean women. "No problem," he said. "You take me, I'm yours."

Avigdor darted after the American phrases Hutch tossed his way. *Voteverright, Fensyzat,* some of them might qualify for import as part of the new Soviet emphasis on consumer comfort.

Standing with Avigdor in the dense press of the bar, Hutch touched the happy Russian on the shoulder and said, "My brother."

"You also," said Avigdor. "Wonderful wonderful friend."

"No, hey, that's my brother. And I fuckin forgot Gloria's birthday—that's the reason they come out here."

Avigdor followed where Hutch was smiling and

winking and shrugging and finally extending his arms. A couple seated at a window table for two, in the quietest far corner of the two crowded rooms, waved at them. Hutch grabbed Avigdor by the elbow and steered him through the standing bar drinkers, past the money-fingered waiters, and said, "Happy happy birthday, Gloria! Case of champagne on order, to be delivered tomorrow! Gloria and Dan, my sister-in-law the birthday girl, this is my best new friend the distinguished Russian journalist and world traveller, Avigdor Valodya, or something like that."

Avigdor cast his eyes shyly downward toward Gloria's knees. Jostled, he pushed his gold-rimmed glasses back up his nose. "Enchanté," he said.

"We're helping world understanding on the personal level in San Francisco," said Hutch. "I always told you I was a public-spirited citizen, didn't I?"

Dan smiled. "I knew we'd hear from you."

"Now we're making a little Cordelia run. We're just on our way to Cordelia's, where I couldn't drag you even if—did you think I forgot Gloria's birthday? Wouldn't and couldn't, Dan."

"Thanks for remembering," Gloria said.

"Hey, listen, noisy, you two having a nice quiet just the two of you, that's what I admire, catch up with you tomorrow—okay?"

"Okay, Hutch."

Gloria had smiling eyes under her brush of bangs. It was a thing Avigdor admired. As Hutch pushed him back through the crowd, he turned to re-admire Gloria's smiling eyes. Hutch was muttering about how a person basically needed not to be spied on by family; he was sure the Russians had problems with spies, too; and let's get the hell out of this place and go somewhere things're gonna be more lively.

"Wife of brother very beautiful, you see so?"

Not quite back to optimum comfort, Hutch hit the

cool of the sidewalk, chuckled, and said, "Can't have her, Vig. Only my brother can have her, plus maybe me."

Avigdor clapped him on the back. They embraced. Staring through the window, Dan seemed puzzled. People always feel it when they are being talked about, especially nervous folks without a whole lot going for them. Gloria did not smile, watched her husband's face. Dan sat very still behind the glass. He knew what the joke was about. He turned away and took Gloria's hand.

Avigdor and Hutch were standing and laughing on the sidewalk near the Valet Parking a little too long. A man with a tight, hurt, congested face, his hands jerkily fisting and unfisting, came hurrying out of the restaurant. Gloria followed him. "Dan! Dan! This is not necessary!"

Dan stood in front of his brother. Although Hutch had surely drunk more, his tie was straight. The handkerchief in his pocket was a rich gauzy tangerine. His Wilkes Bashford suit cost hundreds of dollars more than Dan's. Quality showed. Hutch stood his ground, clenching his fists as if this were a family trait, as if he sensed a crazy assault coming—he clenched and released. Dan shouldn't go rushing around, shaking things up, during a celebration with his wife. "Hutch," he said, "why are you doing this?"

Hutch stared. He was sober. Dan often cooled him down, although he preferred to ride a few drinks to their own conclusions on a special evening. "Who is doing what?"

Dan waited for an answer. Hutch often played at stupid. He liked to oblige when he could, especially his only kid brother. He repeated: "Doing *what*, Dan?"

"This guy. This Soviet."

"Oh shit, man, you some kind of redneck from Mo-

desto? *Soviet* —he's an agent, a *spy*, getting secrets out
of your big brother who knows everything?"

"I am a, I am a," began Avigdor, snuffling through
his thick short nose, pushing at his glinty spectacles, "I
am Russky Rambo from Outer Siberia, Sir. I seek code,
I carry you back to Lubianka Prison—"

"Hey, shut up, Vig, this is my crazy brother. He's the
emotional one in our family," Hutch said.

"Do you know what it means to take him to Cordelia's place? Do you want that in his travelogue about
San Francisco? AIDS, whores, and garbage?"

Hutch grinned. "Brother, maybe you work for the
Chamber of Commerce sometimes, driving them to
and fro, but I'm a *member*. Listen, you got a
nice wife—" Gloria was tugging at Dan's hand. "—a
nice wife, thank you Gloria, take care of the boy, a nice
marriage, a kid, lots of terrific basic American stuff in
there, so let me have my buddies, too."

Avigdor stood with bowed head. He only happened
to be here for the ceremony. He didn't want to get in
anyone's way during family doings.

"Vig is a friend of close personal friends." Hutch
winked at Gloria, just having a little talk with the kid
brother, he'll be right back to normal. "If you had an
average brain, you wouldn't be hanging around my
life and what do they call it, judgmental. Nothing better on your mind, nice wife and birthday and all?"

"Anniversary, not birthday."

"So sue me. Come on, Dan, I had a couple drinks."

Dan stood in the evening chill and looked puzzled
at Gloria, then back to his brother. "Shouldn't make a
big deal about this," he said.

Gloria glanced at Avigdor, still shyly hanging apart.
"I guess you did though, didn't you?"

"Okay. Dumb of me."

"Hey, that's all right," Hutch said. He beamed. He
liked control. He liked getting his second wind on an

uphill run. "You were just giving out some upset vibes, kid."

"Okay, never mind." But Dan didn't move away. He looked at his brother's fine dark eyes and waited. "Never mind, Hutch."

"Okay. That's okay."

Avigdor was delighted to find the real America at last. All these family okays were what he had read about but never experienced firsthand. He watched the white-coated car parker deftly backing a BMW out of its spot in front of a fire hydrant and wondered why he was dressed like a surgeon. When the bumper caught the curb, he understood.

"Can't you foresee the future?" Dan was asking.

"Brother, in my business we don't do that. That's why we make ourselves the General Partner and *other* people put up the cash. So I don't do it in my life, either."

"You can't foresee the past, either."

Hutch rolled his eyes. He caught a glimpse of the time on the steeple of the Italian church across the square. Getting late for Cordelia and Dan was coming at him out of left field. Was he reminding him again about how they used to play together with their bicycles, ride out to Ocean Beach, buy greaseburgers when they were really good, those years? . . . Dan liked to lay that trip on him. What Hutch remembered better: how one got along, that was Hutch, didn't get beat up in a rough neighborhood, and the other had to run to his big brother all the time.

Kids who used to be close, told stories to each other every night, grew up to tell lies to each other—was that Dan's line on the matter?

"Foresee the past," said Hutch, shaking his head, "that's a good one." It didn't mean a damn thing and he shook it off. "If you're asking do I remember things, I do and I don't. One thing I don't is muck around

remembering to no good point. And"—his index finger came out, he grinned to take a little of the big-brother bossiness off it—"and in summary, I don't see the good point around here."

"Okay."

Avigdor grinned. One more American family okay. The night air helped his breathing. Breezes tickled the little knots of hair in his ears. The evening was moving right along.

Hutch tried to lighten up, come down another notch, meet his brother more than halfway. "Hey, Gloria looks terrific. Don't tell her, but I'm sending a big batch of flowers first thing tomorrow, just like I didn't forget your anniversary. My fucking secretary forgot. That's a joke, Dan. I really mean it, nice for you, really *really*."

Dan gazed another moment at Hutch, expecting nothing, receiving a smiling warm-eyed stare in return. Gloria tugged. Dan nodded at Avigdor. They returned inside to their table.

Hutch knew he was going to replay the tape for Gloria. That's what loving husbands do to their loving wives when they have problems with their loving brothers. And of course the loving wives pretend not to be lovingly bored.

And people asked why Hutch never got married.

Just lucky I guess, was what he said.

"Hey Vig, that's so unlike my brother, you wouldn't believe it. Normally he doesn't drink, now I see why—it didn't bother you?"

"Is your brother, not mine."

It was time, although people smelled too much of smoke, and some of them, himself and Viggy for example, might have drunk a little more than they needed, through no fault of theirs, to get on over to Cordelia's. Hutch made his call at the noisy corner booth, gesticulating into the traffic on Union so that Cordelia could hear him better. "It's copacetic, pal. She says come on, this girl Shirley Schwartz got there already and she just loves the Third World."

"Soviet Union is not Third World," Avigdor said indignantly.

"Explain that to Shirley, I'm sure she'll be glad to hear the news."

"Silk sheets she's got?"

"We gave up rayon in this country, man. In California we gave up all the synthetics."

Avigdor shivered deliciously. He had never before known a woman named Shirley. "Thank you, thank you above all, dear friend."

"Save it. Let's both take a couple deep breaths of air so's I'm sober enough to speed us safely to our destination. *Then* I don't mind if you thank me."

Avigdor inhaled briskly, exhaled, inhaled, his mouth damp and open.

Hutch thought it might be the right time to offer his friend a little patriotic propaganda. "We're lax in this country, Vig. Just look at the Statue of Liberty. She's happy. The kind of country this is, you're allowed to have fun."

"Is good." Still inhaling, exhaling, oxidizing the scotch. "Is plan we can learn." But since Hutch was making his little propaganda, Avigdor thought he too should offer an interlude from history. "Hitlerite horde never kill twenty million citizens in your farms and industrial centers. Instead you have bitter shame of Vietnam, now Afghanistan is our patriotic task. In New York I see big dog performance, large lady, engineering very interesting, but everybody tell me: Go to San Franciskeh! In San Franciskeh all copacetic you love it! . . . You say I love it?"

"That's what we say," Hutch assured him.

Avigdor bent to his Hyatt Regency note pad, jotting

swiftly. When he came up from journalistic reverie, another thought appeared in the sudden cool and silence. He cleared his throat of a phlegm impediment. "Brother think you don't like him."

Hutch twitched his shoulders. How to express this with all due modesty and humility? "One guy in a family is always the successful one. That's the American way. We got a competition system going here."

"Maybe he like you too much?"

"Now you got it. How could I live up to that? And I'll tell you one more thing. I said everybody in America's a millionaire, but that isn't necessarily true. My brother has a struggle. Drives cab. I'd help him out, plan to do just that, but it's hard on him. I bring them presents, him and the kid, cute little niece of mine, but he—man, he should be a communist or something, he's so idealistic." And then Hutch looked with dawning light at Avigdor. "You don't look like an idealist to me, pal."

Avigdor tried another American solution he had just learned. "You got it, kid."

They were moving in Hutch's white BMW to their next appointment on the evening's rounds. Hutch drove with the tender caution of an occasional drinker who very much preferred not to scratch his leased white BMW with the augmented interior leather smell (leather scent extender thanks to fragrance technology in a little squeeze bottle stored in the glove compartment). Since he couldn't lean out the window with a whip to lash the Chinese drivers on Stockton, and it was uncool and unclassy to pump the horn, Hutch smiled with that famous benevolent San Francisco tolerance, that treasuring of ethnic differences. With California Zen mellow he said, "Fuckin slants so busy up their own assholes with chopsticks they can't see where they're going."

"Sir?"

"Lookit that one: BABY ON BOARD. A whole god-damn kindergarten in his back seat—and it's midnight." Hutch did not intend lack of gallantry toward the hard-working illegal immigrants flooding in from Hong Kong to take jobs away from real Americans. They were deserving human beings just like any other dumb shits. They came from an oxcart culture, hired one shill to take the driving exam for everyone, used an automobile manual printed in 1906. "Of course, it's only a cultural difference."

Avigdor was admiring the neon agitation, herbal remedy, food, and electronic shops, the doubleparked trucks crammed with goods, everything from muddy live ducks to VCRs in their original crates, the stores loading up even at this hour. "That's America," Hutch proudly agreed.

"On our eastern borders similar problem," Avigdor said. He took note of the traffic, the trudging multitudes. "Tens of millions are waiting, telling they are progressive peoples but they lie. And have Bomb."

"I don't travel that much personally to the outlying areas. I like white sand, a fish-based cuisine—but that cultural difference is a bitch, don't we know it? The major Bombereeno, you say?" Hutch whistled appreciatively through his teeth. "Folks can get killed with that thing. Here, all we see is a little fallout if you're in a place like the Gold Dragon for a late dinner. They come in shooting with those cheapo black jeans, T-shirts with the ethnic stuff on it, don't even blink if you're not the other gang. Hey, you folks're not gonna nuke 'em, are you? Don't answer if it's an official Soviet secret."

Avigdor expressed a degree of diplomatic apprehension. The potato face wrinkled shrewdly, starchy creases pinching up his eyes. His gold frames gleamed when he glanced at the kindly real estate speculator who might really be an FBI agent; more likely, given his sincere friendliness, CIA.

Avigdor jotted down a few more notes on his Hyatt Regency pad. Hutch felt contented. It was always an education to be helpful to important visitors; a person could learn about the outside world if he so desired. Improving the mind due to transcultural contact was a pure lift—no investment reasons for it, unless some happened to turn up; no immediate gain other than, oh, being seen in public with the well-known Russian journalist from the Soviet Union. His lips were moving, savoring the syllables, *My Soviet friend from Moscow, Russia.*

He could have done without mentioning it to Dan and Gloria, however. Tough luck it happened to be Gloria's birthday, or was it their anniversary, and the happy couple took a night off from the battle for existence.

Cordelia's hadn't changed much since the sixties. Natural wood, natural plants, natural people. Cordelia's chin had gotten more bony. She had gone through the experimental cosmetic surgery program at Shangri-La General in Tecate, Mexico. Her hostess gown with the cleavage down to her pupick expressed her sincere intentions—a hostess. Soon she and Hutch left their dear friend Avigdor alone with his heart's desire.

"Your name again, please?"

"Shirley. Rebecca."

"Spell, please. Is Jewish name?"

"Could be."

"Is clean? I think so."

"Government-approved meat here. How's about you, exempt from disease or condition which can be transmitted to another person? Listen, don't consider me a sex object, comrade. I'm just a poor misunderstood California girl."

"Say something in Jewish, please."

"Schmuck."

"That means?"

"It means you have a big one, I hope. Can we see?"

He looked around the bedroom. He had not brought a dictionary. Shirley or Rebecca pinched at the bed with her two Zionist fingers. "Silk. Satin on top, Vic. You ready?"

Then she pinched at Avigdor. He trembled. Who was the meat around here? He sighed. "So now we do it?"

"You got a better idea, Vic?"

Somehow dreams come true never come up to the level of a dream not yet come true. Such had often been the case in Avigdor's career. It was also a frequent occurrence for Hutch, who was waiting for his friend to emerge, discussing this and that and, incidentally, the price of their nightcap in San Francisco.

"I might could give it to you for nothing, complimentary," said Cordelia, "this being a special person in a position to spread the word about my operation in Moscow and all, bring me to the attention of the good-time commissars, and then again I might could charge you the regular rates, because detente ain't worth shit anymore. Plus I don't get much benefit from word of the mouth in Moscow, Leningrad, Kiev, and what other towns they got over there."

"Whatever's right," said Hutch. "I'm treating my friend."

"Suppose I figure the wear and tear on the sheets, looks like the type he won't even take off his shoes, plus all the cleaning and boredom of the deal, plus—"

"Whatever's right."

"Plus whatever's right," Cordelia said, grinning. "When I tell you a girl's Jewish, she's Jewish. Comes with the original sticker, *kosher* in big blue letters. Hey, I'll give him the sauna free. Has he ever had a hot tub? We'll all get in with him—I'll throw in Black Barbara, too—won't that be something like heaven on earth for a visiting Red?"

Hutch considered the deal. "Maybe you got a couple pair of pants somebody forgot, that's also on his agenda. Only kidding."

While they waited and the fun slowed down, his other preoccupation forced its way forward. Hutch thought of Ray Aratunian, the rapid interest payments, the escalations, the telephone calls from Ray. "Cordelia, you got a nice long-running operation here. Don't tell me, but I bet there's some money you can't declare, so I have an investment for you—you can clean it up plus make a legal score."

Cordelia stared at him. "Friend, I have my hustle and you have yours."

"Can I talk with you tomorrow during business hours?"

"For me these are business hours."

"This is so good it's only for my friends, Cordelia."

Cordelia was getting pissed off. "Let's not do your business together so we can remain intimate buddies, okay?"

Hutch shrugged. "Yours is the loss," he said.

"So many in life," Cordelia said. "Our peace of mind together is the gain, pal."

No sweat. Tomorrow morning Hutch would take Avigdor to the Gap as soon as they got down a double cappuccino espresso breakfast. He would load him up to his Commie gills with button-fly jeans; Hutch's treat all the way.

Avigdor appeared wearing a towel and his glinty gold rims. Shirley or Rebecca stood shyly by his side, holding his plump little hand and wearing only a look of modesty. "We are united in peace and friendship," declared Avigdor. "As say your honored cinema artist, this is Term of Endearment."

"Hey Cordelia," Shirley asked. "Where the fuck's my robe?"

Avigdor's back teeth, when he smiled, matched the fine metal of his glasses. He was smiling now. Soon all the progressive world would know how Hutch Montberg welcomed the wandering stranger to San Francisco if he happened to qualify as a dear important friend and international contact resource. For Hutch, friendship was the thing that mattered, because it was lonely on the way to the top.

Even the ceiling mirror had been highly polished, the best.

4

For convenience's sake, although she was seventeen already, Trish still camped out with her parents, Gloria and Dan Montberg, who lived in a cottage behind the Imperial Discount Record Palace out on Geary Boulevard in the avenues. The place was built around a prefab box erected after the great earthquake and fire of 1906. They liked to say, with ironic smiles, that their house was of historic interest—funny little stairways leading from the earthquake box to the several fixer-upper rooms added by various not too handy landlords and tenants. In their own impractical way, they had stayed there, renting, temporarily, since Trish was born. Trish too had made a decision to stay with her parents in their prefab, one-side shingled, add-on box for the past seventeen years. Temporarily. She had grown fond of the siding. She liked to pick at it.

Various deals had come together over time. For example, the discount record palace allowed them to park the old DeSoto bought in a taxi surplus sale in the discount record palace lot. The DeSoto itself was a good deal in pretty good transportation, coming to Dan without having to go through the formal auction situation down at Yellow, where it might have been out of reach, a couple hundred dollars more. Dan kept it running the way he kept the leaks caulked in the house, the roof, the daughter on the wide and broad if not the straight and narrow. It wasn't easy. No one had ever said life was supposed to be easy, except for Hutch. And probably Dan's brother Hutch only meant easy and a festival for himself.

Hutch thought it comical that both Dan and Gloria had pension plans, they could have bought a house, made an investment before the real estate market took off in the mid-seventies, but instead they worried, huddled over their fixed-interest account at Golden West Savings, didn't borrow against the pension plan when they could have broken out of the municipal-loser group and stopped shopping at Sears. Many times he had hinted he'd be willing to help. Hell, he'd come right out and said it: I'll guide your investment.

Trish's education mumble. Early retirement mumble mumble. Maybe take off a year and really do a crash assault on the book, that long habit which Dan trotted out to excuse every dumb caution and settling-for-less in his life.

Poor brother, poor bride who held him up and dragged him down, poor daughter who preferred her uncle because he had an attitude about life.

The great unknown famous writer Dan Montberg sat in his cab, then sat behind a discount record parking lot, a municipal loser. As far as his big brother Hutch was concerned, it wasn't funny at all; strike that. It was tragic. Still, it was in Hutch's nature never to give up. "Metabolic optimism," Dan called it.

"Write that down for your book," Hutch said.

Everything about this life had seemed natural to

Dan when, a young would-be making the big move
from poetry to prose, North Beach beatnik to married
man and prospective father, he also took the step from
temporary driver to regular cabbie, from the pad on
upper Grant near the Bread and Wine Mission to the
cottage in the foggy Irish flatlands of numbered avenues, tract houses, big families, a speedway boulevard.
The Chinese moved in later, but there were still lots of
nice Catholic grandparents among the Hong Kong
punks, the new immigrants from southeast Asia, the
black-clad welfare and foodstamp corner people, the
Aid to the Totally Incompetents. "Hey, Dad," said
Trish, "that would be funny if you said the Totally
Fucked Up."

"Not trying to be funny," he answered, "but in your
eyes what makes that funnier?"

"It's in my ears," she said. "Dad. And you're supposed to be the writer. But didn't you tell me as how
you were a granola before you became . . ."

"An old fart? No, I was a poet. And that was a long
time ago, before granola joined the known world."

She whistled through her empurpled lips. Wow.
Twenty years. Before something that was a name for
departed creepiness had even been reborn as the new
foolishness. That long ago.

Sometimes Trish liked to hear stories about the good
old days, if they didn't take too much of her time.

Now Dan Montberg was forty, still married to the
same wife, with a teenage daughter, and still living in
the cluttered wooden shacklet—everyone looked for a
new way to say it had charm, or at least character—
while he still drove cab temporarily, while he still tried
to finish his novel, which lay about in geological strata
in the room devoted to Finishing the Novel This Time
For Sure. Gloria had a job teaching second grade at the
Han Hu Yin Elementary School just off Clement. Trish
grew up learning quite a bit of street Cantonese, but as

part of the procedures of adolescence, the kids fell into separate Chinese, Korean, black, or white gangs. The Vietnamese and the little Cambodians were just getting organized. "Do you have friends among the other kids?" the friends of her parents asked, and Trish answered: "Do you?"

Generally that stopped them pretty good. Actually, which she didn't explain to them, skin color was a mere detail for Trish. What counted as a negative was the wrong hairdo. Mohawk, skinhead, fluorescent dyes, Lysol bleachings were the okay styles; Trish looked beyond any strict uniform. Ideological Nazis or rigorous heavy-metal punks were, for her, almost as bad as yuppies in knee socks with their streaked blond natural hair in a flip or a Lifestream-trained, cop-modified blowdry.

Trish didn't believe in ideology. She was easy. After all, her parents were readers and thinkers and that sort of thing rubs off on an only daughter, along with all the other crap.

Stupid old folks who thought things were great if you had a few of the right, according to them, ideas. Trish didn't mean to call her parents stupid, slow-moving, up-early, turn-the-radio-down, yell-out-the-window, lock-up-the-money granolas; "Things were better in our days, twenty years ago." Tough shit. Actually her parents were kind of less idiotic than most, which didn't make it easier in the slightest. Less idiotic parents said, "Oh. See what you mean." The others said, "But I thought—" before Trish turned off, turned away, in her little way of staring right through them without blinking and cutting out the volume without even closing down her ears, stuffing the Walkman equipment into her head, because it was strictly and stringently unnecessary to know what they thought. *But I thought* . . . As far as Trish was concerned, even the relatively less idiotic parents she happened to have been burdened with could just leave the thinks out of their blotched, worn-out, mother-and-father faces. She sometimes stared at them just before they started out with the *But I thought* and saw one long bony cab-frayed body of her dad who tried to work two shifts, one for Veterans Hack & Limo and the other at his typewriter, and then the neat, cheery, well-stacked body of her mom, who actually worked out on the bars of the playground at the Han Hu Yin Elementary School so she could keep fit. And the two heads above this double bod of her parents both had the same expression, the one that said, *Trish why don't you . . . ?*

She preferred her Uncle Hutch because he brought her things, used to be dolls and sugarless candy, now it was tapes, arm and ankle bracelets; he was always kidding, and didn't care what she did. He said he didn't believe in worrying because it didn't help. When he caught himself worrying, he said, he punished himself by going to the Winchell's Donuts and eating two sugar-fried grease balls—this was the punishment he had decided on because he didn't believe in either worrying or donuts.

Uncle Hutch made Trish laugh a lot. When she was a baby, and even when she was grown up enough to remember about it, he used to turn her over on her back and growl and tickle until she screamed; he played animal; so did she. They invented funny beast games together. Later Hutch told Trish he used to have a dog called Jesus, and she asked why Jesus? and he said, "Because neither one of them ever took a leak in my house."

Trish liked that, but wanted to know what happened to Jesus.

"He got lost and I never found Jesus."

Trish liked that, too.

"Anyway, I can't afford the time for pets. My time is too unexpected. My things come up at all hours."

And that wasn't funny, but Trish liked that, too. She was seventeen and she liked her uncle better than anybody, even Harry. Don't even mention her mom and dad. Uncle Hutch's stupid brother and sister-in-law, who claimed to be her idiotic parents, worried a lot. So it only proved a person didn't have to take after her relatives.

Trish wondered if she had been adopted as some sort of good deal during the time when granolas liked to worry about foreign wars and abandoned children. Maybe her real parents were gypsies or surfers or musicians from L.A. But then Uncle Hutch wouldn't be her real uncle and that would be a stone loss.

Scuffing down the avenues off Geary, late to school or skipping school, Trish took the time to consider these matters. Some people headed for Golden Gate Park, trees, flowers, buffalos, and grass-covered sand dunes, for their thinking. They lit a joint or swallowed a cap and gathered the nicer things about life around them. They let the other things just float away. Trish had a different idea. Like Uncle Hutch, she took her festival in the city. Not even necessarily turning on, she preferred waltzing among the curbside shambling tonnage of abandoned rustheaps. To Trish they looked like buffalos, dropping their shit in the form of mufflers, tailpipes, gaskets, rusty innards and entrails. Only American cars seemed to get deserted like this in the avenues; the Japanese and Korean cars just kept on running, having no buffalo in their ancestry. Along the street curbs out here in the flatlands, where the tourists never wandered, there was a forest debris of bikes, scooters, skateboards, boxes on skates, and trash in bulging plastic sacks, sneaked in front of someone else's house by resident aliens or resident illegal immigrants who wanted to avoid hiring the scavenger service. Trish's father once looked at the ravaged hulk of a refrigerator, moved from a front porch to the street, and said, "I see we got people from West Virginia, too."

"Huh?" Trish asked.

Sometimes the city trash patrol looked through the plastic sacks for bank statements or other junk mail so they could pin the garbage on some careless Occupant. Inevitably, in due course, the local animals, dogs, cats, rats, and an occasional cute raccoon came foraging, eating holes in the plastic to get at the goodies, growling, purring, cheeping, or clicking front teeth at the bank statements and Occupant mail, tearing at the heap and sending it, after their snack, to swirl in seawind eddies down the street. Sometimes, when the Chinese supervisor interrupted the mayor on her busy round of promoting sister cityhood for San Francisco —Florence, Leningrad, Bogotá—an emergency streetcleaning brigade would be fetched out in their monster machines and orange vests glowing in the daylight. And then the routine began all over again.

"Other cities use public collectors of trash," said the cab driver and novelist who happened to be Trish's father.

To avoid saying Huh again, the girl alleged to be his daughter asked, "Why not us?"

"I guess this is the last frontier. Search me. I guess we're rugged out here in San Fr'cisco."

But Trish didn't search him. She used to like having these walks with her dad, his slow long steps, her fitting her stride to his, taking his arm. As long as they didn't talk too much, she liked the rhythm, something like rocking a boat, feeling a man's stride, smelling him, brushing against the corduroy or blue jeans which he had worn since she could remember. He still liked these walks and Trish didn't much anymore. But since she wanted to be reasonable about things, she had made up her mind to circle the block with him a few more times without complaint before she left home forever.

For reasons she didn't go into, Trish had to admit she still didn't hate these monotonous daddy strolls. Okay, she almost liked them, even if she would have preferred a fast drive to Sausalito or Muir Woods with her Uncle Hutch in his little BMW with the tape deck hard at work. Holding her father's arm at the Balboa crosswalk, where the oriental skateboarders were doing wheelies up the wheelchair ramp, Trish jerked him a little and said, "Okay, let's see how sharp you can corner, Dad," and now it was his turn to answer: "Huh?"

Having good sense, Trish felt it was an unnecessary procedure to explain that she was referring to Uncle Hutch's BMW 450SL if that was the number—no, that was the Mercedes.

Her dad must have been planning a paragraph in the book he had been writing since Trish was born—probably took out the time to conceive her one morning—because he went on about the river of debris at the curb, something deep and moving in the life of a city, blah blah blah. "Some animals produce only fertile decay, dung, bones calcifying, enrichment—"

"Do you have to talk dirty to a poor misunderstood seventeen-year-old kid, Dad?"

"Others leave polyethylene cups and sandwich wrappings by the river, in this swamp with all the stranded hulks."

"Do you have to use all those big words, Dad?"

"Does it seem natural to you, Trish?"

She thought a bit and tried to imagine alternatives. "Hey," she said, "clean up all this stuff, that'd be a trick, and you'd have what? You'd have nothing."

"Funny girl." He took her arm like a happy lover. She marched, smiling. She was surely his daughter, no matter what she sometimes suspected.

"It's my nature," she said.

"It's your nurture," Dad said.

"I guess that's your eastern pronunciation, Dad. Didn't you go to State? We don't say it like that out here in Frisco."

He grinned. "Nurture red in tooth and claw," he said.

She shrugged. "We also talk mostly English out here, ain't speaking Chinese, Japanese, Spanish, or Tagalog. Is that Tagalog, Dad?"

Trish squeezed back at her dad's arm. She pressed his arm as if she loved him. She felt as if she loved him. In a life where the facts seemed to come together for a clever girl, there were a few odd facts which she hadn't figured out and didn't really need to bother with. It still felt good when her father took her arm like a happy lover; it still felt good when she squeezed back at his arm.

It was okay for there to be puzzles and complications in a young woman's life.

Uncle Hutch lived in another San Francisco, money and pretty and white with coke and smooth of transportation. There were hills, there were tourists, there was regular street-sweeping. That was okay with Trish. Out here in the avenues, Trish was content to make herself ready for the big jump to that other, vertical city. But sometimes out here, when the pickup truck and no-muffler motorcycle and Chinese baby racket stopped and she lay awake at night with her hands resting snugly on the strong line between legs and hips, Trish just twisted about uneasily in her bed, not wanting to sleep and not wanting to be awake, wanting to put herself among real city noises, where Uncle Hutch lived. She had an idea about the real city from Uncle Hutch's smiles, jokes, nudges, and the general festiveness he brought during his visits. He was smart. He liked to refine his tastes. There would be glasses with stems that clinked when people congratulated each other, expensive purring automobile sounds, cable cars clanging, the hillside town she knew from cop stories on television and Levis advertisements. It was only a half hour away if she made the right bus connections. It was far from this flat ratty swamp of stucco, siding, and neighbors; it was the place where Uncle Hutch had fun and where, oh, goddammit, Trish wanted some.

Not that her dad wasn't a terrific person. Probably, if Trish didn't have to be her daughter, Gloria would be an okay person, too. Almost everybody has to have parents and probably way down deep, where things were growing in her which might lead to being a parent herself someday, Trish was kind of fond of Dan and Gloria. She just wished Dan could at least give her what the other kids in the neighborhood had, assuming he wasn't smart enough to get her into the life that Uncle Hutch had. And she just wished Gloria could leave her the fuck alone—those lip-sucking looks about the makeup, the stuff in her room, the music, the friends; the hurt looks, angry looks, judging looks —the goddamn mother looks which do no one any good, get only results no one really enjoys. Yet along these lines was how Trish lived.

How this family, Dan head of household, Gloria also head of household, Trish temporary occupant and resident with an itch to go someplace else or make someplace else where she was, dug itself in: that aforesaid falling-down cottage with the Imperial Discount Records parking lot as their port for the clunky,

chunky DeSoto with the prehistoric cab markings that
her dad actually *liked;* he laughed about it; driving cab
all day, he also drove cab at night or whenever he took
his wife or (God forbid) his daughter someplace. A
cottage attached to another cottage full of books on
planks and in crates, so that the first little earthquake
that came along would just drown them all in a tide of
printed boringness. A mother who read some of the
books, read in them anyway, plucked at random from
one of the piles, when Dad drove late and she had
finished her lesson plans. Sometimes, near dawn, Trish
would wake, hoping at least for the sounds of lovemaking, but no, that noise was Dad droning out another
story about the night's fares, the Uncle Hutch people,
the tourists, the rich, lazy, successful people who rode
in the cabs and gave people like him tips; Dad drank
decaf, so did Mom, listening him down into drowsiness
and sleep. Or Gloria slept, Trish felt how her body was
changing, and dad plucked away at his garage sale
typewriter, an Underwood 21 it was, making another
novel—did the world need another?—about a former
beatnik who now drove cab and had his nowhere adventures on the slick streets with a nimbus of fog
around the neon signs. Trish had peeked; Dad didn't
care, no pride at all.

And what, she might ask, is *nimbus*? The problem
about asking Dad was that he'd probably tell her.

Sometimes when Trish got up (was got up) for
school, she found him at the table waiting for her,
scribbling and typing out his endless story. He had
already complained out over a thousand pages and he
had many a rich tourist, dope dealer, pimp, hooker,
drunk, and nimbus yet to go. Seeing her shuffle into
the nook bearing her box of frosties or crunchies or
left-over granola, he rubbed his face, grinned, and
sang a little song. "Here's my Healthy Vegetarian
Song," he said:

This little piggy went to market
This little piggy stayed home
This little piggy had tofu—

"Put it in your novel, Dad," Trish said.

"Already did. That was my night's work, honey."

Once she was thoroughly awake and untalkative, reading the back of the cereal box, he creaked up the stairs to his Underwood and began tossing sheets into a folder or, more likely, after short pauses for reading, wadding, and crumpling, into a metal wastebasket that had *V.A.* stencilled on the side. This so-called novel was shaped like a snake, winding through the nights of Trish's life at home as long as she could remember—a snake whose head no one ever saw. Dad made morning conversation, Trish was a normal person who didn't like to talk at breakfast, Dad tried some more, Trish read the cereal box as if it were her fate, Dad wrote his book, Trish went or pretended to go to school, Dad went to bed for a few hours. Mom trotted off to the One Dumb Slant Elementary School.

Now take the other kids on the avenues. A fireman had hours; so did a cop. Even a Chinese restaurant guy or a Lebanese grocer had hours, maybe long ones, but a limit. A retired beatnik cab driver and unpublished writer had no limits. For the others there was beer, there were normal wheels, there were houses full of kids. There was color teevee everywhere, cable a lot, and enough VCRs to keep things from boiling over when people got edgy in the evenings or on weekends. A few years ago, just before she grew her tits, Trish had to have both a birthday and a tantrum to get Gloria and Dan to junk the black-and-white garage sale teevee in favor of a color sidewalk sale Sony. This family was garage sale to the max, but then Uncle Hutch came through again, so now they had two color teevees—the new one in Trish's own room. If she weren't planning other nonfamily living as soon as possible, a VCR from Uncle Hutch would have been her next project; maybe it still was; but more clearly ahead on the horizon, let's say for her next birthday, was a motor scooter, never mind the helmet, that law was repealed. Riding other people's wasn't the same thing because the other people always wanted to feel you up, top to bottom, as fare for the ride. And truth to tell, a person didn't always need feeling up when she needed wheels—one thing shouldn't call for the other as a *rule.* It should be optional. In general, Trish was not in favor of a lot of rules.

Take the rule about sweets and grease in the house. Trish could eat whatever she wanted without getting fat or zitting up more than anyone else her age, so she didn't see why Gloria would say Yucchy when she followed dessert with a few donuts from Uncle Hutch or a Mars bar with her own spare change. But her parents were like that: granola, tofu, and raw vegetables left over from before Trish was put together, according to their story, one fateful night in North Beach.

No doubt it had been fun for them. Sometimes Dan showed her the Café Trieste, City Lights Bookshop, "Here was the Enigma, here was the Bread and Wine Mission. . . ."

"Hey, I'll bet it was nice for you, Dad, when you didn't have to drive except part-time and Uncle Hutch and you were even, both of you just starting out on life's way."

Dan really hated to take offense with his daughter. He just grinned, turned silent, hurt feelings, rubbed his stubble with his hand—she could hear the crackle —and drove her home from North Beach in the DeSoto which, at least, one advantage of his career, he could park expertly. Plenty of practice. He was a garage sale dad, and even tried to sell his daughter—this was her opinion—the used memories of his historical life as a lean, funny North Beach seeker.

He had sought and this is what he found. The avenues that crossed Geary where Trish temporarily boarded with her parents seemed to make out at the margins on garage sales. Folks bought the stuff—pots, paperbacks, Lawrence Welk records, early digital appliances—from the folks down the block, and then next Saturday they sold them in the driveway to the other folks up the block. Seemed like that, anyway. The fireman with eleven children also sent his older kids out babysitting—thank God—so Trish couldn't be expected to jerk food from the mouths of the hungry Irish city worker and his family. Motorbikes, junkers spewing illegal muck, pickup trucks, and a neighborhood of San Francisco which practiced no birth control on purpose. That was the part that upset Trish. She knew San Francisco wasn't supposed to be like this; Uncle Hutch certainly wasn't.

Of course, a whole lot of parts about life upset Trish at this moment of her seventeenth year.

One of the little things that upset her most was Nazi Harry. He had no hair on his head (shaved regularly), a big black cycle with swastika markings, a membership card in a secret organization. A lot of the other kids her age were still into skateboards and 'ludes, but Harry had real bad wheels and access to mighty powder. He wanted her to leave her dumb school and ride with him on the back of his cycle to Salt Lake City. He had lots of friends in his secret organization in Salt Lake City where they practiced motorcycle combat on the dirt and gravel slopes of the Wasatch Mountains and in Kearns, Utah, where they worked out in the rifle range. He trusted her with the razor bent over a sink, shaving him, coasting with hardly a nick over the bumps in his head. Those were the good parts.

"What's the bad part?" Uncle Hutch asked.

"He wants to make me do it."

"He can't do that, Trish."

"Wants to make me pregnant."

"He can't do that, either, unless you—"

"Oh yes he can, Uncle Hutch. We fight about precautions a lot, but he needs me so much—"

Hutch stopped where they stood near the construction on Geary and said, "Don't."

"Harry's got real strong sperm, Uncle Hutch."

"Don't get pregnant, Trish."

A wrecker's ball was dangling overhead, near the sign that said HARDHAT REQUIRED, and she gave him a lowered sidelong glance. "If I do, Uncle, you'll be the first to know."

He laughed. "Not even second? After Harry?"

"First," she said. "Definitely you're first."

"We better move," he said. The crew in the cabin controlling the wrecker's ball was hooting and jumping up and down, yelling that this was only a test, see if falling masonry could do any damage to assholes, just stay where you are.

They went under the covered walk to look through the fence at the excavation. "Shouldn't your mom and dad know about this?" Hutch asked.

"Hey, but Uncle Hutch, you tell'm one single thing, and I'll—" She held his hand. She couldn't find words. He was moved by her desperation, her silence, and her trust in him.

He squeezed her hand back. "Okay," he said.

Trish and Hutch both loved constructions, especially when they uncovered a tangle of forgotten cables, underground streams, wire casings, sewers and drainages, all the proof of the total simultaneous connection of electricity and shit, water and excretion, power and the poisoned runoff of power. They would stop his automobile and wait for someone to fall in, though nobody ever did; wait for a child to come along and be amazed, and sometimes one came along. Hutch had a funny little quirk about kids. He liked them. Especially if they were strangers, he liked to scare them, talk to them about the underground, unseen, unshelled connections, unless a parent snatched them away or they retreated, pale and wary. Of course, Trish was special, a whole other thing, his niece, his best beloved for seventeen years now.

He had never had a child of his own and probably never would. It worked out that true love didn't come his way, except intensely, temporarily, and since he never knocked anyone up, he had taken to telling them he was sterile. He would rather pay for the abortion; he hadn't needed to. Now he believed it—that he was sterile. Maybe his niece made up in fertility for other people's lack of it.

When Hutch caught a look at Trish's little slip-slide walk, seeing it with the eyes of the guys on the construction project, who were pointing and laughing about the lucky old guy with the tasty little chicklet, he noticed that it still bothered him about Nazi Harry. "Couldn't you do better?" he asked. "This sounds like bad news."

"No news at all. I'm just telling you cause I trust you."

"I mean in the fairy tales a guy rides up, kills the dragon, and saves the virgin. I mean he's out to help her. So they marry and live happily ever after."

"Where you been, Uncle? This is the twentieth or is it almost the twenty-first century fox already, man. What we do now, we kill the virgin and marry the dragon."

She was writing stories for herself like her dad. She was tough and enterprising like her uncle. She was pretty and smart like her mom. Hutch grinned. "And you got a walk all your own."

"Huh?"

But she knew what he meant, that slip-slide walk, a kind of lazy agile toddle, facing both ways. This guy she really respected, older guy, mature opinions about women, Nazi Harry, the first time he met her outside school, he told her she had a real nice gearing in her legs and ass, 'specially the ass, and Trish wished to live up to the standard she had set on their initial romantic encounter. At first she wasn't quite sure what he meant about her gearing, but with practice it all came clear, like using VCR and tape equipment, like working the controls of a fat-bodied Honda cycle.

Okay. Hutch knew about love being a hindrance rather than a help. This clever little girl was a chip off the old block once removed. She was grinning and giving him wink for wink. If she were his own, he couldn't love her more. Since he had no other, she felt like his own. "Promise me, whatever happens, Trish—"

"Hey, but Uncle Hutch . . . Okay, promise."

This was the age of continual risk and trouble. A person could get beat up by her old man, a person could get flunked out of school, a person could get pregnant, a person could get a whole row of zits on her forehead. Yet Uncle Hutch told her life was supposed to be a festival. He also told her trouble had another angle to it; for example, he personally always loved women with skin problems.

"Promise?" she said, laughing and not believing him. But she did believe something about her best and favorite and only uncle—that he cared for her as nobody else did and as he cared for nobody. Hutch knew it, too. This was their secret together. Grin for grin, wink for wink.

Even if life wasn't really always a festival, as Uncle Hutch said it had to be, Trish found that she could even sometimes enjoy getting upset. Hating things could be fun, since it added to the pleasures of revenge. One of the things Trish enjoyed about herself was how she could eat a Mars bar for dessert after a meal of chocolate after a Sugar Pop snack and not get fat. Oh, a zit or two, but no more than when she had her period, and she kept emergency stocks of Clearasil and lotion for one, drying them up and, two, hiding them over. She might complain about things at times, but she was a lucky girl, a bottomless pit of rare adolescent nonanorexic slim. "Hey Slim," her dad said when he caught her in her room with a stash of Walgreen's pocket-sized candy bars—the kind the candy people manufacture for the convenience of shoplifters: "I *know* you got a good body, kid—"

"I was just noticing that in the mirror, Dad."

"Watching yourself eat chocolate, hey, that's great. But what about your teeth?"

"Fluoride, Dad," she said, spitting peanuts, carmelized chips, coconut, chocolate, all formulated chemically from genuine natural petroleum products.

"You give fluoridation a heavy task, honey."

"No cavities, Dad."

"No cavities *yet.* "

"I'm kind of busy, Dad. And don't you have a great book to write during these precious hours at home?"

And then he hesitated. He didn't always obey Trish's good suggestions or advice at once; he took a sad breath—none of these sickly gestures had been passed through the family to either Hutch or Trish; high school biology and genetics explained all this and how it can happen, human beings not being merely the result of cloning or simple splitting of an egg. Trish stared at her dad. He shrugged, closed the door, and let her munch in peace, listen to AC-DC in peace, do her own business in front of the mirror in peace.

She knew what Uncle Hutch would say. He grinned and tilted his lean head at her, and with a gleam of laughter in his eyes, loud and clear, he poked her in the soft part of the shoulder. "You're boosting candy at the Walgreen's, aren't you?"

Mumble mumble.

"How do you get through the turnstile, hey?"

Giggle giggle.

"Don't get caught, okay? But let me tell you something, kid. There's always a risk, no matter how good you are. This is America, so why fuck around with the candy? Watches, radios, and income property are more practical—"

"Can you get zits from income property, Uncle Hutch?"

"It's a family thing, Trish. We get pimples whether we steal or not, and when you grow up it's not stealing. It's speculation, it's promotion, tax shelter it's lots of other things."

"Is it fun, Uncle Hutch?"

He put his arms around her so she could smell the shaving lotion. He changed the handkerchief in his jacket pocket—yellow, purple, once even orange silk —but he always used the same after-shave that smelled of man and spice. "It's a festival," he said.

She punched him on the shoulder—his own gesture returned. He released the hug as she said, "No magnetic strips on the cheap candy, Unk. Non es problema. Real problema is, how do I get the records and tapes through the detector at Imperial Records?"

"Well, how do you?"

"Tell'm I have a pacemaker. Tell'm I'm a seventy-two-year-old heavy-metal freak and turn off the goddamn machine before they got a lawsuit on their hands or a dead heart condition."

He grinned through his dry white runner's lips.

"Put on my Halloween mask and run like hell, Uncle Hutch."

And she grinned and punched him on the shoulder —his repertory of friendly gestures returned with in-

terest—and continued: "No magnetic strips on the
cheap candy is the deal, see, so it's just like the cats and
dogs chewing in the Chinese garbage bags. It's allowed. Real question still is, see, how do I get the
records out through at Imperial Records?"

"Don't want to foul your front yard if you're caught,
Trish. So tell me."

"Send a Chinese kid through doesn't speak anything
but Hong Kong and they're so busy chasing him is one
solution—"

He was bent over with mock laughter. It was silent,
the sound not yet synched.

"Hey, Uncle Hutch, aren't you supposed to be a
grownup, your suits and wheels and all? It's against
teenage law to tell you all our true secrets."

He had his arms around her again, it was in the
rhythm of things, laughter and hugs, hugs and laughter, so easy with her body, unlike Dan. She sniffed the
spicy after-shave and healthy runner's sweat and soap.
He was whispering in a sudden fit of grownup concern, "Don't get caught, Trish."

"That's not my program, Uncle Hutch."

He released her. He studied the grave, pouting,
worried teenage person who had recently been in his
arms, niece to uncle. "I guess it's more fun than watching the laundry dry, isn't it?"

"Wooden know. Mom does the laundry." She lifted
her chin, showing the woman she would become if all
went well—a heartbreaker for certain men who were
overfond of trouble. Just wait a few years. Of course,
by that time her chin wouldn't be stuck with a choco-
lated Walgreen's peanut.

Whistling softly to himself, Hutch said, "Most everybody got lucky with this kid, 'cept a few local mer-
chants."

"Aw, Uncle."

"And I got real lucky, Trish. You're my best little girl."

Sometimes, when she didn't see Uncle Hutch for a while, Trish had the awful fear that maybe he was only a dream. But that couldn't be, she forgot her dreams, the good ones, anyway, and she never forgot Uncle Hutch, even if it was weeks and weeks before she saw him again. And he always did come back to her, wheeling the little white BMW into the Imperial Discount Records lot and honking twice before he jumped out with a present from Italy, France, or Chinatown. She hoped someday to be found eligible to live life as a festival. She was a candidate; she would elect herself.

Out here in the avenues, it was just kids and codgers. She planned not to remain the one, not to become the other. Oh yes. And failures. She planned not to be like her mother or father, either.

Grownups never know how clean the ears of a kid are. Through the crate walls of her room Trish could hear them talking, Uncle Hutch, Gloria, and Dan; all she had to do was turn down the music. Dan was bugged and Gloria was saying, "Maybe it's none of our business."

"That's what I tell him," Hutch said. "I try not to get mad, but if I entertain a visitor from far away, a close personal friend of important people in New York—"

"I suppose you're right," Dan said. "But that guy is a world-famous creep."

"He's a famous Russian journalist, makes a good living at it—wouldn't you like to make a living writing, too? Hey, come on."

"Okay, okay, I agree, it's none of my business."

Trish could imagine Hutch, big about things, grinning and accepting her father's apology. Then he was saying: "She's my only niece, she got to go to a good school, I want you to know she's closer to me than anyone except maybe a brother. I got a policy for her. Remember this name: Missouri Mutual. I want you to count on me for the best school she can get into."

"We can send her to college, Hutch. We've planned for that."

"But I want the best for her. She's always been my little girl. Only the best!"

And Mom was saying, "We both appreciate the offer. If there's a problem, we'll talk about it. We appreciate, Hutch."

Hearing this felt as good as sex while taking XTC with Nazi Harry, but in a different way of course. Trish felt warm and cozy with the sound of Hutch saying, "The best!" even though she couldn't smell his after-shave through the walls. She could almost smell it.

She couldn't sleep that night. Certain drugs did that to her, making her cozy and drowsy and awake—the Ecstasy drug was the main one. But this wasn't that. She limited drugs to weekends and vacation emergencies. She was a cautious person and, like Uncle Hutch, she was looking to make life a complete festival without spoiling it with brain damage.

As she lay there in the crate of her room, amid the accumulation of baby things she had outgrown, blankie, fuzzy-wuzzy from Uncle Hutch, windup record player, and her new discs, tapes, clothes and makeup kits, she listened to the rattle of her father's typewriter in the last darkness before dawn. He seemed to have forgotten that she was supposed to be sleeping. It wasn't time to get up yet, there was a wintry dark in the world, and yet through the walls Trish could see everything in this house in a phosphorescent glow, herself gleaming and restless at the center of it all, and it seemed that her mysterious slash of sex glowed brightest of all through the sheet and quilt. She couldn't sleep. She listened to the rattle and tickle of the typewriter. By putting first one hand and then the other on the source of the luminescence, working them alternately, first one and then the other, she managed to make the light bright, bright, brighter, brightest, and then to turn if off, and then it seemed to her finally that she slept.

5

Gloria thought of the neighborhood as a giant windup toy. As soon as the key of dawn was turned into it, the dogs started working hard at the day's barking. Then the mothers, motorcycles, and junkers went into action; the trucks down Geary had kept things alive all night with their steady brooding roar. There must have been alarm clocks in every house, but what she heard were the mothers screaming at kids, the kids screaming back. Down the alley alongside Imperial Discount Records—"we live in an empire's parking lot"—the alley houses began to shake, as if their springs were being tightened. Actually, these days they were battery-powered.

Because he generally worked by night, slept by day, Dan avoided the regularity of this entertainment. Other late-shift husbands on the block—firemen, cops, a truck driver—also missed it. The wives of the night-working men sang their wakeup arias with a different rasp. Now the kids were fully awake and sore at the mothers who had caused this catastrophe. Sleep had been good enough for them, fully satisfactory; ending it was not. Much of the sound was in Chinese. An operatic vocalization sounded like destruction of the village. Despite the stubborn sleep of the fathers while women, children, and machinery were grinding up, there were still so many of the children, there were continually new ones. There must have been some anxious, tender, silent variation on this behavior which caused the exorable swelling of families. What Gloria heard every morning was family performance, not family privacy.

Just as Trish was central in her own life, probably the crowds of neighbor kids were not mere sleep-disturbing duties in the lives of their parents. Sure of this, Gloria stepped out the back door onto the wooden stairs with her coffee cup and gazed at the shadow moon, the ghostly crescent still visible as daylight took over. Here in the alley stretch of terrain grandfathered off from the Imperial back parking lot, Gloria shook out her hair to shed the last of night, let another day in. When her hair fell across her face, it looked like rain—brown, not silvery light as it used to be. It still turned that reddish silvery color in the summer, if she gave it some sun.

Gloria had a prayer she made every morning on the back steps to the God she no longer believed in. She shook out her hair and she wanted to be a good woman. Not merely good, but a good *woman.* No wonder she didn't dare mention it to anyone, since God was not listening and there was no one else to confide in. For Gloria Duggan Montberg, telling about her troubles, including this ambition she had, was a good example of *not* being a good woman.

She wanted also, explaining her prayer to herself—it was a morning prayer, not a night one—to be a considerate person who didn't lay her consideration on her

family as a burden. She wanted to be a wife and
mother in a world that had changed the rules. She
regretted this fact. She regretted many of the current
facts and habits of her daughter, her husband, her
brother-in-law, and the school where she taught. She
regretted how she both consented to the changed
rules and did not resist them enough.

Being a normal person, with plenty of prayers once
she got around to them, she also regretted the rough-
ening and fraying of her skin, which a short time ago
had been pink and sweet with the softness of youth,
sensitive to the rough tongue of Dan, her lover and
husband, playing on it. How at the same time she used
to tickle and shrink, giggle and cry out with pleasure,
was a mystery there was no more use praying over. Yet
the memory was as vivid as the fading crescent of the
moon over Imperial Discount Records. Why can't a
person be good and also keep the skin she used to own
forever? In California and San Francisco, everything
was supposed to be possible, although perhaps this law
didn't apply to the avenues, Richmond, and the Sunset.

She hoped that as her skin thickened, frayed, grew
tough with time, the desire within, which was untouched by use, might survive. Perhaps she could bear
to be an acceptable person with an average rough-
ened skin.

Oh, her desire, why did it seem forbidden to admit
it? She loved Trish. She loved Dan. That's two out of
two. Gloria wanted to agree with her life.

Gloria averted her eyes and hurried past the
twenty-four-hour Winchell Donuts, which even the
cab drivers avoided except for sugar emergencies.
("We Never Shut. Closed Tuesday.") Distorted by the
glass—so many street people crashed through these
windows, earning a night in a warm dry cell, why

replace them with high-quality glass?—her brother-in-law in his running costume, satiny shorts and T-shirt, was perched at a table on one of the attached pink plastic stools, attending to a paper plate of jelly-dappled puffs of fried grease. His head was bent; he was devoted. Sometimes Hutch joked about his eating habits, entirely San Francisco health except when he binged at Winchell's. All things were possible, by God. A donut shop could never close and yet be shut on Tuesdays. Sometimes Hutch even told the truth.

If she didn't stare, he wouldn't feel her presence through the glass. He did not look up. But then she scanned the acute memory in her head as she hurried on down the block toward her school. At this hour of the morning, after running at dawn in Golden Gate Park, he couldn't resist the Winchell's. Even Hutch, easy and fun-loving, wasn't in complete accord with himself.

She crossed Geary and came back down the block on the other side. She hid in the doorway to the Shamrock & Taiwan Unisex Salon. By this time Hutch was in the service alley alongside the Winchell's, leaning his forehead against the cool brick like an athlete stretching before his contest, except that there were no muscles in the forehead which needed stretching.

He stood up and gasped a little. Now he would hurry home to brush his teeth.

Bulimia, Gloria thought, and in a man; now that's interesting. She might share the news with Dan, but not with Trish. It was not kind of her to see this so clearly, to cross the street and hide in a doorway and consider how she would pass on the gossip. There was no need to explain to herself the good reasons for it. Morning prayers were over; the day was in progress.

The day was in progress; a person could just forget about her morning prayers, but hope some echo of them survived even through her sixth grade English class. Gloria asked Leonard Chung to remain in the room when the other kids clattered out.

"Do you understand plain English?" she said to the lanky twelve-year-old with the beginnings of a darkening on his upper lip. She was thinking: Not only do the Chinese grow bigger in this country, but also they grow mustaches earlier. "I said your paper could come in last Friday. It was already overdue. I gave you an extra week. Now it's late twice."

"Maybe do it next week," he answered.

"That's not good enough. It was supposed to be here today."

"Who says?"

"I said. *We* said. And now I'm asking you: That was plain English, wasn't it?"

The kid stared straight into her eyes. "Whyn't you learn plain Cantonese? That good enough for me, missy."

He meant the insult. He had measured how much insult he wanted and that was what he came up with.

"Okay, Leonard," Gloria said, "we're going to the principal's office."

"Don't think I want to."

"You're going," she said, and resisted the temptation to grab him. "We're going together."

She turned to pick up the sweater she had draped over a chair, and when she did this, in the reflection in the dusty window glass, she saw the boy dip his hand into her open purse. How could he do something so stupid, she thought, and it was not a question. How could I have left my purse open, and how stupid I am, she thought—the sniffles, Kleenex, forgetting the rules for a moment were not good enough.

When she turned back, he was waiting with a grin.

She looked into her bag to make sure. The change purse was gone.

"Come with me," she said. "I want you to come with me *now.* "

With the boy lounging at her side, she told Mr. Franklin's secretary, a gay white male with AIDS, she wanted to see him without any delay. Mr. Franklin was on the phone but would be right off. There would be a little delay. She stood with Leonard, ready to grab him if he tried to run. The boy didn't seem to suspect she might know about her purse.

"You may enter now," said Dennis.

Jovial, courtly, and annoyed, Mr. Franklin stood up behind his Board of Ed Class One Special Issue desk. "Mizz Montberg, what can I do for you on a busy Monday? This boy, what's your name?"

"Leonard Chung. Been in the school fi' years awready, I know *you* name, Mister Frank."

"Franklin," said the principal, and nodded at Gloria.

"It wasn't why I first wanted to bring him in here," Gloria said, "but he's got my change purse in his pocket."

"Wuh you say?" the boy asked.

"Look in his pocket," Gloria said.

Mr. Franklin sighed and turned to the boy.

"You gonna try search me without you got a search warren?" the boy asked. "Come on, just show you—"

And he took off, fleet and easy on his long American high-protein legs. Gloria and Mr. Franklin followed, down the halls to the classroom. Gloria was shaking with rage and Mr. Franklin was shaking his chins and muttering, "This is one of those hard deals, isn't it, Gloria?"

Leonard was in the classroom and pointing to the change purse on the floor as if it were a dead mouse. "Fell outa your purse, woman," he said.

"I think we better call the police," Gloria said.

"Go ahead! Go on! Show you prejudice!" Leonard said.

Mr. Franklin sighed. "Hey, hey, wait a sec. No need to carry on like that, Leonard." He studied Gloria and realized she would not relent, she was determined to make trouble, there was no use trying to pretend this didn't happen. It called for the wisdom of Solomon. It called for all the tact and understanding of a man brought into high office because of his knowledge, feeling, understanding, and the depth of experience with which he was endowed in a time of equal opportunity before the law.

Mr. Franklin kept on sighing, but that didn't keep history from its inexorable advance.

Gloria remembered her morning prayer. Her racing heart beat it out of her.

Mr. Franklin looked gloomily at Gloria, and said at last, since something had to be said and he was where the buck stopped: "Leonard, I think we better talk to your father." To Gloria he added, "You know the police, how they are, didn't actually find anything on his person, the whole goldarn deal we get ourselves into, just a lot of hassle—his dad'll straighten him out." And back to Leonard, severely, as if this were great punishment: "You know where your dad is now?"

"In the restaurant."

"You call him and tell him I want to see him right away and you let me talk to him."

The three of them strolled back to the principal's office. Mr. Franklin dialed nine, dialed the number, and handed the phone to the boy when the answer came in Cantonese. "He's in the kitchen," Leonard said.

"I want him on the phone."

Another melody in Cantonese.

"You don't leave here, son, until your dad shows up."

An operatic aria out of Leonard's face while Gloria stared at him. The boy hung up and said, "Pop coming right ovah. Hey, I'm not your son, Mistuh Frank."

Gloria stared at the boy, meaning he wasn't to move, and Leonard lounged with a tight little smile under his newly American-born little mustache. She had to hand it to the kid. He didn't bother arguing, he didn't bother running.

Mr. Franklin hated to start off the week with this sort of incident. "Sometimes it's so hard to do the right thing, Gloria. That's the bitch about this job."

"The bitch," Leonard said.

Gloria moved closer to the boy. She might pray in the early morning. In the later morning she was willing to fight.

Mr. Franklin made conversation while they waited. "This lingual situation I call it, bilingual, I guess I'm sorry I think it's necessary. First off in my upgrade, I used to wonder, but now I definitely think it's a definite plus in ack, ack, ack—" He leaned forward conspiratorially. "Acculturation, Gloria. We got more'n a melting pot here, Gloria, our pot runneth over. We got these illegals."

"What you callin me?" Leonard asked.

"We got these semilegals from Baja. We got these Spanish speakers from war-torn south of the border. We got the Congress, the churches, and all of Berkeley on our backs. We got the whole southeast Asia, the boats, the sampam people I call them—"

"You got no right to call me that," Leonard said.

The principal applied his slow burn look to the boy. "I'm talking to Mrs. Montberg," he said. Mr. Franklin might be an older man, but he still had plenty of time for interrelationship. He was a busy man in the school administration field, many details, reports, conferences, but school administration was his life and the practice of it his main sport. He waited for Leonard to lower his eyes. When the boy didn't, he said it anyway: "You're acculturated okay, Leonard. You're good with your hands."

There was a raised voice from Dennis, the secretary in the outer office, a shrillness and scuffle, and then the door flew open. A Chinese man in a cook's smock, with blood on his chest—perhaps it was a butcher or meat-chopper's smock—stood in the doorway carrying a large curved cleaver.

"Hey!" said Mr. Franklin. "You can't walk down the street like that!"

"What'd you tell your father?" Gloria asked Leonard.

The man moved toward them, talking rapidly in Cantonese as Mr. Franklin lumbered with heavy agility behind his desk. He was reaching for the telephone, practicing the words Nine One One.

"My pop just come from the kitchen," Leonard said. "He come from the restaurant in a hurry. He don't have no time to dress up for no PTA."

Another flood of Chinese sound.

"What's he saying?" Mr. Franklin asked.

Languorously the boy translated. "Says don't pick up that phone. Says why you pinch me, I didn't do nothing. Says I didn't have no purse, he's my pop he knows, he says why you do that just because my pop Chinese and don't speak much English. Says he a working man, take care of he family every which way."

Mr. Franklin remarked almost to himself, "What right has he to tell me not to pick up my own phone if I want to?"

"I think he has a right," Gloria said. "He just came from cutting meat and he still has his equipment."

Leonard's father was shouting and waving the knife.

"I guess he has every right," Mr. Franklin said. And then, as a responsible leader of the varied little community represented here, he stretched out his arms to those tempest-tossed on these shores from every distant clime of the world, remarking, "With the aid of a

little warmth and compassion, I'm sure we can all settle this problem together, absent the police or anything mess us up like that, including even your typical
social worker. Perhaps, if the idea appeals to us, a small
amount of temporary counselling by a minority group
member of your, not my minority group, Mr. Chung,
which would not in any case interfere with any after-
school activities your son has in mind. . . . He wasn't
caught red-handed. The purse was on the floor. I'm
willing to stipulate that. We only have one witness, this
here nervously distraught lady teacher who is, I assure
you, a dedicated member of her profession—"

Leonard's father sang out, but the blade no longer
flashed in the dust-blown air of Mr. Franklin's office.
Still holding the cleaver, he crossed his arms, shyly
hiding some of the blood spots on his smock.

Leonard translated for his father, doing the cross-
cultural duty of the younger generation. "My pop say
you fulla shit, but now he got to go back to work. I tole
him everything cool. He going back to work."

"That's wonderful. That's *wonderful*," said Mr.
Franklin. "Ask him sometime, you get a chance, just
talking things over, what possibility is they might
bring a culinary workers' union into the Cantonese
Restaurant Tong or Society dealings. I understand
that's a big issue among you people."

"Not for him it ain't," Leonard said.

Beaming, gleaming with administrative sweat, Mr.
Franklin bowed the devoted father and his son out the
door. He rubbed his palms together and looked to
Gloria for confirmation of how well he had handled a
tricky little situation which was similar to those he had
previously faced in Oakland inner-city deals. A person
never knew what could happen in one of these cultural situations. He now planned to resolve the last
little tag end of trouble here by appealing to Mrs.
Montberg. "Thank you, Gloria," he said, "I really ap-

preciate your help. I think you reacted with, uh, great frankness."

Gloria's knees were weak. Fear and rage always tended to loosen the joints. They also tended to do things to the digestion, the heartbeat, and the legs, which were the first to go in this school district. She found difficulty in finding words. She found words, but noticed difficulty in using them. She wanted to tell Mr. Franklin he was a creep and probably the right man for his job.

"By frankness," he was saying, "what I mean by that, Gloria, is how you made it clear your feelings in the matter—after all, a woman's purse is her home— but also you understand the problems in our little community concerning . . ."

"Acculturation?" she asked.

"Chinese folks," he said. "Now that the problem has been moving on upward concerning the young people in this town of my color which I personally happen to be . . . black," he reminded her, "those of us who happen to be of that color . . . black in my case . . . inherit the duty to help our skinny little yellow brothers. See what I mean? Being white and all, a woman, subject to sexism like the middle classes do, you see what I mean?"

"That's got nothing to do with it."

"Gloria," he said. "This boy. This Chinese kid trying to be wild. I was a boy so long ago but I still don't forget. I can't expect you to know, you just see a big old fat man couple years away from his retirement, a *black* big old fat man, Gloria. . . . How can I explain?" He extended his hands with the pink and purplish palms, trying to pull the truth out of the air for both of them. "Gloria, in a hundred years, how much will it matter, child?"

He waited.

"You want to say something, Gloria?"

He had his own griefs. He understood about Gloria's rage. His eyes were asking her only to tell him she understood something of what he went through.

"I've been meeting lots of philosophers lately, Mr. Franklin," she said. "I was hoping you wouldn't get to be one, too."

He gave her a grateful smile. Suddenly she could see the wild boy buried there someplace in all that flesh. "Thank you, Gloria," he said. "It ain't philosophy, just tired."

Gloria went to the Faculty Women's Lounge to wash her face, her arms, under her arms. She wadded up paper towels and did the best she could. She sat a moment, jiggling her coin purse like a bean bag, on one of the two cots covered with grayish sheets, meant for teachers who felt faint. The official public school view was still that women teachers were more subject to the vapors than men, needful of refined withdrawal. The Faculty Men's had no cots, no gray sheets freshly laundered for each school year.

She did not lie down. She removed her blouse and began again systematically, wadding up the towels, dabbing under her arms, wadding up another handful. In the mirror she peered at the flesh which Mr. Chung had threatened to cut. As a butcher he would know the right place for carving, unless there was a different protocol for irate parent only wanting to speak up for his son.

Gloria's body was thickening at this time in her life; there was meat where there didn't use to be meat. Dan, despite his sedentary job, was growing leaner, even stringy, with a paring-down by time. His brother was working on leanness in his own way, developing knotty runner's thighs, pumping away white-lipped on the mayor's Marina running track near the yacht basin along the bay. Hutch had made them come to

the mayor's Marina running track inauguration ceremony and the Celebrity Run. He even got Gloria and
Dan to circle the track with him once, after he had
already done four miles, and they listened as he
proved he could run and drop names at the same time:
"Sure I helped the mayor raise the money"—not losing pace or breath, not puffing—"raise the money for
this track"—breathing regularly, not breaking stride
—"facility, from my friends at City Sports and—"—his
T-shirt soaked through the letters that said YEAR OF
THE RUNNER—"and the Pepsi Bottler TriAthalon
sponsors, uh, I wouldn't let them give me credit"—
exhaling hard, with a little snort—"except a couple
T-shirts." Grinning, turning a little half-stride toward
Dan and Gloria before they peeled off and he continued the celebratory run: "I give five hundred dollars
anonymous!"

Flakes of Chap Stick dropped from his mouth. Herpes simplex is a problem for those who appreciate the
California sun.

"What do they actually do," Gloria had asked as they
watched the crowd of runners, "when the Running
Commission meets? What business do they transact?
They decide to put one foot in front of the other?"

"Maybe Jogging for Hispanics," Dan said.

"They don't say *Jogging*. Jogging is not the word."

"Running," said Dan.

"Third World Parcourse Day. Beats me. Closes the
meeting with a silent prayer that no one ever men-
tions how he's a big man in fitness in this town."

Gloria gave herself a shot of grin in the mirror and
then decided that, yes, she felt a little vaporish. Just a
few minutes on the cot to get the blood back into her
head.

That night, after Trish retreated to her bedroom to
do whatever she did when she locked her door, Gloria
told Dan about Leonard Chung, Leonard Chung's fa-

ther, and Mr. Franklin. She didn't think Trish needed to hear about it. She needed Dan to know. "Remember when we were kids?" she asked.

"Yeah."

"I mean later, the end of the sixties. I mean when good old Charlie Franklin would have talked about his karma. I don't think *acculturation* is any improvement."

"I still see that around town, karma and dharma," Dan said. "I'm driving along and I see Karma or Dharma on a storefront, but this is the law now. Anything got that word on it, it also has the words For Rent, For Sale, or Part of Your Redevelopment Commission Project. The paisley part of it is *gone.*"

"I think I might want to take early retirement, Dan. I'm about worn out."

He lowered his eyes because he knew he was about to lie. "Go ahead, that's fine."

"As soon as Trish gets through school. College. Or maybe she'll want to work first, and then—"

"By that time I'll finish my book. I'll have an agent. I'll get a publisher."

As always, their rule for their life together, Gloria showed no doubts about this long obsession winding its way like a snake through their marriage. "Of course you will," she said. He had written enough for five novels, but they didn't add up to one, not yet. "You're going to have something . . ." She liked to tell the truth when she could: ". . . something unique, everyone knows that."

He grinned and shrugged. "Just about everyone does."

"Maybe I could get a part-time job with the city— doesn't the Running Commission need a former English teacher? To explain to the public why real runners don't say *jogging*?"

Dan laughed uneasily; he wasn't sure if Gloria really

meant to suggest using Hutch to find a job. "He's more likely to be interviewing retired flight attendants who major in Parcourse Management at Foothill College. Because they're looking for a new career track. Are you serious?"

Gloria poured them both more coffee. Whether they drank it or not, this meant the conversation should continue. Something had happened that morning, before her adventure with Mr. Franklin and the Chung family, that had gotten her to thinking. She told about seeing Hutch at the Winchell Donuts on Geary. "What kind of sex does he like?" she asked.

"I think it's the Variety Pack—why? What does that have to do with it?"

She looked at his hands. He had made a joke, but his hands were clenching. "The Variety Pack—does it include anything like love?"

"That's just another flavor," Dan said, "that's the flavor Hutch has a few problems with. So he goes on a sugar binge sometimes after he runs—what're you saying?"

"I was thinking of him in the alley next to Winchell's and his little white car parked next to the fire hydrant—"

"He doesn't pay his tickets. I guess he doesn't have to, it's a point of pride."

"That alley's a lonely place. That skinny boy's body. Those dry lips. He's burning. Maybe besides the pride, there's a soul in there someplace—"

"There is!" Dan said.

"He's your big brother. There must be. Something that makes him go throw up in an alley because—"

"Maybe he just ate too many donuts," Dan said. When they spoke of Hutch, he sometimes just checked out. He went his own way. She understood about a younger brother's brooding; at least she tried to accept it as a condition of their lives; but still Dan surprised her. He wasn't thinking about Russian journalists or donut binges or running tracks or money. He was thinking about why his elder brother had gotten so far ahead of him, had always seemed to start out and continue ahead of him. "He lacks the gift of hesitation," Dan said. "He's sure of himself even when he doesn't know what the hell's happening, where things'll come out."

"It shouldn't work for him."

"This is California, this is San Francisco. It works."

"A lot of times it doesn't."

"People have confidence in such a person."

"I don't."

"Well, you're my wife." Dan gave her that little half-smile from the left corner of his mouth.

"I hate him," she said, "for . . . he's so sure of his ignorance."

"I've always wanted some of that. Oh, I could use it, Gloria. I think he got all the certainty in our family."

"Hate," said Gloria. "I don't mean that. Maybe not hate. I think he really cares about us. What I mean . . ."

"See?" Dan asked. "You and me, we hesitate. Hutch doesn't."

There was a blast of sound from the speakers in Trish's room. Sometimes Trish preferred not to use the headphones, and when she felt like that, she preferred to let her parents enjoy the music with her, whether they wanted to or not. Gloria and Dan waited a moment. Maybe she would turn it down. Dan claimed the heavy metal blasts of sound brought the termites dancing right up out of the foundations of the house, waving their mandibles and bumping each other off the little mounds of wood dust.

Trish had her mind made up. She did not turn it down. Not all the certainty and determination in the family had been given to Hutch. When it came to important matters, Trish seemed to have her own stash.

Falling in love is a populous mystery, all about richness and entanglement, but falling out of love is another mystery and Gloria would have liked to leave it unexplored—a desert, a drought, a heated emptiness where once there were intricate and fertile joinings. The man who was once beloved looks at the woman who loved him and she stares back blankly, dryly, indifferently. A world has become airless, a moonscape of dead lava after eruption.

Ah, she thought, no. It's just time that passes. Those were only feelings we thought we had. Now we understand the feelings have worn thin and they are out of warranty.

Gloria's cool blue gaze upon Dan. She used to see that little half-smile at the corner of his mouth as ironic, as dear, as a shy and clever observer's smile, with secret jokes to share. Now it was a loser's smile. She felt pity for her husband. Maybe she still loved him in the only way possible for old lovers—she cared about him. This only meant she had lived twenty years with his desire and his suffering, his weary ambition. And she was not yet ready for resignation in mere care for him. She saw his sallowness, she smelled his age, she understood him as she understood herself. She knew she understood nobody, nothing.

Oh it's sad, she thought. *They once were in love and they're not anymore.* It's too simple and too much to bear.

She looked at his dear face with the lines and squintings and frayings she always forgot until she summoned him back again, sometimes in the dark, sometimes making love, and remembered. Her breast burned with the desire to hold him, remember, populate the desert again. It was too sad.

Gloria considered whether she should try praying at night, too, as well as in the morning. Oh, she loved Dan, she did, no matter what she thought. She did love Trish and Dan. It was just that, at this time in her life, she loved no one.

6

Hutch disliked to be pressured about matters of principle, such as love and business. Those were places where a man should try to do just what he wants to do, be himself, but take women: art museums and other people sometimes put pressure on him with those old-type pictures, hanging flesh, huge boobs with violet nipples, from before women learned to get nervous, independent, and fit. Hutch wasn't influenced.

Once, on a Sunday afternoon, when he happened to be in a state of privacy and found himself on the terrace at Enrico's, his living room in San Francisco, Hutch had a weak moment. It was a heat spell, one of those September days people aren't prepared for. He invited a woman who was overweight back to his place to see the view, the sunset, try a new Chardonnay. Afterwards, when she sat naked on his leather couch, hot and sweaty, he learned something. A woman like that leaves the mark of a snail. As he told Kenny, the waiter, the next day: honest to God.

It was the last time he violated his principles. Even Kenny understood that love is a place where a person shouldn't listen to anyone, just his own free heart, let the chips fall where they may (careful of diseases, though). When his heart pounded over a long-legged worn-out blond, Hutch liked to practice deep breathing in order to preempt rejection by her. Then, if a Suki said, "What do I want with you, buster?" which sometimes happened, he could still the pounding in his chest—the same pounding he felt when he visited Ray Aratunian—inhaling, exhaling, creating an invisible armor of good vibes all around him.

Zen was great for Hutch. Few knew about his Zen side. He used it when he didn't have time for a run, as now, when Ray Aratunian was exploring options, possibilities—it seemed more like putting pressure. Ray could be more annoying than a fat woman. Ray's group was sitting there without an idea in their heads, but Ray had lots of ideas.

Don't call them ideas. As far as Hutch was concerned, it felt like pressure, the kind of thing he didn't enjoy too much.

"Can you get the bank to renegotiate the loan?"

"You know they don't like to do it on a signature basis, Ray. They say the statutes, after they got their appraisal, the new downtown plan—you know how banks are."

"Yeah. No imagination." Ray sighed. "Okay, how about some income out of it on a temporary basis, like a parking lot?"

"Good idea, I thought of it already—"

"Just, you know, for cash flow purposes. We could help you find a kid, make a sign, someone else, a black guy, wave 'em in from the street. A little piddle here and there might help."

"Sure. Trouble is, Ray, there's lots of parking down there already."

"Then that's not too helpful, is it, Hutch?" Ray pressed his lips together and seemed to be humming a little. "I'll tell you, Hutch, you add the interest to the principal, this exponential is killing us, plus the bank is butting in there ahead, right?"

"You're talking about the increment," Hutch said.

"I think we understand each other."

He waited to give Hutch all the time in the world for a prompt answer.

"My brother needs a good investment," Hutch said.

"Not that it's my business or family, but will you explain this to your brother?"

"Sure. He doesn't understand business. That's not his strong suit."

"You should suit him up, man. Maybe you should take some of your valuable time to explain, even sacrifice some of the important work and play time. Personally, I try to educate myself every day, exponentially, read an H & R Block manual if I have to. That's my heartfelt opinion, Hutch."

Hutch looked at the others. No one moved. Hutch's face was pale and sweating and his voice shot around like a teenager's. "Can you get blood from a stone, Ray?"

Ray grinned. "I always told you this is America, didn't I? How come you don't know where you are, Hutch? I been drawing the map for you."

"You can't get blood from a stone," Hutch said.

Ray shook his head. "Hutch, it would be so nice if you listened to people. I guess you're gonna be talking to your brother the saintly investor."

"Danny, hey, got a previously satisfied client for you —knows when you come on shift."

"It's a small town, Fran."

"Must really like you, Danny."

Face to face, Fran's voice crackled almost as much as

it did on the low-fi taxi radio. She was grinning at him from her communications cage. She was eating a tunafish sandwich for breakfast; he could smell it, along with the rubbery smells of taxi radio equipment.

Rubbing his cheeks awake, scraping palms along the rasp of last night's shave, Dan reached through the grill to pick up the keys for his cab. Fran tickled his palm, scrunched up her nose, and looked cute enough to kill. "I think those FM waves doing brain damage," Dan said.

"Trying to keep up with my drivers' private lives do me enough damage already," said Fran. "Make me a wreck."

The KorVet Garage, a low building south of Market on Ninth, was in a district where most warehouses were no longer warehouses, machine shops no longer made tools, dies, or valves, repair garages had become artists' living spaces or discos or mixed-media laboratories. Next door, the long-running hit, *Audience Go-Go!,* starred a cast which sat in attentive rows, while the ticket-holders were handed masks—black-faced minstrels, nixons and reagans, a Carol Channing for those who wanted to start in show business at the top —and asked to perform a life of their mutual choice. The cast pulled bags onto their laps and pelted the audience with suggestions, insults, and small vegetables. People returned because the show tended to change every night.

For Fran, keeping the radio instructions, personal banter, and the car assignments in proper balance was a bit of performance art, too. She needed her fun. Dan's job would have been a mixed media event, except that it also happened to be how he paid his bills. Now was the time in his life to take things as they were, a way he had been studying, so he should get around to doing so. The Zen of Cab Driving. The Tao of Under-Tippers. He was a novelist who happened to be driving for a while, that was how he preferred to think.

Better to take things as they really were: he was a hacker like a couple dozen others in San Francisco who wished they could be writers, actors, filmmakers. The law of averages being what it was, only a few of them made it to true greatness.

"Hey Danny," said the radio woman, "hear me now, loud and clear."

"That's your way, Fran."

"This request for you by name and number and didn't mention headroom. Ooh, bet you're pretty when you wanna make nice."

"Fran, cut the games. I didn't wake up yet."

But she was still grinning and pulling toggle switches and actually dunked her tunafish sandwich in her cold coffee to make it nicer to chew. "Call come in an hour ago, must of spent a sleepless night thinking about you, wants Danny M. and only him to pick up at the Brasserie in twenty minutes. Sounded kinda cute. I guess you must be cute, too—get your cute ass over there in a nice big Checker."

This didn't happen often, although some of the drivers had old lady shoppers and hospital visitors who were regular passengers, usually strict ten-percent tippers and a general pain in the butt (carry packages, hold open doors, help up stairways). Ten percent plucked in silver from snap purses out of the St. Anthony's Cloisters Sale. And a few of the drivers had, claimed to have, regular women who asked them to drive out to Fort Point or under the Golden Gate Bridge and climb into the back seat with them. They either tipped a whole lot or tried to make it without paying the fare at all—that's what the guys said; personally, it wasn't Dan's scene. He always thought the ones who wanted to be taken under the bridge for a quick sexing were close relatives of the ones who wanted to go over the bridge, *hey stop here driver,* and then jumped out and across the rail before anyone could stop them.

Jumped toward the shore, not the wide ocean, because it was more homey.

Personally, when he saw a possible suicide in his vehicle, he had a practice of describing the bodies netted up from the Bay—no glamorous wispy faces with grieving relatives in the picture, like you'd think, but cops averting their eyes as the stiff (the soggy) was fished out with eyeballs gone and crabs feeding happily on the juicy exposed flesh. "To this," he informed the dispatcher, "I ascribe my Joe DiMaggio record of not a single bridge-jumper."

"Yucch," said Fran, "watch your mouth, I guess it's your imagination, but watch it, okay? And who was Joe DiMaggio? I only follow the Forty-Niners."

"They didn't give a name asked for me?" Dan said.

"Naw, I told you, Brasserie seven-twenty, must of couldn't sleep or up all night just thinking about it, Danny boy. I said sounded cute, didn't I?" She paused and then snickered into her mike. She had left it open for every KorVet driver within range. "Only thing is, it's a man, Danny."

"Great, Fran."

"Hey, wake up. Not suppose to drive less you're cheerful and the urine is free of drugs—management don't care about your brain."

Since he was a former beatnik, a man of culture and a rich inner life, a working novelist, a husband and father who hadn't used speed since 1973 and then only by mouth, never by needle, a person of great forbearance and deep griefs which he generally omitted from displaying to his dispatcher, Dan grinned and did not reply in the words of the morning farewell called for in the taxi industry, his chosen field of commercial endeavor: Fuck off.

"Hey!" Fran yelled as he moseyed down toward his green-and-yellow Checker. "You forgot something, sweetie."

Dan felt for his keys, wallet, license; his city permit with the photo were already hanging in the cab. He had forgotten to ask the name of the fare, but they always had that where's-my-cab, why's-he-late expression on their faces. Non es problema. "What'd I forget?"

Fran yelled into the mike and down the cement cavern toward him. "You forgot to say Fuck off, cunt."

And then static and drivers calling in distracted her from the early morning dose of contagious dispatcher humor which kept everybody on his or her toes or at least on other people's. Fran had worked for KorVet longer than Dan. If she couldn't partake of a little noonsie with him, at least she could hone her skills as a radio therapist. When she retired, with all her commercial FM experience behind her, she planned to go on KPOO with a call-in show. That would be about the same time Dan finished his novel.

The Fairmont lay across Nob Hill with its wings and spires from various real estate epochs, deposed monarch baroque, resort sensuous, Mies-Mondrian moderne, art deco and deco without art. The glassy elevator module crawled tirelessly up and down the checkered shaft of the newest tower. Only city planners admitted vertigo; conventioners admitted to thrills. Dan admitted the crown of Nob Hill was a bit more imperial, spread across its domain, than Imperial Discount Records out on Geary. It made a fellow feel relieved to see the great hotel looming ahead because fares from the Mark or the Fairmont seldom asked to be taken to Hunter's Point, the killing field for drivers, although sometimes they wanted homesick fun, girls or gambling. It was too early for museums; maybe a board meeting or a power breakfast.

The fare wouldn't be Dr. Alonzo, the distinguished former surgeon in his gray flannel pants, tweed jacket with leather patches on the sleeves, cold pipe in the mouth, a cheery, "Good day, sir!" who kept Dan's number and name on a slip of paper in his pocket for when he needed to be returned to the Alzheimer's hospice. More likely some melancholic former spouse or an insomniac remittance person. In recent months Dan hadn't heard from Dr. Alonzo, who once had said, "Call you sir because it's only polite. Your name just escapes me at the moment. But I think it's a good policy to keep up standards, don't you, sir?"

With that funny low-high floating sensation which Dan got an hour after too much wakeup coffee, and therefore seemed to get every morning these days, he steered up the curving driveway past the burly doormen in their Chilean general epaulets and tassels and their helpful tip-promoting smiles. His fare stood waiting outside with a big grin on his face, dressed in one of his best Italian suits, all drape and silken, as if the night before were continuing forever. There was a tangerine handkerchief billowing from Hutch's pocket. Now what the devil was this about.

"I don't want you to high-flag," Hutch said. "This is your working time and I want to pay for my ride."

"Shit man, tell me which festival you're celebrating now."

"Think of it as therapy for me, not you, and I want to be taken someplace—hey come on, it's like a joke, okay? On the level?"

Dan stared from his seat a moment, leaning his elbow on the window. Then he got out and, with the most egalitarian and democratic and American shadow of an obsequious little bow, opened the rear

door for his fare. He stood there with an imaginary
visored cap pressed to his chest.

Hutch smiled approvingly. He paused to take his
memory snapshot of the event, and then opened the
door to the passenger seat in front, pushed aside the
Chronicle, the notebook, the receipt pad, and a couple
of stubs of pencil, and slid in with only a glance to see if
there was any danger of soiling his pants. There was;
the cabs sat in a grit-blown garage. For a special event
Hutch could ignore the risks, since dry cleaning is
always an available option. "Driver," he said, "I'd like
to see Golden Gate Park. Actually, I haven't had the
pleasure of the buffalos since I was a kid—take me to
the buffalos."

Dan gunned the motor and pulled screeching out of
the curved Fairmont approach. "Hey, easy," said the
fare.

"Actually, sir," Dan said, "the buffalo in Golden
Gate Park are American bison. That's the real name
for them. The park was painstakingly constructed on
drifting sand dunes by a Scottish gardener and is one
of the seven wonders of the West, including several
museums, man-made lakes, windmills, what we call
microclimates in the fog and sun strips, an arboretum
which actual foreign tourists travel from afar to visit—
Scots and Italians only the other day—"

"Painstakingly," said Hutch. "Imagine that. Scotch
and Eye-talians. Fancy that."

It was easy to drift into their childhood game of
speeching past each other. Dan wasn't going to ask
what Hutch was up to because he would have to un-
ravel, if possible, a straight story out of whatever un-
straight one Hutch finally chose to tell. That was the
usual procedure. While waiting, Dan described the
Aquarium, the DeYoung Museum with its collection of
oriental treasures (Hutch enacted a frantically bored
tourist's yawn), Hippie Hill with its dopers and histori-

cal connections to the age of hair and paisley and acid (Hutch perked up a little, remembering good times). "Nowadays," Dan said, "there are refugees from Cambodia and Vietnam who hunt dogs, cats, and smaller animals in the park for, uh, excuse me, sir, protein purposes."

"I can take it," Hutch said. "Lay it on me with no holes bar, fella. I can stand to hear what our little Third World brethren are doing to our big fat Frisco wildlife —making steak, are they? Serving crunchy sweet-and-sour rat?"

"And then in the wilderness, where there are tangles of trees and vines and vegetation from all over—"

"Australia?"

"Australia too. Out toward Ocean Beach."

Hutch whistled but didn't say, Fancy that. Dan knew it was implied—he had fallen in love with the words after a double-feature they saw together one Saturday afternoon just after Hutch had begun to shave and Dan hadn't yet. A beginning of mustache, a long wintry Saturday afternoon drill in chic and sex and England; *fancy that.*

"As I was saying, they grow herbs and veggies in cleared spaces in the deep tangles out near the windmills. There are slopes where nobody goes. They grow bulbs, tubers. It's guerrilla gardening. The city gardeners tend to rip it up when they find it, but mostly they get away with it."

"So protein *and* fiber," said Hutch, "a balanced diet. They root around?"

"That's the enterprise of our new citizens and illegal immigrants, sir."

"An inspiration to those of us who are settled in our unimaginative ways, is it not? Rats and turnips—a balanced diet."

"It takes people off the welfare roles, or if it doesn't, it means they have a few luxuries at no cost to the

American taxpayer. They don't plant grass, no cash crops. They're law-abiding citizens of the Mekong Delta."

Hutch fluffed up his handkerchief and glanced at the meter. "Food stamps plus all the legal rats and turnips they can grow. Do you think our native underfolks ever consider such things? Oh, I know all about the occasional garden in a back lot or those garage sales—hey driver, you can high-flag it the rest of the way. I'll make it up to you."

Dan threw the arm on his meter.

"No point in some Mafia taxi mongol getting rich on us, hey? I'll settle with you and we can split the difference."

Dan had read about dyslexia, which was associated with intelligence, he had heard, and now he thought Hutch's funny words, like *mongol* for *mogul,* was a form of impacted wisdom in the ganglia of the brain. Impacted ganglia in the wisdom of the brain. "Maybe it runs in families," he said aloud.

"What? What about running?"

"I might get soft, Hutch, but you might get shin splints."

Click. The game was over. Hutch didn't answer because he wasn't sure if the game was really over. He liked to decide that question himself, when it was important to end it. "Never run on concrete or sidewalks, personally," he said. "My only vice is Winchell donuts that I'll cop to."

"The Panhandle. It's a strip of park that leads into the master park."

"Master park, I like that. Be a good name for a structure. Master Park, no in or out, twelve bucks a day, or monthly rental. . . . You'll never get soft in your lifetime, Dan, not with that brain of yours working overtime." He grinned. "Plus your body. Jeez, man, with a family plus a novel-writing habit to support, why didn't you become a screenwriter, hey? Not that it's maybe too late, is it?"

"Another line is what I'm inclined to," Dan said.

He stopped the cab and, with the motor shut off, in the sudden park silence, he asked his brother to look. Hutch looked but couldn't exactly see what Dan saw, fog hanging in wisps over trees bending away from the salt winds off the ocean. How could he know what to see when Dan didn't give him the information? Puzzled. Hutch asked what was that. High-legged birds were strutting in a line across a meadow. Dan answered that he thought it was peacocks, at least it wasn't ducks. Yup. No hurry to carry on with a rational conversation at this point. It was like being in the jungle, the country, the park, another time in their lives. It was pretty, the fog and those birds with the high skinny long legs.

The smell of sea was strong. From the west, where the salt wind blew, some of the trees had salt-stunted limbs. Hutch was grinning about the long legs on a tired peacock. The brothers were not seeing the same things, but they were in the same place here, they were together. Years before they had been taken to the merry-go-round by their mother. Dan remembered that she called it a carousel and Hutch, although he was older, believed he didn't remember her at all. Later Hutch and Dan used to come out here on their bicycles and watch the birds strut and the thick amazing animals Dan wanted to show him now. "So here's the meadow with the buffalo."

"The American bison," said Hutch. "Knew a Russian once, but I'm patriotic, I'm willing to learn."

Was that an apology?

They got out of the cab and strolled from the park drive down the little slope toward the fence encircling the buffalo meadow. The animals stood there almost without moving, like carved objects in a theme land-

scape, except that a person could see the flanks shifting slightly as the bellows worked, the objects
breathed, shit slid and tumbled behind the tails, just
behind the breathing; the yellowish eyes, moribund,
protected by slime from the fresh salt air which blew
from the ocean nearby, paid no attention to the visitors. They were used to company.

The brothers stood there, watching. Dan liked the
swaying critters—no, they didn't sway, that was his
mind that swayed for them. Their massiveness was a
satisfaction to him. It was unlike anything he knew in
his own life—that mottled hairy presence, those ignor-
ing sly eyes, the wisdom of uncaring. He had brought
Trish out here to see the beasts, smell the air, and then
go to Ocean Beach for a pizza, which was the part she
liked best. She would learn, he hoped; as a child, she
had liked animals.

He glanced at Hutch. "Don't look like any nickel I
ever had in my pocket," Hutch said. "Ain't a silver one
among them."

Out here, at this season, with the valley heating up
east of San Francisco, the fog was sucked in across the
park; thermal inversion, Dan thought and didn't mention; a chill came into the air as they stood, and the sun
disappeared behind streamlets and strips of fog.
Hutch shivered and buttoned his jacket. Dan decided
to wait. Whatever he had on his mind, Dan was in no
hurry. Hutch was his only brother. Besides Gloria and
Trish, there was no other family.

Hutch cleared his throat. "Didn't you used to tell
me, last time we came out here, the summer winter
we have in San Francisco off the ocean, it comes from
thermal perversion?"

Dan laughed. His elbow made the kind of little leap
that was Hutch's trick, made as if to jab him in the side,
but didn't complete the circuit. The brothers only had

each other's habits in embryo. That was still a way of
having them.

"See, I remember things you tell me," Hutch said.
"Must have been ten-fifteen years ago. I was just starting out in the real estate syndication field, maybe a few
years too late for the really big money but you can still
make a payday now and then. You were a veteran
driver and writer and you had a kid already. I had
what's her name, Pauli, the half-oriental chicklet, the
only girl got expelled from Bard College for misbehavior, man I did love her oriental misbehavior—you
were a big expert on Bay Area Velcro Climate."

Microclimate. This time Hutch knew what he was
doing: make the brother laugh, then have his soft attention.

"Hutch," Dan said, "I got a shift to run here. I really
can't play. Can you tell me what's on your mind?" His
brother wanted something from him. With the acute-
ness of a man on the alert against want, Dan stood near
the buffalo and thought with astonishment: Admiration, an audience, and he wants a brother's love, too.

This surprised him. It interrupted the theatrical de-
tachment. It confused him with gratitude and a rush of
warmth. His brother needed him. "Hutch," he said, "I
told you I got a shift to run here. Why don't you say it?"

"Okay. Okay!" But he didn't.

"Hutch, it just came out that way. I don't care, let's
take the whole goddamn day together."

Hutch grinned and poked him. "I keep trying to tell
you. We have to make it celebrate for us. So let's just
see what comes out, okay?"

But of course that wasn't his plan. His plan was to
move around until he felt comfortable. He was impatient, but that didn't mean he was going to hurry. Like
any other good runner, he understood about pacing
himself.

Hutch chose, at this moment, to stand and learn

American bison. He was willing to play with his brother, try another angle on American bison. When he walked, he bent his back in what seemed like earnest stiffness, but it was the discomfort of his health. Running had given him the pared-down look he liked, but it had also given him back trouble, shin splints, knees and hips which did not bounce and swivel as they used to. He had lost his boyish loping stride, although he ran faster than he had in college, when he was carrying the burdens of muscle and adolescence. Now he carried a few selected calcium deposits. The white flakes on his lips were a peeling together of Chap Stick and sunburn. He was told not to lick his lips; it only made the problem worse; he glanced at Dan and licked his lips and Dan did not remind him. It was not a younger brother's duty to lecture a man who was successful in San Francisco and America about the licking of lips, Winchell's donuts, or the failures of linkage with the past and future. When life is a festival, a person has to pay the price, a few calcifications on the moving parts.

Ah, if I even understood him, Dan thought. Maybe it's not even the present he's married to.

If I could even be coherent about my brother, I could put my own things together, my book, my daughter, my wife. And he considered the further thought that everything is connected and a clear accounting with Hutch would be a clear accounting.

Hutch was giving him little smiling sideways glances, waiting for him to settle the discussion which really only included Dan and Dan. For Hutch, the power model, cool, patient, and satisfied, was better than all that eager, I-insight-you, let's-get-into-this style. He's right, Dan thought, folks really don't tell— Hutch turned out to be right about that, although he noised up the not telling with a lot of words.

Today Hutch knew when not to interrupt the silence with jabber. His usual procedure, coming against a bit of quiet seething in the world, was to chatter and tease and make jokes and flatter and send up so many signals that all a person could think was, Oh, what a nice harmless bright skinny fellow this is. And then give him what he wanted, whatever he was aiming, at this moment, for any or no good reason, to get.

A bicyclist dressed like an intricate bug—ribbed helmet, goggles, shiny orange shell, sinewy legs pumping —sped by on the canted curve of drive and turned his head briefly toward them from his four-hundred-dollar, seventeen-pound Gitane Tour de France with the fifty-dollar, fifteen-pound chain draped from the saddle—he turned bug-faced, bug-bodied, with a look of Frisco astonishment: Here were two guys talking in the park when they could be working out! Everyone else had purposeful movements, but here were two guys *hovering* with each other!

Inspired by speed and strength and contact with God the Aerobic that comes with sustained exercise, he screamed: "Faggots!"

The intent brothers didn't respond. A buffalo lifted slow heavy shoulders in slow negligent denial.

The buffalo used to own the West, but could at least still shit all over this meadow. Hutch and Dan didn't have all day, even if they took it. The grass grew in thick tufts, thanks to devoted fertilization, except where hoofs trampled or muzzles munched. The buffalo were natural ecologists. They patiently followed the wear in the terrain. At last Hutch sighed; Dan didn't like his brother's sighs; in the past they were mostly theater, as at their parents' funerals or the birth of Trish. But maybe this sigh was just a breath after holding his breath and waiting. He was looking at the bent orange-shell back of the bicyclist scooting up John F. Kennedy Drive. He was looking at Dan. Then he was asking his younger brother without beginning or ending the sentence with *hey:* "Ever wonder why we were born?"

"Both of us for the same reason," Dan said.

Hutch grinned and poked his brother on the shoulder. The tangerine silk handkerchief billowed like a parachute from his jacket pocket. Dan had difficulty connecting such questions, why are we here and what does it mean, with a tangerine silk parachute handkerchief looming larger than the face above it. But no law said the big questions couldn't be well-dressed with a flowing silk in the jacket pocket. The unmeek weren't specifically barred from inheriting the earth—there was just no special provision for them. And Hutch's taking worried thought, still with that confident grin on his face, was a sign. Dan wanted, how could he not want, to believe in this brother who was kind and teasing with Trish and was his only brother.

"Both of us for the same reason!" Hutch repeated, trying out the line, appreciating Dan's cleverness, even if it wasn't funny at all, as he always did when he wanted to be agreeable. "Hey! I'll bet that means something Zen. I also bet it doesn't answer the question."

"Like everyone else, a couple of future parents or maybe only one of them took a little pleasure—"

"Hey! I'll bet Mom *liked* it, Danny."

Dan tried to remember back before his own birth, even before Hutch's. As usual, such memories were only a movie, only a review of the movie. "Maybe Mom and Dad loved each other. I seem to recall a whole collection of letters, a scrapbook—"

"The question didn't come up those days, hey Danny? Not like now, where you grit your teeth and love onward and upward, right?"

Dan felt his brother was smarter than he let himself be. He liked it when the older brother teasing got smart, liked it less when it was only smartass. "And you, Hutch—"

"Tell me."

"—hold out for the perfect tired blond of thirty-nine but looks twenty-two unless you turn on the lights."

Hutch rubbed his thighs. "The legs don't get any shorter, you know. Far as I'm concerned there's no hassle long as she's clean, blond, and tired. But I'm loyal. If she gets younger and fresher, I stay with her anyway. I'm like that every time."

He fell silent. This was familiar territory, showing all his flags, no matter that Dan's lip pushed forward in an objecting pout. He had no practice at kidding; marriage was a killer. But then Hutch remembered this other question which had come up. "Didn't you say Mom and Dad loved each other? Did I hear you say that?"

"I did. That's what I think."

"Maybe it's only a speculation."

"On my part."

"Yes. Your sort of speculation. Funny, I'm older'n you, but I don't remember that far back." He stuffed the tangerine parachute back into the pocket. "Is that why you have Gloria and Trish and I have . . ."

He paused.

"You have?"

Hutch poked his brother. "I have Suki, Pammy, Debbie, Sharon, and Gretchen, you remember Gretchen, that German girl I think she was?—said she was Swedish. She was so tall I had to go up on her. Laugh, brother."

Dan made a paltry effort.

"When you say that about Mom and Dad, loved each other, it's a speculation, isn't it? You're using your imagination again, only in a nice way?"

Dan shrugged.

"I honor you for it. I *honor* you. It's a good kind

of . . ." *Delusion* hung there among the strands of fog, strips of sunlight, the blunt buffalo.

Dan knew Gloria wasn't sure of him, he wasn't sure of her, neither of them was sure of Trish, and at this moment in her life, Trish hated nothing more than to be accused of caring for her parents. No one would dare. So if it wasn't totally out of line to imagine this good thing of caring in the dead mother and father, it was still—Hutch's lawyer term of art—speculation, merest speculation. Retroactive wish, dream, and, as Gloria would say, prayer.

Not that Hutch lacked hope, either. He always expected the best—the *Besst!*—to come very soon now, maybe after the next IRS audit. They've got computers, they've got Mr. Wong, the demon examiner with most of his points for the MBA. In modern California a person had to face facts in order to evade them. But since the past had no real meaning, it was only gossip, like this talk about their parents; and since the past didn't bear thought, didn't merit attention, it was just Oil of Language, a thing to cut up along with the antipasto; and since a fellow has to get the goodies how he can . . . Everything in the future needed to do the work of memory, nostalgia, desire. Every good thing lay ahead. A person made do with the Suki, Pammy, Debbie, Sharon, Gretchen world. In the future, there would be love and tenderness and fun beyond compare. A cure for the upscale new diseases would come along before Hutch was at serious risk. In the meantime, in the present, just now, in this fiscal year, there was still fun to be had, making out okay.

Hutch was grinning and gazing fondly and boyishly into his kid brother's worn and rapidly aging face (the grit lines, the fret lines, the compression of hopes). At times like this, when Hutch felt the advantage of his large dark eyes, his high flush, his runner's capillaries, his skinniness, his freckles—and never mind an occasional bout with Winchell donuts—he believed he was the happy kid in the family. No matter that Dan was the younger brother. He was heavily planted, like a buffalo over there—a husband, a father, a worrier. He had settled in his pasture out in the avenues and that's all there was.

Hutch had more to come. Expectation, to be continued, was real youthy and California and didn't contradict also having goodies on a daily basis. "—honor you," he was saying, "and if I had a dirty rag stead of this nice clean handkerchief, I'd wipe the shit off your shoes."

He knelt at Dan's feet. "Hey!"

"I'd bend right down like this."

"Cut it out, Hutch!"

"Thought I'd just use my sleeves. Man, if that creep on the Gitane Grand Touring came riding back—"

"Okay," Dan said, "you've got a deal here someplace, Hutch."

"Boy, are you on to me."

Dan was rubbing his shoes together where Hutch had pretended to buff them.

"You do know, I guess," said Hutch, "being as how you inherited forty-nine percent of the brains in the family, I always do everything for a reason. Sometimes, like that Russian spy, what's his name, not a spy, the agent, journalist, Viggy, Vigador—sometimes fun is the only reason for things, but you're my *brother*, kid. So . . ."

Wasn't that nice that Hutch was, for a half a breath, at a loss for words. "So you've got a reason," Dan said. "Fancy that."

"Dan, just temporarily I've got some little problems. It's only temporary till I cash out a deal. Turns out it's not really a problem for me, it's an opportunity for you."

Dan stood there. This time he wouldn't help. Hutch

waited for him to contribute a question, a forehead wrinkle, an eyebrow—nothing. Hutch hated working so hard, but he had to do what's right. "This is only for my best friend and brother. I know Gloria inherited some money—"

Dan was shaking his head. "It's gone. We paid off the debts. Had enough left for the trip to Baja."

"No. Wait. I know you paid off—hey, you play a little cards sometimes?—ate yourself some authentic tacos. Wait a sec. I didn't mention you don't have to actually give me penny one and you can make yourself your kid's fine education, a rest for you, time to finish your book, maybe Gloria takes off from her job—and you don't put up dollar one." Dan was aware of the unmoving buffalo swaying, the shit dripping, the muzzles low, breathing grass. "This is only for a brother I'd do this, Dan."

Then why was he pleading? Why this elaborate early morning meeting between best friends and brothers, if that's what they were? Why all these games and jokes, surprising him at the Fairmont and in the buffalo meadow in Golden Gate Park?

"I don't have any cash, Hutch."

"What about that money market account at Golden West?"

"It's a term account. It's our savings. We get a good rate but we can't withdraw it."

Hutch smiled with renewed astonishment at the huge population of folks who were suckers for government savings bonds, thrift accounts, all those money traps for the working people, while the winners who borrowed from them and thought creatively were building their third home in Palm Springs because they needed a little rest from their second home at Sea Ranch. There were the cab riders and the guys who drove them. There were Wilkes Bashford suits and suits on the racks of good-cause thrift shops on Fillmore. "A term account," Hutch said. He felt ashamed for the family.

"Okay, Hutch, I'm willing to admit you're right. I should have taken some chances instead of thinking nest egg."

"You'd be in great shape right now."

"That's what I just said, Hutch."

"So now I'm offering you another opportunity."

Dan said nothing.

"You just admitted you should have."

Dan had that bull-headed, head-low look—buffalo-headed!—when he couldn't be moved no matter how often a more reasonable person told him he was an asshole.

"You've got your account at Golden West I know about. The *term* account. Both the school pension plan and your driver layaway, whatever they call it, like a goddamn Christmas Club, you can borrow. For my only brother I'm offering you a sharp quick turn upward, Danny."

Now how can a man just rock back and forth like that, not even answering? It was because he knew Hutch was right and he was wrong and he still couldn't see his way.

But a metabolic optimist doesn't give up. When something blocks the road, he just keeps on running, up the obstacle or around it or whatever it takes.

The kid looked exhausted and Hutch hadn't even gotten his second wind yet.

"I haven't even gotten to the whole story yet, Dan. Let's think about the basic deal. The beauty part is you don't even have to touch your hard-earned pennies you got squirreled away here and there. Think about something else for a minute. I've only got you. You guys are my only beneficiaries on my Missouri Mutual policy—who else, Suki? Sharon? Whatzername? Trish is my only heir when I die, Dan. You got to hear this story."

Dan said coolly, his chest tight, "What I have to do is get back to work."

"Why, you know, I got no other heirs or heiresses, so you can bet you and Trish are in my will." Dan lowered his head. He didn't want to hear about it. Goddamn buffalo. "And I got my insurance policy covers you in case I, anything happens to me."

Dan looked his brother in the eyes. "Nothing happens to you, Hutch."

"Could. Who knows," Hutch said. He made a shooting gesture with his finger. "Got you all covered . . . Missouri Mutual Plan."

Dan didn't want to hear about this. It was a hard issue to go against. Hutch took his advantage and did one of his famous double reverse twists, reminding Dan that he had his troubles, too, despite all his expertise in financial planning.

"You know the kind of people I got to do business with normally in this town? People with cash stowed in paper bags. I call them the paper bag capitalists. It's not Pacific Heights Wasp people, it's not nice folks like my family—"

"I'm not your regular money person, Hutch."

"You're not a regular investor, Dan, but you got resources, an employment record, you got a credit rating, that means you got resources—"

"What kind of investors you deal with?"

"You don't want to know them—boy had a liquor store in the Marina, now he's an entreprenoor—hey, better you don't know what you missed. Put it this way, Dan. Sometimes people drive me to breaking my diet. Gloria saw me at Winchell's this other morning. You can tell her I saw her, too. Listen: here's the people. I got one woman with a vowel at the end of her name, she said the Mafia runs the Italian race like the Pope runs the Catholic race."

Dan laughed.

"And she got a vowel at the end. Don't even know her own kind! Man, I mean not too smart, but she got some money from her daddy in the ravioli factory and that's her way of telling me she wants the money not only cleaned up a bit, laundry they call it, clean, press, and alterations, but she definitely wants the right return. She knows from that, man."

"I'm sure you got her point. I'm sure you did it."

Hutch bent suddenly, picked up a stick, and threw it at a buffalo, which didn't move. In his distraction and concentration on the matter at hand, he had temporarily forgotten that buffalo don't run and retrieve sticks, as some dogs are known to do. He looked Dan full in the eyes. This took some effort. It wasn't his habit. He had trouble with the operation, looking his brother full in the eyes. "Danny," he said. "I have a little difficulty here with the ravioli money. I really need another investor."

"What are you saying?" Dan asked.

"I'm saying," Hutch said.

Dan watched the stick near the erect swaying carcass of the trapped buffalo. "Bison," he said, "that's the other word for them."

"I'm saying," Hutch said, "you got no problem, you got credit, you could co-sign."

"Pardon?"

"You and Gloria, you're a family, you both got jobs. You wouldn't have to put up any money. You could make some. You have a residence you lived in for a long time, a kid in school, a regular situation. Hers is a city position."

Dan was having trouble getting it. Hutch had to carry him every step of the way.

"City job, a definite credit asset, like a term account."

"I don't understand."

"It's not complicated. Are you putting me down, trying to pretend you're just some poet with your head in the clouds? This isn't too hard for a medium-smart fellow, Dan. You're my only favorite brother." Hutch was breathing through his mouth. He was skinny and his flanks were moving like after an eleven-mile run. "You just have to co-sign a note, that's all."

He knew enough to make his case and then let people enjoy nature. The cooldown phase was important after a long run. Look around, stretch a little, keep the peace. The park was filled with birdsong and the sounds of grass growing, clouds moving, sand dunes shifting, hidden underfoot by the artful greenery. The buffalo stood absolutely still. They never seemed to move, not even a nice stick could tempt them, but then they lumbered forward, to another spot, and shat anew. Here and there the green was suddenly rich and verdant, thanks to buffalo-intensive fertilization. And then one day they would simply topple, an avalanche of brown, a thundering rumbling fall of gristle, fat, and meat.

"Hey?" Hutch was asking. "Why don't you say something? You act like you don't hear me, brother. Did you hear me?"

"I could co-sign a note," Dan said.

"Right! You're listening! I could factor it, but they take too much. Oh, they sure take, they're good at that, Danny. I could borrow, but I'm extended already. That's business. So I think to myself: what's the best most advantageous and helpful way to get out of this deal whole? Get into it and make it work for me and my family? Right! My family! Way to go, Hutch, I said to myself after working it up on paper and in my night thoughts—way to come out whole for everybody."

So that's what it was all about. "What's the bottom line for me?"

"No real exposure when I tell you this. Bottom line, Dan, is no dollars and you end up a part owner. I'm just a little overextended with the vowel people. So it's a Hutch-given opportunity only for a brother. I want you to be not just a happy father and future great novelist, Dan, I want you to be an owner, a co-partner."

"Co-partner?"

"I'm emphasizing to make myself perfectly clear. All you have to do, Danny"—here it was, here is what the surprise call, the run to the Fairmont, the visit to the American bison came to—"all you have to do is so simple—*write your name*! You're a writer so you know how. Your blessed full name which is in part the same as mine. For a brother! Your name with its unblemished credit, Dan, costing you nothing—a virgin name is all."

"No."

"I want you to, Dan."

"I can't do this."

"Talk to Gloria. Goddammit, talk to Trish, she likes me. She might want to be secure in the future, maybe well-off, too. You got to sit down and let me show you the papers and all you have to do is *sign* it and then you're finished, Danny."

Dan began to speak, but Hutch raised his hand and said, "Don't answer yet. You think you answered but you didn't. I know you through and through, you're my brother, don't say that yet. I got a buyer on the property, I know the redevelopment plans—it's the City, man, it's a sure thing—it's not public information yet, that's both the advantage we got and the little problem—but I can't tell the bank and the bank says money's tight, fuck, I already know that, they say I'm overextended, I don't know that—I'm *extended*, man, like the Zeckendorfs, like maybe Bob Fraser and the Pritzkers and even Gerson Bakar was one time, that's not overextended, if you don't take chances you don't meet Miss America, sometimes you make a mistake but you find Miss Daly City anyway, and listen, I can't tell the bank about the deal I got cooking, it's just a little matter of integrity they wouldn't understand or some loan officer trainee cooks on a hot plate at the Y would go to Jerry Adams at the *Examiner*, hey, try to follow me, Danny—"

How the running worked to extend his breath. How Hutch could let all this pour out and keep the color in his face and not faint from hyperventilation. How he kept smiling and pleading, and how rare this was for the member of the family whose deals were always so far ahead of the dumb taxi-driver brother. Dan felt a rush of warmth and pity and pride that his brother came to him.

"You got to talk to Gloria, right? It's her money, too, not that it's anybody's money. It's her decision. She lets you fuck around your book you think you're writing and she makes the money decisions, right? I can go for that. I know you through and through, just like you know me—say, you were right about that Russki creep, you know that?"

"Gloria will have to agree—"

"Not if you talk to her, Danny, say it's important, there's not much time, I'm family, people don't have much family out here, it's your big chance, I'm *it*—hey?"

And Dan said, "No."

Hutch looked startled. It was the look of: Last thing in the world anyone'd expect. "You won't just write your name on a piece of paper for me?"

"It's not my money. There's got to be a risk. It's

Gloria's in Golden West. It's our kid's education. I got peanuts in my pension, I'm a driver, it's all we got, Hutch."

"You actually have money and you're saying no to me, Dan?"

Dan nodded.

Hutch looked happy. "Fancy this now. I thought all you had was credit." He turned his laughing dark eyes on his brother, grinned with surprise, grinned into his face, happy as happy can be, and said: "I'm up shit creek."

7

_____

"Hey little kid, wanna ride in my foreign car and a donut?"

Just as if it were the most normal thing in the world for him to be hanging around in the afternoon at the entrance to a high school that didn't even have the prettiest girls in the city, unless he had gone really deep into ethnic, a true Third World explorer, she looked him up and down while the bells clanged, signalling Drama Club, Computer & Video Phreaks, football practice, disco and crash dancing for recent immigrants, AIDS and Herpes Actionatorium, teachers' meeting, and to Trish, go home. She wasn't into extracurricular; she provided her own. _Wanna ride in my donut?_ she thought. She took in the two-toned shoes, brown and white, with perforations so the bugs could crawl out, the ice cream suit, the felt hat from Anthony Enterprises where a person could also buy THIMK signs and rubber turds. Trish was not going to be surprised when someone tried that hard. She took in the costume with one rapid scan, up and down. Her computer processed the material and put it on a chip with a blink. She didn't bother printing it out. "Why the fuck're you dressed like that?" she asked.

His little snapbrim hat bobbed. The red, white, and blue feather quivered. He tap-danced lightly, up and down a couple of stairs marked Entrance/Exit, bringing his hand to his forehead in a smart salute. "It's the Uncle Hutch Show!" he said, "starring your favorite Uncle Hutch plus featured this afternoon as his special guest . . . Trish from south of Geary!"

She was already relenting. "Aw come on. I already saw Halloween on the spectacular. You don't look like no comedy luminary."

"Luminary! Hey, nobody ever called me that before."

"I'm about ready to call you something worse, you don't stop that antenna from jiggling."

He came off it. He skipped down the steps. He grabbed a handful of the fake felt hat with its Korean patriotic fancy feather; he flipped the hat into a pile of soda cans and pizza rinds overflowing a litter can. The hat was only for the moment. He had given thought to making her shake her head over crazy Uncle Hutch. Trish definitely felt herself relenting.

"Hey Trish, that better now?"

She loved the way he looked when he had just stopped smiling. The smile was gone, but the face still had an aftersmile glow on it; sort of a vanilla smile, not too wild, just right for an uncle. They both knew the wildness was there. One thing a kid Trish's age was told to study, even if it's impossible to learn, was *Later, later, the good stuff is for later.*

"This is not teevee, honey, it's more like real. Life is supposed to be a festival."

"Don't I know that."

"Good girl. Enjoy to talk to you, Trish. This might be

none of your actual business, but since you're a smart kid, you're my only niece in the whole goddamn world, and things are important to me—" He did a little reprise of the tap dance because he wanted to start it back a moment, reached for the Korean hat, which was gone; did a comic double take. "It could be important to you too if people see it the right way. I want to level with you, Trish. I got to confide in some loved one I can trust. How about some coffee?"

"But Uncle Hutch—cappuccino?"

"Is there any other kind? Are you bargaining with me? Have a double, kid."

No question; Uncle Hutch deserved to get his way, especially when he went to so much trouble to make sure it was also Trish's way. She liked the way it looked, her arm linked with her uncle's, on the way to the little white BMW snugly parked at the fire hydrant. His Policeman's Benevolent Association sticker seemed to prevent tickets about half the time, and since he only got towed about once a year, courtesy of some unbenevolent policeman, he had to think it was a reasonable business risk.

She fitted her step to his. It wasn't difficult. He was a great dancer, and they had been dancing together since she was a baby. He used to carry her; now all he had to do was press, lead a little, let her press and lead if she was following the beat in another direction. It was okay with him if she had her own ideas. He preferred running his life with dancing, games, surprises, fun. He was a grownup kid, like Trish. He realized other people might have the same preference. Maybe there was something to that inheritance stuff, chromosomes, only they didn't know the paternal uncle genes were dominant. Like uncle like niece; that would be a terrific discovery which Trish had made years before anybody.

He jabbed her with an elbow as a Chinese kid pedalled by on his no-speed bicycle, wearing a stupid felt hat with a red, white, and blue plastic feather. "Yucch," she said. "That's the one likes to jimmy open the *Chronicle* boxes for quarters. Bet his head smells like sweet-n-sour pizza."

Uncle Hutch usually paid attention. Just now he was paying less attention to the festival on the sidewalk than to a thought he was continuing. "You get some of that good cappuccino in you, made with real Italian expresso, not Brim, plus maybe a healthy strawberry nosh, I'm going to lay it out to you like an adult so's you know all the facts." Not so fast. He hummed a little. *Not so fast.* "Hey, whyn't you bring any your school-books home with you?"

"Cause I'm smart, Uncle Hutch, like you. I can do all my work in study hall."

"Just like me."

"Plus this isn't much better'n Enterprise High School anymore. I can talk myself into the clubs like I'm eighteen or over or talk myself out of trouble or just talk till people give me what I want, just like—"

"I been eighteen or over myself a few times, I fully dig what you're saying."

She made a face. *Dig.*

"Whatever's necessary," he said. He held the car door open for her. "Whatever feels right. What is called for in this difficult—"

"Bucket seats," she said.

He backhanded the door with just enough follow-through so that it made its satisfying clunk.

"Fancy that," Trish said.

He took her to the Love Boat on Clement, just a few blocks away, far enough so she could feel the BMW airstream rush on her face before her cappuccino and cake, before her sugar and caffeine rush in a café which served the neighborhood population as an immigration station on the road from dim sum to Ameri-

can bar drinking. The local kids also used it for homework and sociabilty purposes. Coffee refills were free
at the Love Boat, but a person had to pay for every
new cappuccino or espresso. Anybody could immediately identify the big spenders. Hutch was the big
spender from Telegraph Hill.

He went up unasked and got the cinnamon for her.
He dusted cinnamon over her cup like a waiter turning a pepper mill. He had already taught Trish about
such things, but on her own she knew to smile because
it was cinnamon, not the pepper mill rotated by a
waiter named Kenny.

Their shared smiles were silent. This was a temporary condition. It was one long smile between uncle
and niece. Trish knew Hutch had something on his
mind. She liked that. She didn't mind waiting. No
hurry, no sweat, and she had heard about foreplay,
even believed in it a little, if it didn't interfere with
her programs. About the length of the hourly station
breaks was about right.

She had already lived a long life with Uncle Hutch,
the great love of her girlhood, which ended with the
advent of foreplay, although girlhood itself could be
considered one big giant overblown forefumbling. "I
can wait," she said.

Hutch grinned. Read her mind.

"Had lots of practice," she added, and grinned back
at him, and then they were still just smiling and having
a great time like the other great times she suddenly
remembered. Thanks to Uncle Hutch, waiting for
things wasn't really so bad, no matter what all her
friends said. They were immature.

Trish and Hutch didn't even necessarily have to be
grinning at the same things, so long as it was each
other doing the grinning. For example, Hutch was
looking her straight in the raspberry preserves
jammed into the tight little crotch of gum between

her teeth. He truly admired firm young periodontal tissue, the unetched teeth, the purplish tongue, the rich mystery of a kid's mouth with all those busy salivary glands which knew how to spurt without even thinking and the whole-throated love of such a person. It wasn't just calcium and fluoride, flossing and education—it was goddamn hardly any yesterday and a whole lot of tomorrow. But he was strict about remembering his responsibilities as an uncle. He held it, held her eyes, and said, "First time in my life, honey, I might need something extra from you—probably nothing, but *might*. It's just a little precaution. You be on my side."

"For what?"

"Just too boring to go into details. But be on my side when it comes up, honey, okay?"

"Hope to die, Uncle Hutch!"

"That's not necessary," he said, sighing a little. He put his freckled brown hand on hers. "I want you to live forever, just like me."

Trish fastidiously used her fork to retrieve the last brown squiggles of crust and raspberry. She was president of the Clean Plate Club. Maybe this was another skill she had inherited from Uncle Hutch. Being able to wait, yet getting all the good tastes right now. Anyway, a person who has been appointed to live forever needs her nourishment to get through the commercials. With the points of the fork still prickling her tongue, she said, "I have two uncles."

"Hey, who else?"

"You're both of them, Uncle Hutch. You grow another face sometimes, but you don't lose the first one, you just stash it."

"In my condo? In my *closet*?" he asked.

"There you are. That's it right now. One of them is old, like Mick Jagger, you know? Still jumps around a lot, but *old*."

"And the other one's a boy?"

"That's also Mick Jagger on the *Sympathy for the Devil* album. I taped my friend's mom's. When he was hot, you know? He was real?"

Hutch captured her hand again. There was nothing more for the fork to find. He pulled at her hand and wrapped both his around it and they giggled at the tangle of fingers. "Maybe I do it with air brushes," he said.

The jukebox was playing something without words that anyone could understand, *wanna goa funna dooah, brokeah mah heart,* but at least it wasn't rap. Two Korean girls were sharing a sponge cake—boringest thing at the Love Boat—and doing their algebra together, stroking away at matched hand calculators. They were learning how to spend money while doing their homework, just like Americans, instead of going to the library—*libary,* Uncle Hutch said. Smoke coming out of the *chimley,* cute Uncle Hutch said.

Trish noticed that her uncle was the only person in the place over eighteen, but because she would be over eighteen herself someday and the subject had already been covered, she decided not to mention it. In fact, she would mention the opposite. "It's like a date," she said. "That's the thing I always liked about you."

"You *know* what life is," he said, inclining his head toward the two Korean girls now lining up figures in their ruled notebooks. "It's not getting ready to work for the IRS—"

"Huh?"

"—or a bank. You and me dated when you were four years old and I first started my fitness program. Hey, remember when the Parcourse? Now I suppose you run around with other guys."

"Run around," she said, making a bad-smell face.

"Dates." Sometimes she could tell he came from another time, like Mick.

Hutch took her criticism in stride. He was thinking. "When you have a date," he asked, "this is a riddle, that means someone you go out with or someone you go home with?"

"Out with."

"Good! Means you're straight. So you got a terrific chance of never getting AIDS."

"Thanks for all that upbeat hope and data, Uncle Hutch. Sometimes you're better'n anyone."

There was a boyish trembling at this ambiguous flattery. Since he was not sure she believed anyone on the planet before the twenty-first century could be any good, and she would have to reserve judgment on them until the new century came along, he didn't know how far to take the compliment. But when she said he had two interesting faces, that was better than two boring ones. He was loved by a girl like Trish, his only niece, her only uncle, and it wasn't a law. She didn't have to. There were no rules, but adoration counts.

She noticed he had sugared his espresso and then left it untouched. She decided not to say anything, but he must have followed her eyes. He sugared it again. It didn't make sense to start over like that. He didn't drink from it.

Uncle Hutch needed her for something and it was up to Trish to help him find the way to talk about it. She would do her best. When disco was in, she was Miss Shake-It of her junior high school, and in grammar school she always led the snake dances. "Plus," she said—plus from what?—"I'm feeling kind of yucchy, throw-uppy." Trish had a whole laundry list of things to tell Uncle Hutch. Conversation with him was an add-on game. "I hate math, but they tell me I'm good at it and they want to put me in the class with a lot of boys and Chinese girls. The Korean ones are all named Blah-Blah Kim. Plus, they say they need a girl of my, you know, extraction. Plus Dad is upset about his book. He's written about a million pages—no, rewind erase, a thousand—"

"You're supposed to be good at math."

"That's arithmetic, Uncle."

"Gotcha. Right. So?"

"Plus he doesn't see how to end it. I'm not even sure he knows how to *continue* it another thousand pages."

"I don't suppose that's your problem. Sounds like his problem, Trish."

"He's my dad."

"Oh yeah."

"Plus, Uncle Hutch . . ."

She didn't say it. Plus what?

"Plus, he wants—Harry does—still wants to make me pregnant."

"Don't let him. We've gone over that subject. There are things you can do."

She smiled shyly, slyly. "Harry says he's still got strong sperm. Says it's up to him. Says it's so strong, he wants me to decide."

This didn't make anything but teenage sense. Hutch decided he and Trish should pay close attention to each other's recreations, as they once did. What she used to like best about the Parcourse was hanging from his arms and squealing, not part of the official Parcourse routine. Then she used to trot after him and study his bar stretches with solemn wonder. Her eyes were so large. She still had nice gleamy eyes, but the face had filled in around them. He forgave these changes.

Hutch loved her like a swain. She had always been his pet, his delight, his mysterious little girl whose staring blue eyes, when she was a baby, he could meet without flinching. From the beginning they could look into each other, unafraid. Looking into a person's eyes was not one of Hutch's strong suits. He shut his eyes when he made love, unless he was peeking up through a jungle tangle of hair—he liked to peer at that—but when he looked into Trish's eyes, he felt as if he was making a kind of love. It was better than a jungle and a tangle. Heading his way upstream through the crotches of San Francisco was a job God and hormones had handed him twenty years ago; he still did the best he could. But a delicious delight didn't come that often into a bachelor uncle's life. And he loved her not just because there was the slightest chance she could, in this emergency in his life, be useful to him.

"Thanks for being so terrific, Trish."

"Maybe I do it with air brushes," she said.

"At your age," he said.

She thrust her chest to the future.

"Hey, you ever need anything, a breast job—"

She laughed. There were other priorities in her life. But this was California and she was willing to get used to the idea. "Smaller," she said.

"Right! The times are for small. I liked small before it was in."

"Mine are *huge*."

"But nice. You'll settle down. A girl's body at your age, hey, it kind of explodes."

"But Uncle Hutch . . . You used to say anything more'n a handful—"

"Is a waste." He finished for her. *"Used* to say."

"Now everyone says it."

"Smart girl. You're a smart modern person of today. Hey, forget breasts, how about the nose? I know the besst plastic man in Pacific Heights—studied with a Nazi in Brazil!"

"Hey, cool."

He grabbed her nose between two fingers, screwed an imaginary monocle into his eye, and did it in teevee

movie accent: "Werry goot. Ve give you liddle more of
iggle look . . . *Eagle*," he translated behind his hand.
"You like zat. Liddle not zo much hawk, liddle more of
iggle, my beautiful buffalo."

"Buffalo?"

"American bison," he said. "Get hip, girl."

"You get with it, Uncle Hutch."

"My proud beauty. Zo arrogant, zo cruel, zo desir-
able. Ze zirty-two-bee nose, not zee zirty-zree-see."

"You're awful!"

"You like it? Hey, but the folks at home are stringent
about improvementism, sweetie. We'll have to wait. In
the meantime, continue brushing your teeth."

Hutch reached over with a fingernail and flipped a
raspberry seed out of the crotch of her upper front
incisors. He didn't play around with back teeth, the
canines or molars, in public.

She pouted. It was about waiting, not about brushing. She was a willing brusher. She didn't litter, either.
And she never went out with Chinese, black, or Mexican guys who carried ghetto blasters unless they were
willing to turn it down in residential neighborhoods.
Unless they looked really cute in their body shirts.

She did her gums, too.

"Hey!" Hutch seemed to be remembering something. The day was going fast with the late slanting
afternoon sun through the window of the Love Boat
on Clement. Since life was a festival, he could see
powdered sugar floating in the air (otherwise it might
look like dust and cockroach wings). The jukebox was
playing some kind of new synthesizer version of that
old standard, "Chariots of Fire," which was synthesizer to start with, and maybe this made Hutch want to
get out on the Marina for an extra three-four-mile run.
He needed to cool out.

He stood up. He slapped a couple bills on the table

without looking at the check. "Got a couple stops to make. Carry you home, honey?"

"I'll walk."

"No, carry you home. You want that, whyn't you say what you want? Always level with me. Just remember your promise, okay?"

Trish looked puzzled. What promise?

But if anything came up about Uncle Hutch, he could count on old Trish with the eagle no ❭ and the neat, naturally perfect tits.

Some of Hutch's friends thought his running was an addiction, like alcohol or drugs. Hutch's doctor told him he was ruining his knees, tendons, and back. When he didn't run, he felt a flood of yearning emptiness, an ocean of regret washing over him, and his body was chilled and shaking, unable to bring him down into the relief of sleep. Not even women could do this for him. Coming sometimes left him staring into the dark with jagged nerves, seeing jagged lights, wondering if all this stupid bouncing and thumping had given him a detached retina. Sometimes he didn't come at all, but like a woman could pretend and just slip the needle out—they liked that, didn't they? Didn't even notice.

So an orthopod only saw joints and shin splints; he didn't see how much a man needs to run. No matter what his friends and doctor told him—and what did they know?—Hutch knew he had to run. It wasn't because he was addicted. It was because running was good for him and he liked it. He liked the shoes, the shorts, the T-shirts, the company out on the Marina running track. He liked the worn skinnies, the jet-lagged stewardesses, the good folks with the tachometers, the wrist weights and the lead belts, the people whose lips moved as they ran, counting off steps or laps or heartbeats or winning arguments with the ghosts of former lovers. He liked runners, their spirit, and he liked himself when he ran.

It was natural. In the wilderness hunters run, the prey runs, the strong run after the weak and gobble them up. Even a coyote sprints a little to eat out the belly of a fallen creature. Man is the animal that runs on two legs. f there were no running, what would there be? Man is the animal that runs on two legs wearing the best New Balance shoes. Addiction only occurs if a person runs when he should be doing other things. Hutch only ran when his body and soul told him he should be running.

That was a nice chat with Trish and it felt good, did the job. No jagged nerves and funny darting lights on his eyelids. Yet he wasn't quite finished. There was another stop he should be making. As soon as possible. He should be taking care of business with Gloria. Right now.

On the other hand, his body spoke to him and he was attentive, listening to the message it sent, which was why sometimes less-aware folks thought he wasn't listening to their sad stories: He should be running.

He should be taking care of business.

He should be taking care of the evening, the sweat, the rush, the heart and arteries.

No reason why he couldn't run later, in the cool and damp, in the dark, with the occasional light from a patrol car playing on the pumping skinny legs. Yes. That would work out fine. The commands of nature could be postponed for an hour. Life was a festival and his body agreed to a new date. Hutch was in control.

When he carried Trish back in his little white BMW that she liked so much (good niece, good friend), with the plan of then heading for the Marina, changing into the running stuff he kept in the boot for just such an emergency, fix up with a three-four-mile evening series of slow jog, sprint, slog jog, maybe another sprint before the cooldown, there was no trouble at all in changing the plan. Dan was not home. Trish headed straight for her room. Gloria was alone with a pile of student papers at the breakfast-room table that served this family as a dining-room table and sometimes as the place for Gloria to sign off some of her work for school.

Now was the time to talk with Gloria. "Hey sister-in-law, you got a minute?"

She looked up and there was a space of no reply. He could see for himself: a thick heap of lined yellow sheets, some white, filled with childish handwriting; a red pencil in her hand, another stuck in the hair behind her ear. He was thinking: Now talk about addiction, who needs to carry a spare pencil behind her ear, in case she runs out? It was so unattractive in a woman who once seemed kind of cute . . . But he said only, "Shame to let that breakfast coffee I see on the stove go to waste. Lemme sit with you a minute, hey Gloria? Then I got some stuff I have to do myself."

"Please," said Gloria.

For a moment he hesitated, but then he knew she meant, Please sit if you must. He grinned. "Hey Gloria," he said, "everyone drinks too much caffeine these days. Could you make me a—no, a frozen o.j. from concentrate's fine."

She had read his mind about the pencil. She untucked it from her ear; she played with it, tapping one pencil against another, a regular percussionist of impatience. "I've got these papers for tomorrow. I make my kids do a theme a week. If I don't get them back tomorrow—"

"I got some papers myself for later, Gloria, know exactly the spot you're in. Hey, won't take but a minute, fella."

His sister-in-law Gloria didn't like to be fella and he knew it. Stupid of him and he knew that, too. She wasn't a fella and couldn't get it through her dumb female head that he only meant she was as good as a fella. So he made up for it with a big, big Hutch apology that always worked on the chicks he really liked, who could feel his good will and his deep personal sense of brotherhood and sistership: he winked. Then the quick oral follow-up, his one-two punch: "Say Glory, you look great. In fact, terrific! Been losing weight?"

Might as well have both the o.j. and the cold breakfast coffee, since he was sure to run later and work out all the bad caffeine vitamins from the coffee while turning the good o.j. vitamins into dissolved cholesterol and tension. He'd knock the sticky stuff right off the artery walls. He downed the juice Gloria handed him, rinsed the glass himself—good guest—and then poured the cold coffee into it. Good brother-in-law, at home with his relatives.

He sat down briskly and said to Gloria, "I want to talk with you about this first because before I go into the details with Dan, I know you're a big part of his decision-making process, being a wife and all, being the underline *the* wife, Gloria, and as far as the important money decisions in this family are concerned, well, you're as shrewd as they come. So the deal is something like this—"

"He told me," she said.

"He told you already? I asked him to wait till I could explain it more fully and lay it out. He told you already?"

"He told me," she said, "and you want some more orange juice? The answer is yes."

Hutch beamed. He knew what she was saying, but he tried it his way, double reverse twisting it: "That's great, great! I knew you'd see it like that, a chance for security plus a little fun and extra—"

"The answer about the orange juice is yes," she said. "The answer is no about investing."

"Glory, listen! Wait till you understand! I just want to give you an edge to spare, because you're my sister-in-law and all, because Trish is my heiress, because—"

"We don't have the edge to spare, Hutch. We don't have the edge to risk."

Hutch was breathing through his mouth. The idea when running is to keep the breath coming easily and to be able to carry on a normal conversation. A runner should never have the blood burning in his throat and panic in his knees, as Hutch had now. The words that came out should be paced normally, with no gasping for air. He waited a moment till he could get the words and the breath organized. "I've been doing goddamn well," he said. "My connections go first-cabin in this town. San Francisco is still a place where it helps to know the right people. I know them, I take pasta with them, I run with the healthy ones and they're really pretty goddamn healthy, Gloria, the besst, watch their weight and their diet . . ." He struggled to get back where he wanted to be with her. "I've been worried about you. My brother, what he wants to do with his life, that book he's been throwing himself at for ten years now—"

"More," said Gloria. "But he's a terrier. He hasn't given up."

"And Trish, my only heiress."

"That's good of you," Gloria said.

Hutch came to his ace move. This was the one he saved for the crucial moments with Dan, Gloria, and Trish, and he used it only one-on-one for maximum power down the final stretch. He stared at a space above Gloria's nose, just between the eyes. No one in the world could swear they knew the difference between looking someone in the eyes and meeting that place where lots of people plucked their brows. He fastened his eyes sincerely onto the dark points of hair in that spot. He lowered his voice. "This deal is only for my family," he said. "This is only for them."

"I've already discussed it with Dan. I wish we could help you out, Hutch. It's just too dangerous for us."

"This deal is only for you," Hutch said.

Gloria said nothing. It was the hard part of a conversation for Hutch—when the person he was arguing with said nothing. He had never figured out the correct response to silence, to withdrawal, to nothing. He thought of telling her he would do anything in the world for Trish, but she already knew that, she already knew he would say it, and it came out too easily. Sometimes he wasn't sure it was true, especially when he wanted to use it, as now, but sometimes, maybe always, he knew it really was true. He thought to go back a step, start from the beginning.

"I've always wanted to get my family into investment, only this one violates the rules, being more like a windfall. It's too easy."

Gloria sighed. She had practiced patience with Hutch for so long that now she seemed to have her own investment in it. "We're not into windfalls," she said. "How about survival, Hutch? We're more into that."

Hutch refused to feel insulted. There was no use in it anyplace, he had found, especially with family and good friends, the lunch boys on the terrace at Enrico's. Being insulted was like jealousy; it did nobody any good. He operated on the theory that Gloria liked his guts even if some of the evidence indicated the contrary. "Survival's a sure thing these days, unless you give me atomic Russian blah blah blah and you're not gonna hand me that. The question is: quality of life. How's your quality of life, Glory? Do you want a real quality of life like my family deserves or do you want—"

"Quantity will do for the moment," she said, "adequate quantity for a start."

"Hey, Glory! You're not some kid just starting out!"

"Let me repeat, Hutch. I want to be left out of any and all sure things."

"Are you mad at me, Glory? Did I ever do anything back to you?"

"Bad," she said.

"Bad? What bad?"

"You said back. You meant bad."

He poked her with his elbow. "Hey, a Freudian! I slipped! But whyn't you think back, or think bad if you want to, and tell me."

She looked at him while he hummed and nodded and didn't meet her eyes and smiled at his knees and at his pants hiked just a little above the ankles. She wanted to be fair. She wanted to say what was right. She had to admit . . . What did she have to admit? "You're a devoted uncle," she said quietly. "I think you really like Trish. I think it's nice that she can count on you."

"So then?"

"So then it doesn't change this matter, Hutch. Look: I said you like her. I think you really love her, Hutch. So try to understand we're her parents and we have to watch out for her."

"No?" Something stopped him from saying, I watch out for her when you don't; something stopped him from using this weapon. "No?" he asked. And it was his turn to remain silent, a silence composed of his need, his hunger, his stubborn hope, and also what he could not say about Trish.

Gloria had no answer to this unfamiliar space of no words, no pokes or nudges, no further appeal. Hutch was thinking that he wasn't stopped yet, nothing could stop him, stopping him only made him more determined not to be stopped. She was smart not to argue anymore. But he was smarter. He was doing what she did, only better: not quarrelling with his beloved sister-in-law.

He'd get her yet.

"Here's Dan," Gloria said. Hutch watched his brother walking from the parking lot of Empire Records, through the little place in the fence with the path trampled through fernlike weeds and clots of dried Richmond District mud. It would be interesting to have a woman looking out for a man, saying, Here's Hutch, as he pushes through the little white gate of a blue-and-cream-painted, orange trim, Victorian someplace on a good street of Pacific Heights—maybe a dog, also glad to see him—a kid—unlikely he'd inflict this on himself, no matter how nice it might be to dream of that expectant *Here's Hutch*. . . . Dan had the stoop of the workingman. He was carrying something. There was nothing on his back or in his hands. He was carrying something in his chest. His seamed face, the downward leathery creases, looked too tired to express surprise.

"Waiting for you," Hutch said. "Been talking with Gloria about that little matter. Want to consult with the family, you know? Get all your input?"

"I thought we decided," Dan said.

"Hey, she says the same thing as you, but sometimes you put a couple heads together, you get something better along the lines of an action point of view. No harm in discussing it out, is there?"

His smile meant to be helpful. When heads bump, this is the smile that results, so long as the smiler is not one of the heads. Dan stared at Hutch and wondered if a person can be lovable without being likable and if that was what being a brother entailed. He had heard of people working to make the right connections, get their way early in the morning, the power breakfast, the power brunch, and he said to Gloria, "Hutch and I went out to Golden Gate Park on my shift this morning. We had a power buffalo watch."

"What?" she answered.

"Pardon?" said Hutch.

"Tell you what," Gloria said, scooping up her papers. "I'm going in the bedroom to finish this stuff. You can finish your power brotherhood meeting out here —got everything you need?"

And she left without waiting for an answer.

The brothers watched her go and then silently watched her absence, the place where she had been. Dan sighed, as he sometimes did when Gloria left the room—it was a habit Hutch had noticed about his brother because it was like his own habit about women in that it was very different. When one of Hutch's tired long-legged blonds got up to make a telephone call, freshen her makeup in the Ladies, discuss with a friend, Hutch sighed because now the weight of proving was off; he could tease and smile with his own friends, flirt with the new tired blond across the terrace at Enrico's. When Gloria left, Dan sighed because he missed her, because a part of his strength had disappeared and he mourned over its shadow.

"That was very unforeseen of you this morning," Hutch said.

"Unforeseen?"

"Just to leave me swinging slowly in the wind like Richard Nixon or some creep like that."

"Richard Nixon?"

"Hey! Remember him?"

Dan made an effort. He guessed he did. He knew what Hutch was saying: They saw the buffalo together, they used to see the buffalo together, they used to ride their bikes through the park together, how could Dan forget? How could he say, Trish, Gloria, as if those words meant he didn't have to help his brother out when his brother was in a jam and in so many ways it was a great opportunity.

With an effort, Dan could figure things out. Figuring them out didn't make them easy.

"I saw Trish after school, too," Hutch said.

"You've had a busy day with my family."

"You'd be my only family even if—"

Even if he didn't need us now.

"Even if I didn't need you. I talked to Trish, I didn't explain too much, I listened to her. I talked to Gloria and she doesn't like me too much." He winked at his brother. "Maybe because I'm not too likable. So what else is new?" He opened his mouth and showed his perfectly repaired teeth in a happy grin. "You're the likable one, I'm the one tries to be likable, only succeeds to a degree, we've always known that, don't we?"

"You do all right, Hutch."

"Looks like it sometimes, hey? But I have to work at relaxed. Sometimes it's not the easiest thing. For instance example, this project. What I want for you, all I want for you is to come with me talk to my people, listen, see for myself—"

"For myself?"

"For *your*self is what I was obvious. The problem, the window of opportunity. Then report back to Gloria, okay? Because listen to me now is all I'm asking. You got me for an only living brother or relative, you know what I'm saying?"

"Gloria. Trish."

"Okay, so blood relative. Okay, so we can presume Trish is a blood relative, too. You know what I'm saying, blood from way back, get my drift? Brothers?"

"That's not hard to understand. Also I don't like some of your jokes."

"Hey, hey, sorry. I'm a lonely guy, I have to make myself laugh sometimes." Dan could almost hear the anxious flush coursing through his cheeks; he didn't have to see it. When the salesman revved up in Hutch, he proceeded in a series of short sprints, not long easy lopings. He joked. He apologized. He chewed his lips; that permanent chapping, sun and baked saliva, must have been painful. "I'm absolutely filled with sorry, Dan, but didn't think you'd be difficult. You realize you're being stupid and pigheaded—cancel that. Middle-aged, scared, cautious—cancel those, too. You make me sad for you, Danny. You're being, stick with my first idea—*difficult.* And that's really and truly unnecessary in this beautiful opportunity of ours together."

"You make that clear."

"So. You force me to repeat myself. Say, you know another reason I never got married? Not yet, anyways. They nag. First they do everything you like, up down and sideways, just how you like it, they study that, and then they say, Hey, little guy, that's not my thing. And then they repeat themselves, just like I'm doing to you. Why don't you help me be my best self, Danny?"

Dan was remembering saving money with his brother by walking to the Saturday afternoon movies at the Four Star. He was remembering playing the double feature back at each other when they walked home, and how good Hutch was at taking the parts of Englishmen in India, sheriffs in Arizona, space captains from Venus. He liked games. At eighteen he spent part of a day in the armed services, helping the psychiatrist discover he had a problem and a few hundred bucks to spare. The money was for an hour's therapy, plus a letter, and since it was only the Vietnam War, nobody was the loser. When I was in the service, he liked to say, air force, that long afternoon . . . Gretchen, who was Swedish or German, Linda, Sharon—not Suki—most of them laughed every time he told the story. Not every woman nagged.

"Your best self," Dan said.

"Everyone got one, brother."

"It'll cost me to see it again."

Hutch shook his head. That wasn't kind of Dan. One thing about Dan, his best self was supposed to be kind and here was a definite, clear, right-on failure of that quality. Hutch had lowered his head, he was shaking it, hiding from Dan the little grin because he knew he had just taken a slight advantage around the turn on the track, cornering him worth a half step or more, because Dan would be brooding and regretful over letting something nasty slip out. Hutch raised his head, the grin erased, and looked straight into the space between Dan's eyes where the unplucked eyebrow hairs grew together.

"We been hiding from each other too long, Dan. Do you remember when you were a bachelor, some of those midnights, nobody, nothing, just your own self? Try to see how my life is. I pet your kid, sweet kid, your Gloria is a real sport, too, I won't say I'm an orphan—I can always call you and go for a drive—but when I have to think about things at night and watch the dawn come up . . . These can be difficult times in old San Francisco, man, less you find yourself a brother to share your troubles and joys, hey."

Hutch knew one of his advantages was the genius for just riding over obstacles, wearing people out with friendly jabber, doing the conversational parcourse, a skip up or around if no one was watching and then right on through to the next challenge, waiting till they just let him have his way. And he also knew his problem was saying too much, wearing people out. Occasionally he succeeded in finding the right silence. He searched for the correct expression of nothing. It would help if he could look his brother in the eyes. People are sensitive; there could be a marginal differ-ence between eyebrow hairs and eyes. This was an important occasion and Hutch made the effort. He mobilized his strength. He gazed across the table and found, with a shock like that of an icy shower, the connection of his own dark eyes with the puzzled, curious, weary gaze of his brother. So that's all it took. It was possible after all to connect a merely moist physical object like eyes without touching them; not much harder than making love to a person who refused to speak kindly.

Hutch said in a low voice:

"Just put on a suit and come meet these guys with me. Just give me moral support. That doesn't mean you have to do anything but listen up and learn, Dan. Think of it as research into the real world. I'm not asking so much—super valuable for a future novelist. Just straighten it out with Gloria you got to do that for a brother. Hey, no obligation, that's my word-of-honor promise, okay?"

Accidents usually happen when the weather is wrong for them. One day in this heat, the hottest day of that autumnal summer which is the freak habit of San Francisco, and that was the day the shorted-out fridge chose to defrost in murky rivulets onto the linoleum. A biochemical miracle, sent from heaven, on just the best day for it, proving something—maybe that God chose to test Gloria by leaking food all over the floor. She stood there laughing. She didn't believe God wanted her to waste either a prayer or a curse. There was no reason to cry about lettuce turning brown, Bonnie Bell frozen orange juice going soggy, a rock cod's eyes going worse than rheumy. Lysol could take care of the smell, Jergens Extra Dry skin lotion would help the hands, and there were bigger things coming out of the late 1980s.

Trish liked a whole bunch of things about her mother. Gloria waited a while before she got upset, and a bad fuse in the fridge was an upsetting event she could put off worrying about indefinitely. Therefore Trish even liked helping her clean up, although her mother *did* point out that it was also Gloria helping Trish, since the household belonged to all of them, and if Dan had been home, mother and daughter would be helping him. They were in this mess together.

"I like burgers better'n fish anyway," Trish said, and Gloria shot her a look of: The fish was for Dad and me.

Gloria stuffed a wet bunch of old *Chronicles,* smelling of orange juice, fish, and Lysol, into the trash. She stood there rubbing lotion onto her hands. "He looks like a prince to you, doesn't he?" she asked, and Trish knew she was referring to Uncle Hutch, not Dad, because in their family that way of saying *he* always meant the same thing. "Just try kissing him. He turns straight into a frog."

"Mom, what the fuck?"

"Is that your way of asking me for the reference, dear? I mean he wears nice suits and smiles but watch out."

"He's Dad's brother, isn't he?"

"It's nice of you, honey, to think that proves he's a real swell guy—dude?—like your dad. Will you help me sort out the rotten stuff from what we can still use?"

She was stacking cartons and containers on the sink. Trish picked up a yogurt carton with two fingers, smelled, and said, "It says good till October twenty-one."

"How does it smell?"

"Smells like end of November and it's only ten or eleven October."

"See what I mean about labels, honey? So many things make stuff turn bad. Dump it, dump it, and will you get the Clorox behind there? I want this musty smell *out.*"

Gloria and Trish set to work at rescuing the remnants of food, cleaning the fridge and around it, and Gloria looked at her daughter and said, "It was only a fuse. Not the worst thing that can happen to us, is it?"

"Hey, look at this, Mom. This stuff is bleaching the floor."

"Neato," said Gloria. "You can see it happening. Hey, Trish?" Trish looked up. "You know what? You're not so bad, honey."

Trish said to the white grain of wood as she scrubbed at it and pressed a cloth into the corner: "You're not so bad either, Mom."

When Dan came back from the union meeting, he gave Gloria the usual news: a tribe of chiefs, no Indians among cab drivers; the union was a debating society in which the subject of debate was always the same—not enough money, not enough benefits, too many regulations about pickups at the hotels and the airports, taxi zones filled with creepy civilian cars, harassment about high-flagging and rear taillights and any goddamn thing they thought of just added to the stomach troubles from too much sitting in traffic. . . . A waste of life. And no one dared mention the cozy deals between union and management.

As Gloria knew, he was thinking about something else. "I just told Hutch the least I could do was put on a suit and come to meet his people."

"That's a promise," Gloria said.

"What?"

"When you put on a suit, big boy, that's a promise." Gloria knew it was time to lighten up and deal with what was coming down anyway. "Hey, do you like the ring of that? Hutch's people?"

When a refrigerator defrosts unasked. When a daughter grows up too fast. When a husband is putting on a suit and going to meet his brother who could easily bring trouble.

Dan went through it again. This committed him to nothing. It hardly needed all this heat. He could hardly refuse a little conversation, a cup of coffee, with his brother and the money people if he didn't refuse to talk with his brother and a Golden Gate Park buffalo. "It's in the nature of being a brother," he said.

Gloria had her lips pressed together in a white line. She smelled Clorox and Lysol, a sharp bite in the air. Her hands itched. She knew there was no reason not to love and treasure a man who was in thrall to another, especially if the other was not a woman, not a rival for her bed. Yet she wanted her husband free. "What do you know about the nature of other brothers?" she asked.

"My own is what concerns me, Gloria. Look at it this way: Talking to those people should be *interesting*. It's a world I know nothing about. Sometimes I think KorVet Taxis, plus my book, isn't the whole world."

"Plus your daughter," she said. "Plus your wife."

Some people, Dan thought, must have other rooms for arguing in. Kitchens and basic discussion weren't tied together for other families. Maybe they had separate dispute rooms, away from food and sink smells. "I can't just say no without even hearing it out with his people. I don't have to say yes."

"His people. That's the trouble."

"I can talk to them and then say it doesn't look right."

"You can say that? Dan, if he gets you wrapped up in this thing, all his funny moves, his games, his winks, his tricks, you're his. That's how it's always been."

"Remember the Russian? I didn't let him get away with that."

"Didn't really have anything to do with you, either.

That was just out there. And I think you surprised yourself."

She was right about the Russian. What he did wasn't so great and he liked it too much. "I know how you feel," he said. "But that shows. Things are different. I'm a big boy, Glory."

"You're his little brother, Dan."

"His! Listen, I'm on to him, I've been on to him for years. But he still . . . why don't you trust me?"

"I trust you, Dan. I know you. That's what he says, too: *Trust me.* But don't make a mistake, okay?"

She turned away when he put his arms around her. Her body felt stubby to him when she did that. She had only added a few pounds, but that's how it felt, how it would feel to Hutch. Dan had noticed Trish's calculating study of her mother's neck, shoulders, arms; he could see the resolution in her face, that she would never let herself go as her mother was doing. There's no justice, he thought, just doing the best we can. "When?" Gloria asked.

"We made an appointment for tomorrow. I'll talk. I'll listen to him. I'll listen to the money people. I won't do anything without you, Glory, I promise that. I swear it. You're the best thing in my life, honey."

Gloria just stared. She would not let him get off free even when he told the truth.

In her room, Trish was playing the music loud so they would know she couldn't hear. She didn't care anyway. She pressed a glass between the siding wall and her ear in order to hear them, only because she believed in not knowing what she didn't need to know but knowing everything about what concerned her. She needed to know about Uncle Hutch, money, and her parents.

On the whole it had been a good day for Trish. She liked being with Uncle Hutch. She liked cleaning up the kitchen with Mom. And the great thing about a pregnancy is that it doesn't just give you until tomorrow to do something about it. You have days and days, weeks, months, practically all the time in the world, so there's no point in worrying about it today, as so many of her friends did, because usually it just went away suddenly, one afternoon after school, with an ache in the tummy and a warm wet rush.

8

Hutch had a secret about the tired blonds. He liked to
sleep with them. After they performed their service
for him, he liked to curl up and tuck himself against
them; and in the dark, with no eyes to pry out secrets,
no bills or telephone calls, no Enrico's terrace friends
to show how successful he was, he could simply fade
into sleep like a slide into warmth. If she wouldn't
wake, if he would never wake, it could be perfect.
Closeness could be imagined. It was the sensation he
used to feel in the heat of pumping his bike up the
slope of Geary toward Ocean Beach, his brother close,
nearby. The spokes flashed and his body felt flooded.

Sometimes, when she was a saint, a tired blond saint,
he liked to sleep with his hand cupping her mound,
her hands lightly around his cock or under his balls, so
long as she wasn't liable to twist with sudden bad
dreams. He curled and liked having her there, whatever the saint's name was.

But they always woke, they asked questions, they

wanted breakfast, they needed to explain that they were thinking about falling in love. "Do you like being together, Hutch?" a Linda had asked, and he had answered, "I'm together, how about you?"

Tears came to her eyes. He didn't mean to hurt her feelings, but when he slept with a woman, for a while afterwards he only wanted to tell the truth. "Hey, listen, let me just hold you and we'll close our eyes, okay?" he said. "I mean it. Just hold you, okay?"

"Say my name," she said. Couldn't leave well enough alone and let it happen.

As far as Hutch was concerned, a man like Avigdor was at a primitive stage in the lust department, hookers and stuff, especially when you consider the minor herpes problem and that major AIDS thing. And Dan was at a practically holy stage, it reached the peaks of sanctimoonie, as Hutch called it, locked into a marriage that would have been the most boring thing in the world except maybe for Dan's liking it that way. So Hutch's job was to find the proper middle path which kept the fun and yet made things right. Hutch looked high and low for Hutch's festive way in life, in old San Fran, and it wasn't easy; some friendly tired blond who could be guaranteed clean, though there's always downside risk, yet fully fun.

Not so easy. The night didn't always work out according to Hutch's plan. For example, having studied a good book from a friend at the Zen Center, he tried to practice advanced lovemaking with Suki Read after a day filled with various distressing hurry-up messages from the bankers and an article in the *Chron* about the real estate market and his back hurt a little because of running too soon after the last bout of disc trouble. He was in Suki's nice bed out in Cow Hollow. "I have an idea," he was saying.

She raised herself on one elbow. Already she was

suspicious. She didn't trust men who suddenly, before they made love, said, *I have an idea.*

"This idea, just hold me, don't move, I don't move either—"

"What?"

"I mean, like this, I'm in you like this—"

"I know how you're in me."

He stroked her cheek, along the line of the nice jaw; ran his fingers lightly over the tuck scar behind her ear; showed sweetness and discretion by not reaching to the parallel scar behind the other ear; said soothingly: "Hey, listen. I read this book. Don't rock like that."

She turned her face away into the pillow, consulting her own thoughts. Then she looked back up at him. "You just gonna stay there?"

"I thought we'd turn on our sides and get comfortable."

"I'm comfortable."

"I mean, for this thing where we're really close—"

Suki interrupted with annoyance. "I know what you mean. You think I'm not informed? This is some sort of Hindu yin and yang crap where the guy keeps his vital fluids—"

"Right. That's part of it."

"—gets to keep his vital fluids, buster, and I just stay plugged up all night?"

Suki was a tired enough blond, but sarcastic. She hadn't yet learned that sarcastic words don't win fair gentleman. And until he found the perfect tired blond, Hutch guessed he would have to take care of his own soulfulness all by himself.

The conference with Ray Aratunian was brief. Ray was one of those persons who could relax and lay back and shoot the shit one minute, and the next minute he was all business. Ray's changeable character, which

Hutch tried not to think had some ethnic meaning, because prejudice is wrong when you're trying to do business with people, keep on wonderful terms, make business a continuation of all the other good things in life . . . Anyway, Ray made Hutch feel a little less festive these days. Probably his handling of Suki had suffered as a result. And certainly his handling of Ray was not all Hutch desired for himself.

Ray was, that's the word, a control freak, and if there was anything Hutch disliked, spoiling this climate where the weather was always nice for running, it was one of those. Control freaks. People who just didn't relax and let the festivity come their way.

Now all Ray wanted to do was review the deal with the man he called his partner—Hutch felt he was no partner of Ray's—and tell his partner what he expected and not listen to any of the shadings and qualifications that make life more attractive. Ray was droning along with his little speech, boring himself, boring Hutch, reviewing and reviewing, making Hutch's stomach churn. "Let's review our deal, partner. Normally we don't do deals with distinguished persons like you because it's not our line and we hate the crap that comes with you. We prefer offshore, factoring a shipment through Miami or Baja, we also still do a little work for people with ordinary debts—people go to Nevada and come back a little shorter than they used to be. So that's kind of how you walked in our door. You weren't so much short as over your head. Remember you came to us?"

"I remember," Hutch said.

"And what you said was, you said you only needed this sum till you laid the project off on your stable of regular investors. It was just a short-time deal. You said the regular mortgage people made you sign a personal note already so you couldn't go back to them and you couldn't just walk away from the project either, all that responsibility you feel to your regular investors plus maybe the stuff about you'd hate a trial for misrepresentation or felony fraud or whatever they like to call it these days."

"I thought it'd just take a couple of weeks, a month," Hutch said.

"But it didn't. We're not trying to confiscate you with the interest, Hutch. Nothing to confiscate anyway. You said you have all these buddies just begging, lining up, and you only needed to get the paperwork out—"

"I don't think you ever fuss with paperwork."

"Personally, you're right, I hate it," Ray said. "In this office we do without. We avoid it. We just understand what's ours. The clock is ticking, Hutch." Ray shook his head sadly. "And what with the clock ticking and the interest compounding and the clock ticking some more, and Hutch, you may call us loan sharkers or anything else, but just try to recall in your little heart of hearts that *you* came to *us*."

Hutch was willing to work it out. "I recognize we got a problem."

"*You* do, Hutch."

"Wait. Let's not rush ahead and forget our goals. I've been thinking."

"Good. I'm glad you've been thinking and feeling. I think you're a thinking person, Hutch."

"Okay, Ray. I want to share my concerns. You wouldn't believe how rental rates for downtown offices changed overnight. . . ." Hutch perceived that Ray would believe, but it didn't seem to be an intimate concern in Ray's life. It might be better to move right along to the nitty and the gritty. "Okay, never mind, so the problem, Ray, the basic problem here is the monthly payments while my deal matures. That just puts a pall on things." Ray seemed to lay back and roll his eyes at the others, his colleagues. There was no

Paul in this room. "Listen, Ray, this is an outstanding deal but it's taking a little time I tended to underestimate. It's ripening slowly but surely. The climate for investment property in this town has turned a little slow right now, not bad, just slow due to the changes in the tax laws and a couple big companies moving to Marin and down the peninsula—"

Ray lifted and waved a hand slowly. He wanted to enjoy Hutch's song, this speeding-up aria with the voice being so convincing and going a little high as it speeded up, and he was sure this stuff was fine in Hutch's normal line of work, lining up investors, but it happened that this particular aria didn't mean much to Ray Aratunian. They were supposed to be talking about Hutch's debt, not about climates for investment property. The waving hand didn't even look as if it were chasing a fly. It actually looked tired.

Hutch paused. He was aware of the climate in this room. But the reason he thought of himself as a success was that he was not a quitter. He had this metabolic optimism, as his brother called it, because his brother didn't have it. He waited until Ray's hand fell back onto the arm of his chair and then he began again. "Some deals take a little longer, Ray, so suppose we just add the monthly payments to the principal, the balloon, and that way you get a bigger balloon payment and I get the little more time I need—"

"Hutch," said Ray, grieving. "You didn't listen. We're not such a bank. Such a bank wouldn't do such a deal for you and that's why you came to us."

Hutch thought this over. He tried looking Ray in the eyes, above and between, at the caterpillar line of hair between the eyes, making man-to-man contact, but Ray was thinking about other things. "You said you got a brother needs to place his capital, hasn't got no investment writeoffs. We agreed about that, too. Now we need you to remember what we all agreed. Otherwise, Hutch, it just gets difficult. I hate to have to point that out once again."

"I understand," said Hutch.

"Preciate your consideration," Ray said.

It was almost visible in the air of the room, with Ray and his colleagues all sitting around in glum silence, not bothering to look at Hutch, just waiting in their sadness for the simple, unfestive point to get through to him. It was abstract, like arithmetic, and yet it was heavy in the air. No adding monthly interest to the balloon. No more extensions to the already extended final date. Accept the extra penalty payment, separate from the monthly interest payments, because Hutch needed to learn a lesson and that's how these bankers ran their bank.

Cash out the deal now, Hutch.

Clarity didn't seem to fill them with energy and joy. They drooped as they sat comfortable in their silence which made Hutch uncomfortable. Probably they drooped because of their cholesterol, their lack of consideration for their bodies, their coffee and bad eating habits, meat, all those heavy sauces, no aerobic exercise, a certain lack of the California and San Francisco spirit.

Just pay up, Hutch.

Ray sighed and began again although he clearly felt this meeting had gone on past its end. He didn't so much begin again as attempt to sum it up logically, in simple and easy-to-understand language, for the benefit of a slow-thinking partner. "Hutch, we here at Vecchio Investments are beginning to wonder if maybe you'd like to stiff us."

"I wouldn't do that, Ray."

"Hutch," said Ray, full of grief and fatigue. "Hutch, Hutch. Hutch, you *can't* do that."

9

Dan was happy! Sometimes the anarchy came together. For him it didn't need what could send his
buddies down at the KorVet garage into a knock-on-
wood Big Spender act, wine and takeout all around—
some suave Third World big tipper asking the driver to
carry a bag into the lobby of the Huntington and then
sticking a Ben Franklin or two into his hand, sharing
the wealth he had stolen from the folks in the rice
paddies or the oil desert. It happened regularly to one
driver or another every few months, like the lottery,
and over their morning thermoses of coffee the drivers tried to guess what might be the advance notice.
Fawn-gray gloves hanging limply from one hand, an
antique cane from London, a share-the-wealth cologne were all good signs. Best profession: middleman.
The surest signal was a new girl hanging on the Third
Worlder's arm, nineteen years old max, a perky number who really dug helping a fellow cool out after a
hard day's middlemanning. It must really get tiring to

go flying back and forth between the emerging young democracy and the team of ex-CIA technocrats who had access to a research library filled with surplus shoulder-held missiles. An attaché case full of coke didn't hurt, either.

This wasn't how Dan Montberg looked for his ship to come in. He just liked driving, liked his freedom, liked his wife and daughter, liked his dreamy immersion in the long book he was writing. It wasn't only a fit of coffee elation that swamped him with hope. The mood came on when everything was not merely *going* to be okay; it was there right now. Happy! Okay.

He rushed home with ribs from the Tuscaloosa Triumph Rib Joint out on Haight, announcing, "Time for a little grease, team!" and Gloria and Trish knew he liked to picnic on the floor, on newspapers spread on the floor, pigging out on hot sauce, jokes, and being a family no matter what.

At such times he understood what Hutch meant about making life a festival. What the devil else was it about? And Gloria, smiling, Trish, laughing, all of them teasing, this was better than Hutch's tired long-leggers.

"But Dad, what's got into you?" Trish asked.

"Nothing! That's the beautiful part."

Gloria poked their daughter and said, "You remember the last time, don't you? I think it's his hormones."

He switched on the tinny kitchen radio, whatever music came out—by God, it was the Byrds from 1969 —and grabbed Trish. "Hey Mom! I think he wants to dance."

"Better do what he wants," Gloria said, and then he grabbed her, too, and Trish gave herself permission to enjoy the crazy dad who was only crazy now and then. She would have given him permission, had he asked, to be crazy more often. But at times like this she could see a little of Hutch's knack in her father.

Dan whirled them, bumping against the walls, dodging the indoor picnic, smelling his wife and daughter, letting them sniff him, his hot breath, and then letting them go. He fell back to eating ribs, grabbing a newspaper to wipe his mouth. "I don't know anything," he said.

"Well aren't you nice," Gloria said.

"I mean it. Got my wife, got my kid, got my jobs to do—don't need to know!"

"Maybe you'll learn, Daddy," Trish said.

"Hope not! Hope not!"

Dan didn't care how they teased him. They were laughing about all the things he didn't know, death, war, murder—"Sex!" Trish yelled. "Money!" said Gloria. *"Us!"*

"Hey! Don't teach me, gang!"

They were with him. He wasn't a sagging career driver. He wasn't alone. It was a blessing how, in family, happiness would flood over him like a weather, not pleasure but happiness, joy in his wife, joy in his daughter, the awareness of a thing going on, his family, now, then, forever. A house in the avenues, a functioning DeSoto, a telephone, teevee, and miscellaneous electrical goods, a school for his daughter, garbage collection that was moderately reliable, medical insurance all around, good health anyway—in El Thirdworldo, where Mr. Suave Big Tipper came from, the Montbergs would be ranked with the gods. In many corners of San Francisco, where welfare or AIDS or loneliness or mere quarreling destroyed lives, theirs was still a life of great luck. What a deal. When he dreamed of lovemaking, he dreamed of Gloria, and when he woke, she was by his side.

If she didn't know, he wasn't going to correct Trish about this matter. Gloria knew. But sometimes even people who were very close, like Hutch, knew nothing of the good deals they had or were missing.

When the ribs were gone, and they were tossing the bones into the styrofoam bucket, and they were licking their fingers, picking at the special Tuscaloosa Triumph slaw with their fingers and licking them again, Gloria had something to say. "The boy wants to talk to you, Dan."

"The boy?"

"Your brother."

Trish hated for the fun to end. For her mother to end it this way wasn't fair, because her dad was a boy and fun some of the time, he really was, give him credit, although Hutch was always *really* there for Trish, always fun, a man *and* a boy. Judging by the squint her mother was giving her dad, and the way she crumpled up the newspaper with the spilled hot sauce, sticking it into the bucket, the fun was suspended for now. People weren't supposed to end the fun so abruptly.

Trish guessed she had her homework or something to do.

Later, when he came down, alone and awake after making love, Dan remembered that he was in jeopardy with Gloria, he might not be a writer, he might just get old and tired, his daughter would go away, it would all come to an end. And yet he had just been alive. And yet it was all worthwhile.

Then finally, curled against his wife's back, feeling the freckles even in the dark, he thought about printing her back as a poem, a poem of freckles, and made a startled laugh at the thought. *Wuh?* Gloria asked from dreamland. "Just falling asleep," he whispered. "It's all good."

Hutch was in the driver's bucket seat. Dan was sitting alongside. Hutch really cared about his poor schmuck of a kid brother. Despite the inadequacies of others, all was copacetic with the world.

Dan had a hand cupped to his ear, although the motor noise from a BMW was nothing more than a sweet whisper, sweeter than Suki's whisper for sure. Probably the wind across his elbow in an open KorVet clunker, plus the constant traffic noise when he was making an airport run, was doing no good to his hearing. Out of kindness about Dan's problems, Hutch raised his voice a little. "I wanted to be, you know, considerate. Insulate you from the other investors, not get in the way of your life. You got a real life going for you there. You know, not to interrupt the flow—"

Hutch liked talking from behind the wheel. He could chat straight ahead. He liked the low accompaniment of the motor of a leased BMW, a sweet hum indistinguishable from one bought with time payments but a whole quantum leap ahead in business considerations and IRS creativity. He liked the intimate confidentiality of two people, really close people like Dan and him, in this small lease with option to buy space. For punctuation he could sniff the leather, so pungent when he first climbed in, then rapidly weakening, like a romance with one of the Enrico's terrace tired blonds. He kept his eyes on the road. He purred along like a fine German engine in Dan's ears. "—if you're writing a great book or something. I know it doesn't help to be bumped out of it."

At times even Hutch could be bumped out of his main business. After all, the plan was an upper, here in California and everywhere, for Trish and him, for Dan and Gloria, for all of them. Dan was squinting up at his sudden grin. He looked puzzled but it wasn't appropriate to distract him with explanations. Hutch was thinking about how he could freshen up the leather smell with the Skotch-Leather aerosol can in the glove compartment, something a person couldn't do with Enrico's terrace ladies. He hadn't found a Tired Blond aerosol product.

"This is an interruption no matter how we think about it," Dan was saying. "It's not just signing a paper. I can't believe it's that. Gloria doesn't want me in this."

"And well do I understand her concern, that marvelous wife. She's perfect for you, I've always thought that. She's only protecting your interests, hers and the kid's. That kid is my heiress, Dan, down in my will in black, white, and Technicolor. I absolutely agree. Trish —what else is there? My only niece. And that's why I have to take your time to see and hear for yourself."

Cut it short. Hutch knew his flaws. Sometimes he went on too much. Better to give the other person the space to work himself into what Hutch wanted him to do.

Dan wasn't speaking.

BMW motor. Silence. Like looking a person straight in the space between the eyes. Wait.

At last Dan said, "It feels complicated."

Now they were on again. "All deals are complicated. That's the nature of deals. That's dealing. But the rewards—" Hutch took one hand from the steering wheel. He glanced over at his brother in the unfamiliar business suit with its narrow lapels. Hutch had dusted the shoulders with his hand and warned him many times over the years about leaving clothes too long in the back of the closet. They became useless. Style marches forward. "The rewards of a good deal," he said, and kissed three fingertips at the traffic light. "And it's not too complicated to put out a signature, crazy as that sounds. You'd be surprised the dummies get rich, just stumbling around in the right spot at the right time."

"I need to know what I'm doing."

"That makes sense. Empires have been gained for the shake of a hand and a signature, Dan. You're the

scholar in the family—was it Rome or Athens? I can't
think of them right now."

"Hutch, I need to know."

"Right! Don't I agree? Isn't that why I asked you to
meet the bankers? They're a little different, Dan,
brace yourself for that. This is absolutely on a need-to-
know basis, we call it, because I have nothing to hide,
so you're coming to the meeting, right now that's
where we're headed, isn't it? Hey, gimme a break."

They were caught in that downtown financial district traffic at California and Montgomery which
makes a person curse and sigh, first one, then the
other, in an order depending on temperament. The
lights were changing; the little red and green pedestri-
ans were flashing on and off with no results; a Pathways van driver was flinging himself against his horn
and giving the finger to an Eskimo bag lady with a
Cala Foods shopping cart. *Walk* meant nothing at this
hour and this intersection. *Trudge* meant nothing.
Only the Eskimo woman and two skinny speed-freak
messenger people on bicycles, screaming whooee
warnings, were able to break through gridlock.

Hutch made a serious effort. Neither cursing nor
sighing, he emitted philosophic conversation. "You're
going to learn some things about investment, brother
of mine. You remember how important I am about
keeping fit? Well, in business, even in San Francisco
SFO, sometimes you got to do business with overweight people."

"Your standards," Dan said.

"They may not live so long, they may not smell so
good when the going gets rough, but sometimes they
hold the lease, the option, the loan, you got to deal
with them. Some of them are smokers."

"There is no justice, is there?"

"Sarcastic. Oh God, your sarcasm, Dan. Never learn,
never change. Just because your life's pure and mine

less so." Hutch was shaking his head. He certainly wasn't going to get into an area of old rough roads with his brother, not now. "But listen up, brother, I learn from you. Running is pure. Not much else, but running really is."

Dan wondered how Hutch had learned from him, since he wasn't a runner. The final gridlock was postponed one more time. As traffic began to move, the Eskimo lady abandoned her shopping cart and charged the Pathways van, spewing great rich gobs of spit at the driver. He almost got his window up in time. It was a contest of froth versus finger; the van driver cursed and jabbed his middle finger into the air; the Eskimo lady responded weakly to metaphor, but silently covered the van with saliva, lumbering after it like a seal over ice, until the traffic picked up speed.

Hutch was thinking about the purity of running and not wasting one's vital energy on futile animosities. Dan watched him pull into a lot with a big FULL NO SPACE GO ELSEWHERE sign blocking the entrance, pluck a five-dollar bill from the change compartment as the attendant came trotting toward them, yelling, "Hey, fucker, can't you read? . . . Thanks, mister, just leave the keys."

"Not much in this life is pure, Dan, 'cept family feeling."

And not always that, Dan thought.

The way a man sweats, one of his entrepreneur friends had told Hutch, tells what he's holding—a good straight or just a bunch of limp cock. Larry Klotz, he had a way with words, being in film and all, but it was a useful comment for a man who sought success in another difficult business. From then on, Hutch had decided to sweat thin, spicy, and clean, turn himself into a healthy runner, keep the pores easy. He ran to get used to the right way of running. He intended to avoid plumpers and doctors. Unclogged was the ticket. Today, however, he wasn't sure the sweat was coming right; he preferred to sweat in jock strap, satin shorts, T-shirt, not in one of his good Italian suits. He rested there just a moment in the bucket seat. In a moment he would jump out.

Dan stared at his brother. The happy boy was at bay; the animal was cornered and his teeth were showing. Beneath the alert health there was something like the fate of everyone else, those who grow tired, old, and regretful.

Hutch's eyes darted toward Dan and then away. He didn't want to be caught with a look of supplication. Dan thought: I can save him. Only I can do it.

Still sitting there, Hutch said, "I'm sure you have very real concerns and doubts. I'm ready to allay those concerns."

"You're a regular surgeon general's report, aren't you? Come off it."

"Only kidding. Trying to sell you, Dan, you *know* part of my job is selling. But you don't make it easy."

"Okay."

"Dan, just buy me time. We'll both do good—this I promise. You supply the time and I'll do the rest."

Only the kid brother can save him.

"I give you a brother's word," Hutch said. His cheeks were shining. There was an exaltation of sweat and the reflection of the yellowish sky outside, lights from the city, fog from the sea reaching all the way into North Beach. Soon it would burn off, or maybe it wouldn't; whatever was right. On Hutch's pared-down runner's face the nose stood out like a beak with vulnerable trickles of blood beneath the skin; the capillaries were broken from running, not drinking; from allergies and steaming them out; from the years.

When he climbed out of the BMW, he did what he always did: cocked his ear for the nice clunk of a balanced door as he shut it with a graceful flip of his hand.

Good machinery was likable. Hutch liked to look at it, keep it shiny, visit a quality car wash; liked to use it.

Dan remembered riding their bikes out to Ocean Beach. During that time before ten-speeds came in, there weren't even many three-speeds, bikes didn't make much sense in San Francisco; but the Montberg boys were willing to fight the hills. Then they locked them together and climbed down below the dying amusement park with its Laughing Fat Lady and half the food stands were shut but there was still plenty of smell of taffy and hot chocolate and oil from the stalled Ferris wheel. They bought greaseburgers and ate them on the beach with containers of root beer. If they were rich that day, they also bought It's-Its, ice cream between cookies, layers of chocolate, crumbs, cream, and sugar, providing a thick, satisfying aftertaste for the return back up Geary Boulevard.

They chained their bikes together on the slope of beach, but kept an eye on them and on the surfers in their gleaming black rubber suits. They took off their shoes and felt the warm sand between their toes. Hutch swore he would someday get rich, get laid, life would be a festival, girls and money and laughs; virginity would be just a memory, and so would stealing coins from their father's pants; and Dan confessed he not only intended to write a book but had started it already. Hutch whistled. "Hey, admiration! That fuckin notebook with your homework? Hey, fancy that."

And the first Aquarian kids in their funny Goodwill costumes were chanting with a guru down the beach. And the pre-guru ones, the post-guru ones, or the dope-guru ones were toking or freaking out or turning their Aquarian cartwheels into the water. At age fifteen these brothers still had each other, had heard the Jefferson Airplane from the sidewalk in front of the Matrix on Fillmore, and hadn't yet paid their way in to the Fillmore Auditorium for the Tower of Power, the Grateful Dead, and the nights of LSD rituals and rock weddings. They knew Space Daisy before she met Lee Quarnstrom. And Hutch had learned already what life must be.

Playland-at-the-Beach: now it was all condominiums. Even in this early sunlight of the San Francisco crusade, Dan had noticed the network of veins on Hutch's nose. Later he learned they were capillaries, everyone had them, and his own were hidden, maybe because of a lower level of blood pressure. He watched the signs of pressure in Hutch the way other kids studied their parents' eating habits, noisy chewing. His brother chewed tactfully.

Today in North Beach the fog was burning off, which it was supposed to do, and there was glare off the massed windshields in the parking lot. Hutch squinted. In his eyes was a place he reserved for no one. He didn't like Dan looking at him in there. It wasn't personal; it was a reserved parking spot. Today, since this was a serious business occasion, Hutch didn't wear his favorite tangerine parachute of silk billowing from his jacket pocket. Instead he affixed a little red ribbon to his lapel. He had seen it downtown on Sutter near Brooks Brothers and liked it, and then found it again in a shop on Polk. They assured him it had nothing to do with Mao or the Russians. He awarded himself the Legion d'Honneur, just like a man who stayed in the best small hotel in Paris, France, one frequented by nothing but dusky oil billionaires, blotchy arms dealers, and red-ribboned gentlemen, all with girls that fit nicely with the money and the ribbons.

"Hey, you know what that is?" Dan asked.

Hutch took a rubber Pluto nose out of his pocket, a shiny black-and-yellow mask, and slipped it over his face. "I'm a star," he said.

"You gonna rob the bank?" Dan asked.

"Go fuck yourself, too, brother." He stuffed the mask back into his pocket. "Hey, let's get some laughs around here. Come on."

Even if Los Angeles seemed to be fulfilling its ambitions, San Francisco was still the financial capital of the West. Because Hutch used words like *loan* and *bank*, Dan thought they would be visiting an office in a stately Roman temple or an aluminum-and-glass skyscraper, humming with electronic machinery, lots of busy striding back and forth. But *bank*, it turned out, was just an expression. The office of Vecchio Investments was in a low brick courtyard, past a shuttered Mexican restaurant on Pacific in the Barbary Coast area between the financial district, Chinatown, and North Beach. The words VECCHIO INVESTMENTS on the door were not followed by the names of loan officers, fund managers, experts in trusts and real estate development. No vice-presidents around here. When Dan stared at his brother, Hutch paused with his hand raised to knock. "Banks make nothing but red tape. They're just like the government, all overhead. These guys it's just a handshake and you've got a go. I've had it with banks up to here."

The hand now rapped gently.

Sometimes paperwork might be a helpful idea, Dan was thinking as the latch slid, a chain fell, and someone opened the door. It was a short, hefty, dark-haired woman in a shapeless black widow's dress. She was not a secretary or a girlfriend, more like someone's old sister; she was someone's older sister who kept an eye on things and stayed in mourning because there was so much to grieve over. "You're late, Hutch. Who's this?"

"I said I was bringing my brother. He doesn't look like my brother, but he is. The traffic was you wouldn't believe and that's why I'm maybe seven-eight minutes late."

"Don't make no difference." She left it unclear whether she meant she didn't mind if he was late or didn't care about his excuse for being late. Dan thought he smelled Mexican takeout. If so, it didn't come from the defunct La Puerta across the courtyard with its heavily stained dark Mission beams and railings the color of refried beans, and the sad little last-ditch sign, *We Serve Luncho.*

The office where the partners met was too small for the four men and a woman, or perhaps the people were too large for the room. When dapper Hutch with his Italian suit and undapper Dan in his lumpy Sather Gate clothes entered, there was a small amount of reluctant shuffling. Two card chairs, stencilled *Vecchio Catering Enterprises,* were unfolded. The partners in Vecchio Investments were drinking glasses of wine, as if they had already toasted some success. Without asking, the hefty lady poured black coffee from a thermos and handed paper cups to Hutch and Dan. Maybe she also managed the catering division.

One of the men grinned at Dan, shaking his cheeks. He had a happy astonished smile. He was thick and short, stumpy in the arms and legs, alert and clever in the eyes. "For your sake," he said to Dan, "I hoped you wouldn't show up."

"Pardon?"

"But you did. I mean I have one position for myself. For myself I take the normal position about getting return on investment. But I can't help it, it's like a disease, sometimes I put myself in the other fella's place."

Hutch looked startled and fidgety.

Dan said nothing and waited.

The man, Ray Aratunian, shrugged and proceeded to business. "So we have this here proposal to save your brother's project. It might even work if he makes a lucky lunge. Then your brother will come out whole and so will you. And we'll be happy, he'll be very happy, you'll be satisfied, everything will be pretty and nice." He was more and more amused by what he was saying. "Mr. Dan, you wouldn't be here if you were likely to listen to me, so why should I advise you what to do?"

Another Vecchio partner spoke, an emaciated dark old geezer with a wispy tail of beard—a cluster of hairs from a cherry mole—hanging just below his lips, drawing attention from the mouth, which seemed to be turning inside out, a pendulous heavy lower lip, fresh and red. He summoned up the strength for a question. "We get down to business or we just fart up the room? I didn't do that last one."

Everyone shrugged. They didn't do it either.

"The clock's ticking, ain't it?"

"Tick-tock, you're right," said the laugher. "Hey, I didn't drop the bomb."

The geezer's lower lip was still working itself in the wrong direction. He was sniffing furiously and pushing the air goodbye.

The laughing partner, Ray Aratunian, agreed with his general point of view. "Time is money—"

"Air, too." The old guy stopped pushing at it, subsided suddenly, closed his eyes, snored once and then stopped.

"—which is why we are all gathered here—both time and money running out. Our patience is infinite, we are known for that, so we don't want to foreclose the property. That only makes things difficult for everybody. Unimproved land south of Market must have looked like a good deal, which is why Hutch bought in, and some time in the future it'll look like a good deal again to some other farsighted individual or corporation, but in the meantime Vecchio Investments is not in the business of waiting on line, hat in our hand, when the foreclosure doesn't cover the loan, couldn't possibly, the new tax laws, south of Market overbuilt, the vacancy rates a regional and national disaster—no recriminations are necessary at this point, that's not the Vecchio way of doing business. You didn't think ahead, Hutch. You lunged."

"Who did it again?" the old guy asked drowsily. He waved his hand twice, and then let it fall.

"We're not in the business of being taken by a speculator who lunges because he thinks he knows what's happening and solemnly promises to pay a good rate of interest along the way plus principal in the form of a balloon payment which is now coming due. Right, Hutch? So since no bank or savings and loan is available, given the circumstances, the possible dream you sang to us, Hutch, when you brought us into the aforesaid property . . ." He sighed and shook his head. "Which is where a new investor comes in."

Dan stared at his brother. He didn't have money to pay these people off.

The senior citizen, pretending to sleep, surreptitiously lifted one buttock. He preferred not to be blamed. He was deep in the golden sunset years. He preferred to blame.

"Hutch promised us a new investor. Someone with confidence, someone who brings confidence. Something to guarantee we all come out whole." Ray shook his head joyfully at Dan. "I guess you're the new investor, hey?"

Dan heard the faulty heartbreaks in his brother's chest, like a scurrying of small scrawny limbs, pattering and dancing in fear. Hutch folded his arms, he was smiling. Pressing the little beast back took all his effort. Maybe Dan only heard the echo in his own chest. Courage had always been one of Hutch's tools. He used it sparingly. Occasions were now coming up. When they pedalled their bikes up the long slope of Geary, coming away from Ocean Beach, his heart used to thump with mere exertion, not this panic. The ferret pawing in his chest was nurtured by his life.

Ray Aratunian's eyes kept their smile. For him too life was a festival. There was a row of thick lashes that gave him a look of flirty girlish laughter, a generous face, nose, lips, bluish cheeks—altogether Ray was a well-set-up overweight man. The seams in his tan suit were cracked and threads showed. It was from being wide and moving around in his clothes. The suit was made of cloth—not cotton, not wool, just plain cloth, something spun out of materials which came from deep out of the ground, had hung from a rack, now stretched over Ray's shoulders and thighs.

"If you insist, Danny, I got the papers right here in my briefcase." His briefcase was some sort of plastic with the words *Armenian National Home, 1000 Yrs of Progress* embossed on it. Dan had a lot of respect for ethnic loyalty. Ray believed in laying things out, whether his adversary was a Turk or a human being. "But you know sometimes those old sayings, Danny, our ancestors weren't so dumb. Never let yourself get fucked in the ass unless there's a real percentage in it. You look at the papers, I insist. Read every boring word of the boilerplate."

The word startled Dan. Hutch started to speak, but with Ray's help it wasn't necessary.

"It's legal. It's just printed there. But Danny, a lot of learning is a dangerous thing. So take your time."

He nodded and handed over a sheaf of paper.

"Please," he said helpfully. "It's all bullshit."

Hutch just smiled and let Ray do the explanations. For Hutch this took great concentration. But Ray was good at it; he had a nice quality about him.

Dan held the papers and let his eyes run over the first page, then another. He knew the printed papers with the typed insertions and the little circles for initials were not what it was about. This was the rest period of due deliberation. He could feel Hutch's shallow breathing, his need, the pattering of the ferret's paws in his chest. Ray understood about such things and believed in giving him all the time he needed, so long as he took it right now, this minute or the next.

The boilerplate did not get his attention, but laughing Ray Aratunian did, and the sleepy old man with half-shut eyes, and the hefty woman who had returned to help. The skinny nervous kid with a long neck, his head darting swiftly from face to face, just sat there. His head swiveled at signals the skinny kid was supposed to pick up. The body came with a neck-extending option. His complexion was nervous; the raw places would make more scars if he didn't get antibiotics into them, stop picking, maybe grow a little less alert, cut down on chocolate, keep his fingernails out of the eruptions.

If Ray Aratunian asked him to get angry, the kid could do it fast.

Hutch was doing the right thing now. Silence. Dan felt his brother's effort, hope, and need of him. It was the right move for Hutch.

The sleepy man, not actually asleep, maybe only dozing, was focused on results and effluvia. He grew bored waiting. The process did not interest him; process and procedure made his eyelids heavy—his partner's laughter, Dan's hesitation, Hutch's anxiety. None of it was more interesting to him than the nervous turnings of the little zit-infested head of his bodyguard. And that didn't interest him, either. The sleepy man had lived through other people's healthy tics, knew the final rest was on its way for him. Therefore he wanted his money now. He didn't enjoy the working out of deals as much as he used to, and he had never really enjoyed it. He glanced with gloomy boredom at the pingpong swivelings of the nervous stalk of neck. He sucked between his teeth with a noise like something hidden in grass. He was asking, his associates were asking, they were all asking on his behalf for Hutch to cooperate for his own benefit. They could make do with a negotiable signature.

These were not friends Hutch had picked because they liked to run, like him, on the Marina. It was another set.

Ray understood that the important thing in negotiation is to sit there, not get impatient, sit and wait no matter what damage it does to some flabby stomachs. The important thing here was to sit and wait and give Hutch's brother all the time he needed to digest his brother's distress. While he sat, his own stomach easy in its doings, Ray liked to pass the time with a little pleasant and educational conversation. "The nice thing about credit," said Ray, "it was invented in Venice by Venetians. Credit always makes me think of those canals, those statues, the gondoliers. Those carvings, they used to do great trim, outstanding custom work. It's beautiful at any season of the year, even though it's kind of damp sometimes. Winter's a bitch."

"I didn't think it rained on Venus," the bodyguard said, suddenly endowed with contemporary human intelligence. "I saw a movie once they claimed it didn't even have atmosphere."

"You want another liquid refreshment?" the hefty lady asked.

"So how could it rain?" said the bodyguard, his stalk of neck turning from one to the other. "Nothing to breathe, nothing to hold the molly-cools."

The hefty dark lady was a close relative of the sleepy man, perhaps of the boy, too—a sister or wife, a daughter, perhaps even a mother, respectively. On this occasion she was here to help.

"I know you're not kidding around," Hutch said. "I take the matter seriously, that's why I'm here. I was a little late through no fault of mine."

"You got a bad habit being late," said the sleepy man. He seemed to be oscillating into wakefulness. "But this time you brought over this nice guy. This boy Hutch got a nice guy for his brother and I like that, I got respeck for it."

Ray turned his huge happy thick-lipped smile full on Dan. "You see what he's saying? Yunnerstan? Thinks you're an idiot—see?"

The old guy murmured, "Wasting time. Going noplace. Let's get there."

"But now I'm into this," said Ray. "I'm studying human nature."

"Someday I want to go to Venus too," said the body-guard.

"You see, Tommy's learning to comment and par-ticipate," Ray said.

The former sleeper called them to order. "This ain't night school here."

Dan was thinking: I don't need people like this. What am I doing in this place?

Hutch is here because he has to be.

I'm here because Hutch has to be.

The frequent sleeper was not disconnected from himself. He was here because he was here. Even his lips retained connection when he deigned to part them in speech, joined by ropy links of saliva. "Let's can we get to the," he asked. He didn't need to finish the sentence, *business,* before the twisted yellowish ropes pulled his lips and teeth back together again.

I'm in the afterlife, Dan thought, heaven or hell, and I don't understand what the choir is singing at me. He didn't know anybody here. He was lonely for his brother.

When their eyes met, Hutch shrugged and quickly glanced away. He reached for a plastic cup of thermos coffee which he lifted to his lips, as if he planned to drink. He touched his lips and put the coffee down.

Hutch did not seem to be enjoying the business meeting. Dan told himself: decide nothing now.

This may also have been a meeting room for the defunct Mexican restaurant. Dan admired the rough Mission beams with knotted, deeply stained Mission supports. It was an odd clubroom for a cab driver and not-yet-published novelist who wanted to recapture a time in his boyhood, long bicycle trips through Marin County, all the way to Inverness, with his older brother.

The sleepy man was snoring again. He was not really asleep. His head had fallen, his esophagus was soft, his breathing bubbled. But he was full of surprises, sneakily shifting in his chair.

"Personally I'd put up my own money if I had it!" the young bodyguard said with an eager chirp, looking around for confirmation of his initiative. "Looks like a good deal to me! You could count me in if I had any loose savings account to spare!"

His exclamations did not disturb the sleepy man. Ray said happily, "Shut up, hey?"

"I mean it!"

"I mean it, too," said Ray, not laughing.

The old guy woke up. "So we got one?" he asked. "He ready to write his name?"

The smell of Mexican takeout, which seemed so persuasive when they arrived, was dispersed by their breathing. Metabolism created smells but also took care of them. Now, as they got up to leave, the hefty woman fixed Dan with a very bright, angry, almost sexy glare. "Mister," she said. She did not include Hutch in this address. Her eyes were fierce on Dan. "Mister, you decide quick. I don't like waiting on line."

Again Dan felt a dizziness, the Mexican Mission courtyard twisting and dipping like a ship in strong waters; he wasn't sure where he was. Now the sleeper was only the philosopher here; laughing Ray was a helper; the boy was just an infected kid; and the hefty lady seemed suddenly in charge.

Ray put his arm on Dan's. He was steadying him with a warm farewell. "This is just an episode in your brother's life," he said kindly. "Might even be a crucial episode in a life made up of episodes. But on your behalf, my new friend, make sure it's only an incident for you. Would you please do that for me?"

He passed a whole lot of jovial through the air to Dan, his lips parted, his teeth stained and brown but useful for proving that he kept most of his own teeth. The thick seam along each cheek disappeared when he stretched his mouth in laughter. Laughter healed the cheek seams, but not the stretched ones in the tan all-cloth suit, the threads pulling away, the suit evolving when he leaned toward Dan. "Do that one little thing for Ray, will you?" he asked.

The door shut. Hutch and Dan felt the discomfort of leaving a group behind which was surely now proceeding to evaluate them. The brothers strolled silently down the short hall and through the Mission courtyard which led to the street.

The sun was skating around on the tiled surfaces of the closed Mexican place. *We Serve Luncho* had disappeared into bankruptcy, but California sunbeams were still bouncing between mosaic glaze and burnished dark wood, a dance of heat and light, sheltered by walls from the wind and the fog off the Golden Gate. Emerging into the glare, Hutch narrowed his eyes like a hero telling his story to a new woman. He remembered air battles. Dan felt heavy, as if he had eaten too much lunch. Information and noninformation overload was acting up in him. There was too much blood in his stomach. A grown person can't just lie down when he has a problem to meet. "Okay, Hutch, they didn't tell me enough."

"From their point of view, they said what they wanted to say."

"*You* don't tell me enough."

Which way was the lot with the car? Hutch looked up and down the slope of Montgomery. "I'll tell you more," he said quietly. "I don't want to promise you great riches, though it just might happen, the market shifts, no one can predict, you'll do great. Is that what you want me to tell you?"

He paused. Dan waited. Hutch sighed and knew he had to move on a little.

"What I can promise is I factored with these people, I thought it was only a couple months. You know what I mean, Dan? I mean they could really hurt me if you let me down."

Sometimes Dan thought of starting over without wife and daughter, without furniture or history, in a room on the flatlands south of Market like his room on upper Grant when the shadow of Jack Kerouac still walked that sloping street. He remembered the vision of himself as a doomed young poet alone in the foggy swirl of San Francisco. Doomed to what? To cappuccino and lost loves? He had believed in this dramatic, repetitious waiting for the past and the future to come together as a form of heroism. He had found Gloria and learned there was also something a person could construct every day in marriage, escaping the prison of times gone and to come. He was a husband and he became a father.

He used to dream that a poet began anew from disaster, needed loss and disaster, and that this was the way for him. Now it would be different: industrial warehouse flats instead of an Italian settlement on a hill; his grizzled regretful forties, not the dewy ignorance of his twenties.

He had not yet cleared the smoke out of his head.

He still had a wife and a daughter. He was past the middle of his life. The bills were coming due. He was not allowed to search out a heroic disaster for selfish, fantastic, daydreaming, boyish reasons. A person's dreamlife could be as ignorant in the middle of his life as at the beginning.

Hutch was a greedy dreamer, too.

Dan hoped he was not being merely ignorant. He wasn't sure shared blood with his brother was a wise guide to correct procedures. He tried to present the facts to himself in a businesslike way. His family was larger than it used to be when they bicycled out Geary Boulevard toward Ocean Beach to watch the giant Laughing Lady and bite into It's-Its. Following the old loyalty and yearning could be the right path in his imaginary world and the wrong one in the world he was offered. He had even discovered the pleasure in his anger with Hutch about Avigdor; excessive anger, a sign of other enjoyments and decisions from the real world in which he was growing older. He had wondered why that deliriousness of rage, almost a tantrum, felt so indulgent and delicious. At this time in his life more was available to him than his childhood, his intentions.

If that wasn't so, he might as well spend the rest of his life hanging out with the other cabbies at Sophie's Home Cooking near the taxi garage, explaining how everything would soon be wonderful, there was this couple in his hack, they asked if he would come with them to their fuckin Presidential Suite at the Fairmont —the usual cab driver's poetry. But he didn't need this form of poetry. He made his own. He knew about a present responsibility. He had a wife, a child, a hope of work to do. Gloria and Trish were his flesh, blood, and obligation.

But so was Hutch. Hutch had always been so.

Stubbornly Dan pushed ahead with what he believed he had to do, no matter which corrupted and childish parts of his imagination distracted him. It was his fault if he had grown up dreaming in San Francisco. His big brother had fed on dreams, too—of turning slowly, dizzyingly, in the Carousel Bar at the Fairmont in the company of an important late-night talkshow-confirmed band singer.

Hutch had updated his ambitions. Dan still dreamed of his book about their childhood on the edge of the sparkling hills of San Francisco, their yearning to leave the Richmond for the international glamor village where the hundred-year-long operetta called San Francisco played itself out in sexy restaurants with the sexy legs and buttocks of clever women, the sexy money to be made, fame to be achieved. He saw how close his dream was to Hutch's. He had also discovered unexpected loves, Gloria and Trish, which came without consideration. His only brother remained embedded in the boyish nostalgia. It was not an improper procedure for Dan to go on loving a brother. It was not a thing to measure and quantify; love was supposed to be a passion; fear, anger, and the risk of loss were a part of it.

It wasn't Dan's job to be prudent and businesslike. He had always given that job to Gloria. In the past she had accepted the assignment. Now she was asking: "Do you know anything more about it?"

"A little bit. I'd say he's in trouble."

"Is it up to you to get him out of it? Without knowing any more?"

"They don't foreclose property. They foreclose people."

"Without knowing what it's all about?"

She had a right to be businesslike and pissed. It was her job.

"He says he's sure he can pull it off with just a little more time and then we'll be in a different situation. I mean you and me and Trish, some kind of cushion, security."

"In exchange for some kind of insecurity."

Dan said very slowly to his wife, "He needs my help —*our* help. It's not actually our money. We don't have to put up anything. He says it's the deal of a lifetime and he's only giving it to us because we're family. Since we don't have any equity yet, it's our best chance to get some. Money is freedom, Gloria. We can use some of that."

She drummed on the kitchen table. There was a humming vibration of rapid fingertips. She looked at the walls, at the fridge with the messages to Trish about her kitchen duties, at the spider plant in the pot on the sill with the yellowing *Chronicle* underneath to catch Dan's careless watering. A child who wants to avoid doing things does them carelessly, explains with sullen silence or talks too fast, as Trish did, as Dan was doing now. She hated it when he played stupid with her. What he was saying did not cover the matter and he knew it. "We're not putting up cash, true. It's just our credit, right?"

"We don't use it anyway. We're letting it go to waste."

"Hutch said that, didn't he? Didn't he?"

Silence from Dan.

"Do you see our credit out there rotting on the back stairway? Which, by the way, is going to kill somebody if you don't get out there with a hammer and nails and some fresh boards."

"I'll do it, I promise."

"That's great. Will you promise something else?"

"Anything."

"Not make me listen to Hutch's bullshit secondhand out of your mouth, Dan."

He waited. He knew how her eyes migrated during their quarrels when she didn't want to fight and yet was about to. It usually happened in the kitchen. Up till now she respected their bedroom. Her eyes went from the wall to the fridge to the spider plant. She gathered her grievances on her migration in the kitchen.

He braced himself for the harvest. She was collecting one thing at a time, preparing to hurl the tangle at him. He didn't like the shrug he had offered her. It reminded him of Hutch's way of letting a burden roll off with no hurt on any side. It didn't work for Hutch, either. He tried his best good-fellow grin and said, "Okay."

"Okay what?"

"I'll fix the stairs. I know Hutch likes to say things . . . Okay."

"That's eloquent. That sure wins the old lady's heart. That'll stand up in court."

She had drawn back before. She might do it again. It was Gloria's way and had kept them going for nearly twenty years. She knew he loved her and she only needed to understand how much he needed their life together, how much he wanted to make his life entire and complete, including all of them, the beginning and the end of life. And he only repeated, *"Okay,* you're right."

"Listen, don't you work hard for your money? I know I do. Don't you say you're gonna get piles from squeezing down in your cab and then sitting in front of the typewriter in the middle of the night when some people are nice and warm in their beds?"

"Tell me," Dan said.

"I know I work hard if you don't remember. I grade papers with thirty-five in a class should have twenty-five. What kind of security and freedom are we working for if we—"

"We don't have to lay anything out. I explained that."

Gloria was grimacing with rage. "You're not that dumb. I've lived with you too long to think you're that dumb."

"Well, if I sign, Hutch knows he's responsible, and if I help him out—"

She slammed the door with her foot. From her room Trish yelled: "Going out or coming in? Hey, keep it down, I'm trying to tape my group."

Dan winced. He thought a moment and all he thought to say was: "I love you, Gloria."

"You know I . . . I love you too. But if they come for it, for whatever you're signing away, if they come for it, Dan, that will be the end."

"What are you saying?"

"The end. The end for us."

"I don't understand. Why would you want to do that?"

"Sometimes people have enough. Having enough, sometimes that's all marriages are about."

"That's not right, Gloria. It's not right to threaten."

"I'll divorce you, Dan."

"He's my only brother."

"Did you hear me?"

He turned away. He might have said, I'll have to take that chance. He might have said, No, please, try to understand. He might have said, Don't threaten, you have no right.

But she had a right and he knew it. Because they knew and trusted and loved each other, both of them understood this was why he did not answer her.

10

Hutch was sitting with his chair pushed close to the pretty person whose hand he was holding. She was talking and he was listening and he was nodding and nodding to her. Then he was talking and she was nodding. They were looking into each other's eyes. They saw no one but each other. He saw nothing except her, but he felt the envy of the others—those who wanted what he had. The air of Broadway was blowing envy gas.

"Hey, Hutch! Shaving points on the Washington High basketball game?"

Too bad for those who let themselves be eaten up by what they weren't smart enough to get for themselves.

On the other side of the terrace, a group of the Enrico's bachelors who called themselves the North Beach Lonely Hearts Club was having its regular Friday afternoon lunch. The subject was generally why this collection of legal, financial, artistic, and presentable middle-aged genius heterosexuals, most of them at least once divorced, therefore certified as both experienced and hopeful, could not find, each for each, the perfect young woman. One of the philosophers among them, Frank Curtis, noted the word *perfect* and commented that here was the problem and the joke. The others laughed about the problem; they mourned about the joke; Frank was happy to have crossed the Bay and contributed to their wisdom. "Perfect! Oh, perfect!" The Enrico's terrace boys were accredited seekers, listed in the National Registry of Fully Board Approved Lovelorn. Their adventures of the week provided much of the occasion for fun at these Friday lunchtime summit meetings.

This afternoon, however, they were laughing about Hutch Montberg, who sometimes joined them, over there across the terrace. "Doesn't see us, he's unconscious," said Larry Klotz, a screenwriter. Since he was also a Jungian analysand, Larry's word "unconscious" referred to Hutch's anima, karma, or space-time soul, no one asked which.

It meant he had eyes only for the girl.

It meant he was up to his usual tricks.

Hutch was bringing good news to the young person at his side, his chair touching hers, the fingers of his big male paw masterfully entwined about her cool and slim ones: "Hey, the important thing isn't just get through your life. Anybody can do that in San Fr'cisco. But your life is all yours from beginning to end by means of what I call continuation. You got to worry if your mother says sign up secretary school when you *know* you're supposed to go for, I don't know, top model. Okay, then take the time to worry, but say to yourself, Wait a minute! Hey! The beginning and the end of my life are mine, right? So if I don't make it a festival, who will?"

"Me?"

"That's pretty good. I like that. That's the same thing I want for you—a festival."

She broke into a delighted grin. *Continuation* was a terrific philosophy of life. Continuation of the festival. She was up for it, she could go for it, even if it wasn't all that serious, like word-processing class or smile-at-the-customer service industry. If those were serious, who needed it?

She could make better money in the Cablecar Lounge at the Quality Inn, which Hutch called the Quantity Inn. All she had to get was an I.D., push up the boobs a little, say her birth certificate was coming from Stockton. Hutch had already told her he found one sort of crooked front tooth a real turn-on and his birthday present for her would be to get it straightened. Maybe some night this other thoughtful millionaire type, a dude like Hutch, might happen to notice her and she wouldn't even have to work up gradually to top model. A lot of these millionaire types had their own model agencies.

Trish modified, modulated, the smile toward the shy and cute Hutch liked best, giving him an extra peek at the tooth, and said, "Fancy that."

Hutch appreciated being teased. Life was their little game. They kissed lightly, sweetly, just bumping lips in the late lunchtime air with practically nobody paying attention to them. So tenderly.

The men at the big table were applauding, but these two didn't necessarily need to notice.

Larry Klotz needed to make his friends laugh. "God, what if we were all like Hutch? Looking for Miss Right?"

"All still looking for the same girl," said Ferdinand the Bull Lawyer, "but not a one of us finds her. You know what? Hutch might not be the only strange one around here."

"Speak for yourself, Ferdinand. I got a Hungarian psychic says she's been sighted—"

"Who?"

"Miss Right! Pay attention and stop drooling over that teenie-tiny with Hutch. She's been sighted shooting her own movie elsewhere, at this very moment, probably in Malibu, with a guy'll turn out not to be Sir Anthony Stunning-Right, either," said Larry. "Hutch's story is in turnaround. Only that there chicklet"—he lowered his voice, but it was a principle among these pals that there could be no secrets—"only that there chicklet over there, hey, is too young even for me."

They all laughed. It was Hutch's turn to be cut up, since he wasn't at the lunch today. Instead, he was Exhibit A, nuzzling the cute little person across the terrace. Probably voices wouldn't carry in the lunchtime hubbub. It didn't matter. Friends and colleagues were supposed to communicate about each other on a Friday afternoon.

Solemn Frank Curtis, the philosophic journalism teacher from Berkeley, asked for permission to offer his own deep-think analysis. He needed a little attention from the grabby San Francisco types. Frank had given up pipe-smoking, a shame in a way, even if his collection of pipes did tend to offer a touch of lip and mouth cancer in return for the thoughtful prof image. Time to reward Frank for his Friday drive across the Bay Bridge; it would only take a moment. "Let's listen to our boy," Larry Klotz said, "and then I'll puncture him with a well-chosen word. Frank? You got it."

Frank cleared his throat. He kept it brief. He thought Hutch was the perfect Homunculus San Francisco, the forever-springtime lad, filled with selfish hope and affection. He may have been scrambling for his cash flow these days, but he also needed his friends and family and that was the next thing to liking, perhaps loving them. "All his friends say—"

Ferdinand's magisterial finger was wagging *no* at him.

"What's the matter? You're interrupting."

Ferd felt sorry for Frank, so smart to be so dumb. "No. You got it wrong. Hutch don't got no friends."

"What about family? He's always carrying on about his brother and sister-in-law, he talks about that niece of his—"

"Sure he likes them." Ferd was ready for this line of argument. "Okay, Frank, let's stipulate he was a child once, before he became the boy he is. Your Honor, Persons of the Jury, I ask you—on national holidays, Christmas, alternate side parking suspended, who the hell doesn't like his own family?"

"He really cares about them," Frank said. He was irate. This was important to him.

"You should be writing op-ed pieces about the changing of the seasons, man, and the gathering of the clan by the hearth. For marshmallows and port. But you still don't get it. Hutch doesn't have friends. He doesn't have family. He has *customers.*"

"I don't believe that. In his heart of hearts he's sincere."

"In his heart of hearts, Frank, he's a classy boutique. He treats his customers to every amenity, smiles, drinks, full-length mirrors, kind words—hey, even a free shoeshine. And then he sincerely takes from them."

"Cynical, *cynical.* You always think the worst, what is it? A professional deformation of lawyers?"

Ferd was nodding enthusiastically. Right, right, a professional expertise. He continued, still wagging his finger. "No, better than takes *from* them. Just *takes* them."

Larry Klotz laughed. "Lighten up, man. He's one of our closest pals. He's one of us."

"He's pretty smart," said Ferd, now thoroughly

warmed up—but he put his hand on Frank's arm as an apology—"almost smart enough to make people think he's not taking, they're *giving*. But not altogether smart either. The boutique has to run a sale now and then because he sees a chance, you know, like these restaurants see a chance to sell a little coke, clean and press some money, specialize back of the kitchen near the alley in a little South American laundry work—"

The others were suddenly silent and interested. "He does that?" Larry asked.

Ferd loved getting the jury to sit up and listen. "Does what he has to do, according to how he sees it, from the point of view of the only person who matters. The only person in the whole wide world. The rest are shadows—"

"Nope, you got it wrong," Larry interrupted. He was frowning. He knew *nope* wouldn't stand on appeal and he was up against a strong lawyer. Nope wasn't a great defense and testimonial to the character of his dear pal and colleague in the bachelor business, Hutch Montberg.

Frank had taken to mouth-breathing during rude analysis of the personality of others. His habit had been obscured when he kept a pipe close to the source of his own comments. But he was following along with Ferd; he really didn't find Ferd too complicated to follow; he agreed with him. "They're not shadows. Other people are necessary. They're providers."

Ferd extended both arms. He shot his cuffs. This was a triumph. "Now you got it, fella," he said.

For the sake of completing the investigation, Ferd cut into any applause that might be his due. As an attorney, Ferd hated grandstanders. If the applause came, he didn't necessarily phone the newspapers, although he did miss the wife he used to keep awake by confiding, in modest rumblings at night in the dark, about how he saw the truth before most people even had a glimmer. So now he turned to Frank. "Didn't he ask you for an investment, too?"

"More like a loan, it's supposed to be. *This is just for my friends.* You also get that one?"

"More like a competence test for morons, wasn't it?"

Watkins, who was also a lawyer, thought Ferd was being simplistic. He said a person might want to take a chance. People bought lottery tickets, didn't they? A person might be fond of Hutch because of, oh, frequent propinquity. Shared psychopathy.

"Wow," said Larry. "Love that vocabulary. You're both tenderhearted and legal, what a one-two shot."

Watkins pressed on without heeding Larry's kneejerk sarcasm. The laissez-faire freedom of Friday lunch also meant the lonely hearts needed to forgive their brothers' weaknesses which came from too many trivializing commuter flights to Beverly Hills. But Watkins summed up his argument in favor of maybe lending Hutch some money in language that even Larry could understand. "A person might think, What the hell?"

"Right, you got a great point there," said Frank Curtis. "One time I washed a wool sweater in hot water in the laundromat just because I wanted to see if this time maybe it wouldn't shrink. Just because they did every other time I tried it was no reason to assume—"

"It shrank!" cried Larry Klotz, and Frank asked if anybody knew any needy small people because he had a drawer full of tight little sweaters for midgets and Ferd asked if a moral dwarf would do and everybody was laughing about the problems of Hutch, the problems of bachelors at the laundromat, the problems of love and money and friendship in general, of the meaning of life in a time when people were getting just a little older; the problems of the Lonely Hearts lunch bunch.

The Friday boys now let themselves go. This was just for fun. If the quartet had been missing one of them instead of Hutch, perhaps the missing one would have gotten the joyous roasting Hutch now received while he was busy sending sweet hutchlings into the ear of the innocently punkish, very young creature at his side across the terrace. He's so pretty, he dresses nice. Hey, he's Dracula's advance man. . . . For Frankenstein with all those bolts and rough stitching he has nothing but contempt. . . . Our boy gives bloodsucking a bad name.

Laughter. Enrico Banducci himself came steering his belly forward to ask, "Having fun? Having the angel wings? You fellas better try the clam chowder. I opened the can with my own hands, a fresh can for you fellas."

There were women lunching alone on the terrace, but the boys had no eyes for them. There was angel-wings pasta on Frank's plate and he was gently inhaling the gentle bits of dough filled with chopped something-or-other, avocado and shrimp it might be, but he looked at his plate with surprise when Enrico brought the subject up. Their good buddy Hutch was on everyone's mind and it was a feeding frenzy at his character. "We might be being a little hard on him, you think?" Frank asked. "I mean, just because he's got that little underage thing with him—what's underage these days? I don't care about his lustlife."

"Hey, that's a word," said Ferd. "You're a true wordsmith, I call you, wait till you get your turn. Are you in Berkeley our next lunch, maybe you got a faculty meeting at the school?"

Frank knew what they would cut him up for. For hopeless love, for solemnity, for boring. Well, everybody needs a flaw. He had learned to forgive himself a bit of high-I.Q. dull. And they'd nail him for Suki again. Okay, he determined to proceed with the subject at hand. "He must be in a strange mood if he's willing to settle for a sexy young operator with the original sticker still on her. What happened to all the tired ones?"

"They're at the Tired Blond Convention in Las Vegas."

"You're interrupting, Larry. This is getting to be a bad habit of yours. Maybe when you're pitching a project to some penguin-shaped producer it's okay, appropriate, but here you're with your intimate fellow seekers—"

Larry folded his hands together in front of his chinny-chin-chin and bowed in a gesture of Zen submission.

Frank sternly waited. Then he shot a glance across the terrace at Hutch before speaking. "He must be desperate."

"Right now I might settle for a young dewy myself," Larry admitted, "out of desperation plus the pedagogical desire to teach which I share with you, Frank. . . . How does he do it?"

"Never gives up," said Ferd. "You got to admire that."

"Oh we do, we do," Watkins said without taking a poll. Nobody objected to Wat's judicial decision. Rumor had it that he wouldn't say no to a Superior Court appointment.

They all paused a moment for a refreshing peek at Hutch's graceful moves against the dewy punkette. She wasn't really a punk; there was just a shadow of it in the water-sharpened hair. Maybe she was only a respectful child and her mother was a punk. "Tireless," said Larry.

"But he finds them—tires," said Ferd.

Larry and Ferd now got a little thing going, a little pingpong game. "You supply the car," Larry said, "he steals the hubcaps."

"He'll even buy the hubcaps, long as he can steal the car from you." Ferd's face was reddening. This was his best time in days.

"Hey, he wants it to look nice. He'll steal some wire wheels, too," Larry said.

"Naw, don't bother to do that. Get you to give him the wire wheels. Cause he promises you a free ride."

Frank interrupted the sport. "It doesn't make sense."

"You ever look at the big-time takers? Hitler, Stalin, Napoleon? Does it ever make sense? And they never fall." Ferd was in earnest now. He was committed to winning his case.

"They do. They always fall," Frank said.

Slow burn. "You call that a fall? When everybody else falls so much further down?"

Larry thought they'd gone too far, even for boys just hanging out on a Friday. Lunch was almost over, anyway. Time to come back to earth. "Hey, hey, this is only old Hutch with the pretty smile. He's having fun. He's no Hitler."

"In San Francisco," Ferd said, "we do the best we can. He does all he can. And you're right: he doesn't care about hurting people. He sure doesn't want to hurt anyone."

"Good Ferd. Good-hearted barrister."

Ferd grinned. "He just wants to help himself. Can't hurt anybody, can he? When anybody don't exist?"

The boys fell silent. The happy vaudeville of the Lonely Hearts Club sometimes brought them down to pensive. They divided the check without playing the match game for who pays. The problem in this discussion was that they knew there was a bit of Hutch spread around their table and the more they abused him, the more they laughed, the more they pleasured each other with the joke and gossip, the sadder they got.

It was like some kinds of sex.
It was like most of the sex they knew.
But the boys truly loved each other.

Hutch's life, like every experienced bachelor's, was
an orgy of missed chances for supreme happiness beyond that of anyone else—the perfect girl in her re-
stored Karmann Ghia alongside the stoplight (a
whisper of baroque music from her speakers); the tall
colt he bumped into in the rain on Union Street,
knocked her umbrella out of her hand, didn't think
fast enough ("Let me buy you a coffee and a sword
cane for protection from men like me" was what he
practiced saying for the next time); the woman in the
parking lot with the serious puzzlement on her brow
who asked where he got the wax job on his car and he
neglected to say, "You like wax jobs? Let me take you
there right now" ; the one whose racket strings broke
while he was watching her doubles match at the
Golden Gateway courts—he lent her his racket and
then let her get away, swinging her tush, one of those
blonds who can play three sets under the October sun
and still smell like heaven—let her get away with only
a bright and dazzling "Thank you so much."
And that was only one fall season in San Francisco.
The years passed with trivial successes and these
tragic failures. Losses didn't put a halt to the continuation of festival. Losses were the origin of renewed
hope; hope was what expectation and confidence
were all about in this land of forever-springtime,
smelling like heaven if a person kept his nose in it. The
woman who would complete him, make him whole,
was probably dreaming of someone just like Hutch,
wasn't she? Wasn't she alone, like him, and making
do with others, and deserving better? Deserving the
best, with a white BMW 325is?
Then why couldn't they meet?

So it was a happy life. Each day at lunch, on the terrace at Enrico's, held the promise of finding the ultimate tired blond but sometimes making do with one who worried about her mother's upcoming lecture and wouldn't look tired enough for another few years.

He couldn't understand his friends over there on the terrace, those guys who let their beards grow out when they were turning gray—how much would it cost them to shave and slice a few points off the public score of years? They let bellies hang or go lax, they let their hopes be reconciled with reality—what the fuck was reality but what a person made it?

Eventually everybody's got to do business in broad daylight. Hutch had nothing to hide. He didn't want people to look too closely; he helped them avoid looking at what was none of their business; but that didn't mean he had anything to hide. His birth certificate was plain, out for inspection upon legal demand or subpoena. The gray in his beard was securely contained within his skin; all a woman had to do was keep him from shaving a day or two. And the belly: muscles held it up, a banjo tautness held it up, pure will and a regular morning run can win against gravity any time. On the terrace of Enrico's his life was an open newspaper.

Hutch had heard about introspection, which he understood meant taking an estimate on the inside prospects of things. He knew about that option. Considering his own insides was close enough. He took great care, usually ate right, did his best to think right on every feasible occasion. Aerobics went without saying; running was as natural as breathing or making money. "I'm kind of interested in being alone sometimes," he told his brother Dan, "a person gotta. You can't just escape, you know. I like to stay home by myself in my condo sometimes, put on a videocassette with some good movie, and just sip a couple lites and really think about things."

"You do that?" Dan asked.

"Well, I lied. It sounds better that way. Actually, I sip a grapefruit juice."

Dan laughed. "You'll live forever, won't you?"

"That's the plan."

Life and age, even in California, needed to be controlled by clean living. Hutch had heard about a tumor of the uterus which stimulates certain alert germ cells and grows teeth and hair. It had a name; he forgot it. Fortunately, only women have a uterus so Hutch didn't have to worry, but the thought only went to prove that introspection was no fucking good. Something wasn't real just because it was true. Those teeth and hair didn't help. What was real was what helped Hutch and the rest was somebody else's problem.

When Hutch made love, he yelled and died. And then came back to life, grinning sheepishly. "I've made a mess," he said.

He wondered if it was the best loving a tired blond had ever received, but didn't ask; he waited till she told him. Sometimes she did. That sudden faint, that sense of drowning in an ocean, a blackness, which was somehow a pleasure even though a death, it was odd that people made so much of it. Hutch liked it when the women occasionally screamed and died, too.

And liked best of all to shower immediately afterward, not remain in the sticky mess; then to dress nattily, take the lady, if it was that kind of afternoon, to sip a cappuccino on the terrace at Enrico's with everyone surely seeing by the pink cheeks, the confident lounging, that the small death had been accomplished. Some women preferred to dig for their own yell, a cuddle, a sleep—well, for Hutch, whatever was right was okay with him. He just didn't stay around long with the ones who couldn't see it his way. In general, he didn't hang around too long with any one person.

But when it worked, both sky and street glowed. North Beach had that clear damp San Francisco shimmer. Hutch often succeeded, made his mark. Of course, the discontentment flowed back by the next day or two, and sometimes the woman seemed to act insulted because he no longer knew her nor wanted to know her.

She hadn't saved him after all. Only Hutch could rescue Hutch.

"I got this letter from Harry's mom in Texas or Chicago someplace asking if I was having an adultery with her son. What does she think I am, an other woman? Harry says she's some kind of religious fanatic."

"What's he telling her, anyway?" Hutch asked.

"If I was to write back, I'd say I was getting it on with her baby—you think she might like that better, Uncle Hutch? Is that an adultery?"

"I hope you're not going to write to her."

"Just kidding, Uncle Hutch. Writing's my dad's thing. Personally, I'm like you, I enjoy face-to-face living. Harry might be a creep sometimes, but we get together—"

Hutch whistled. *"Having an adultery."*

"Sure knows how to talk about fun, don't she?"

They sat together with these and other thoughts circulating in their heads, then with no thoughts, just a good feeling. They ate their desserts. They communed. Hutch felt close to his niece. He took one of the nuts from her sundae, grinned and held it between two fingers, raised it for permission before popping it into his mouth, and said, "You'll see how people didn't learn to have fun in this country. I really had to study."

"Teach me," Trish said, taking his hand.

"You learned. You're learning. You might even get

ahead of me," Hutch said. Trish was one person he felt secure about complimenting. It could even be a sincere compliment without weakening his position with her. "But aside from that," he went on—it was complicated—"I guess it's okay, but Trish? Just don't wreck things for yourself."

Trish looked at him amazed. Now how the devil did he always get to be so smart?

The girl on the terrace at Enrico's with Hutch, whose hand he was holding lightly and affectionately, suddenly took a bunch of his fingers between hers and squeezed. "I'm pregnant," she said.

He didn't have an immediate answer. He didn't ride on with a joke. He sat there, feeling her hand kneading and twisting against his fingers.

"Honey, are you sure?"

"They tell me the test is ninety-nine percent. I'm sure."

"Trish," he said, "you don't even want to tell him he did it, that's why you're telling me and not him. But you know I'll stand by you."

"Hey, those guys still waving at you, Uncle Hutch?"

"Yeah, I know them. You hear what I say to you, Trish."

She looked into his face. "You said you'll stand by me. I know that, Uncle Hutch. I know that about you." He pulled her chair with a clumsiness he normally did not allow in his life. He tipped it close and put his arms around Trish, chair, her tears. The boys, standing up, were shooting their grins across the terrace, proving their points to each other, this lunch a great success with its floorshow of Hutch and his weepy young chicklet. But Hutch and the girl weren't noticing.

"Don't feel sorry for me, Uncle Hutch. These are just selfish. I'm crying because I'm happy because I've got you."

11

Hutch put his favorite tangerine handkerchief in his jacket pocket, billowing like a parachute from the region of his heart. He wasn't sure if his mission was a sensible one. He decided to visit Harry in the San Francisco skinhead headquarters on Haight.

When he locked his car, he folded the antenna down, removed the stereo rig, poked the code on the alarm, which was more or less normal procedure, and gave his white BMW a long fond look of goodbye. He shrugged. Sometimes a person might lose his best wheels ever, but had to take that chance.

He stood in front of what used to be called a crash pad. The downstairs stores were empty, but the sidewalk was a menace to his shoes. Everybody needs somebody, people liked their pets around here, and pooper scoopers had not yet made the long trek from Nob, Russian, and Telegraph, the hill country, and Pacific Heights. The dog walkers of the Haight believed in a more natural life and anyway, only a few teenage

runaways came around barefoot anymore, foggy as
things tended to be. On the corner where Karma Lik-
kers used to supply a local need, the sign said Future
Home of Chotchka Office Supplies, but the iron grill-
work was hanging open. No sign of the Chotchka folks
making renovations. When Hutch put his hand on the
grill, he could feel vibrations from the music upstairs.
He dusted sharp rust flecks off his hands. He wondered
if this trip was necessary. A careful-living real estate
investor with many responsibilities to bank, lenders,
and himself was preparing to discuss the pregnancy of
his niece with a kid who spent whatever money came
his way on new tattoos and a fresh head shave.

The bell didn't work. Perhaps it worked, but the
music was too loud and the speakers gave out enough
buzzes and rings of their own to distract anyone. Since
the door was open, this made no difference. Hutch
walked up the stairs, blinking to get his eyes going in
the dark, feeling a bit of soreness in his knees. When
he ran in the morning, he just ran through the pain
barrier. Climbing, as the heavy metal music pounded
at him, a singer shrieking strange syllables, Hutch
wondered if Trish and Harry ever looked at each other
fondly, listening to this, and said, *Our song.*

Very likely not. Hutch worried that perhaps he no
longer understood modern romance procedures.

He pushed open the door with its handlettered San
Francisco Skinheads Welcome and Stay Away sign. He
stood above a half-circle of bald men and half-bald
women in studs, black leather, boots, or bare feet,
nodding out to the music. Some wore earphones; some
didn't. Prickles on a girl's scalp weren't much of a
turn-on. "Hey," said one young man, rising and standing close enough to Hutch, "what's that perfume you
wearin? You break open a page of *Hustler* for the perfume?"

"You're Harry, aren't you?" Hutch asked.

The boy looked around this deafened universe. No one moved. "Guess I am," he said.

"I'd like to talk with you."

"That's what we doin."

"Is there another room where we could be alone?"

"Other room occupied just now. Hey, don't you notice? We're alone."

Hutch sighed and took a breath. "Okay. I'm Trish's uncle."

The boy grinned. "Trish?"

"Trish. Trish Montberg."

"Oh, *Trish*. That Trish. So?"

"You know why I'm talking to you. I don't know why I'm talking to you."

The boy was having fun. "One a them statements got to be right on."

"Do you have any thoughts on the subject?"

"Thinking ain't my strong suit," said the boy. "Other things I do."

"You plan to do anything about this?"

"You mean money? Don't have no money."

Hutch wasn't sure that money was the only question. "Maybe see her through this," he said.

The boy was amazed. "Through what? Man, I'm a busy person. What you want me do with that chick?"

Occasionally Hutch found himself in similar situations. It was like going to the bank for more money when there was no money forthcoming. The boy had no idea how Hutch dared to want what he wanted and now Hutch didn't, either. "Tell you what," he said, "you ought to think about taking responsibility for what you do."

"I'm healthy, man. I take care a number one."

"That's a beginning," Hutch said.

"Anybody says I got AIDS they gonna have to deal with me. I don't shoot up no more. When I used to use, now I always use the disposable ones. I pass the test, man. And my little herpes shit, I try to keep my hands off anybody when I get my little herp or two. I don't believe in getting it on even if it's nothin more'n a pimple burn and itch a tad."

He stared at Hutch.

"You got any more questions?"

"You answered a couple of them, maybe."

"*Maybe?* I look sick to you?"

"Well, you offered an answer. I guess that's all I can ask," Hutch said.

"So what you want from me? You want to give me something, I do what you want me to do you ask nice?"

"No. No," Hutch said. "No, I guess not."

"Ciao," said Harry.

The boy pulled his ear in a sudden wax attack. His expression was one of wax itch in the ear canal. He could not believe this perfumed dude with the orange snotrag tucked into his pocket. He was also getting tired of the conversation; long conversations were not his strong suit, either. "Lemme splain," he said. "I got strong sperm. Far as I think, she should have the kid. If she don't want it, why she get pregga-nunt? I think she tole me she was taking the spermkiller medicine."

"Maybe she was."

"Like I tole you a hunnert times, I got strong sperm, man. I think that's why she likes me."

"So do you have any plans?" Hutch asked. He found himself meeting the boy's eyes. To Hutch this was an interesting experience. He was meeting them on behalf of someone else, for Trish, and that seemed to make it easier.

"Plans? Planning ahead?" the boy asked.

"Yes."

A soft and friendly grin emerged on Harry's face, stretching the swastika tattoo on his cheek so that it looked like two crocodiles wrestling. For the first time Hutch noticed that there were tiny crocodile heads on the swastika. It was careful and professional artistic work. "Plans. Sure," Harry said. "Plan to throw you down them stairs on your fuckin head less you leave bout two minutes ago."

Dan scanned his brother's face. "I think there's something you want to tell me first."

"I'd appreciate if you'd sign that paper."

"What is it?"

Hutch shook his head. "I promise it's got nothing to do with this deal. Something else, promise. Word of honor, brother."

"What is it?"

"Nothing I can say now. Sometimes you and I both need a little, uh, introspection by ourselves. Someday maybe, on a basis of need-to-know. Promise, Dan."

"It crosses my mind, Hutch—"

"And a long and winding path that is. Listen, Dan, I'd like to swear nothing bad will happen. I offer that freely."

Hutch would *like* to promise. That wasn't the same thing. Dan sighed and reached for a shadow cigarette. He hadn't smoked for nearly ten years, but when he got into one of these family deals, family frets, he reached. He buttoned his jacket pocket again. "Who can promise nothing bad will happen, Hutch? That just makes me worry, you saying that."

"I mean I wish you only the best. I'm doing what I can. You got to sign, Dan, it'll give me time to complete the deal. We'll both come out good. This is really our chance, Dan. Sign now. Your brother needs you."

The papers were spread out with neat pencilled X's where Dan's signature was to come. Dan stared at the neat pencilled X's. Hutch was smiling, his deeply tanned, freckled, sun-wearied face filled with hope and encouragement.

Dan remembered another cabbie saying that in ev-

ery family there was a winner and a loser and Dan
answered no, it wasn't so simple, you couldn't always
tell, they could be both winners and losers. And brothers could change positions, too. Nothing was so simple
in family obligation and the confusions of family love.

He wondered what would happen if he wrote his
signature with his left hand. It would come out wavy
and unreal, maybe not even legal.

He knew, he really knew, he believed with all his
heart that his brother wished him no ill. On the contrary, the brothers wanted and needed and loved each
other in ways, sure, that were different; had to be; they
were different human beings. He could not explain
this to himself or to Gloria. He felt it more strongly
now than ever in his life, more even than when they
were kids. Someday he would try to explain to Trish
about the sister or brother she did not have and about
what it meant to him to have a brother.

Rapidly he took the pen and, squinting a little,
signed with his right hand.

As promised, Hutch gave Trish a ride in that little
BMW 325is she loved so much. He slid the button-
controlled roof open to the midday sun, because she
liked that, too. As promised, he was taking her in his
automobile to the clinic. But he said, "Don't even
thank me. I'm happy if that's the word to do this for
you, but a few things. One thing. What is this, this, this
individual?"

"Harry? He's my skinhead. It was only one time,
Uncle Hutch—maybe a couple times—nothing I expect from him."

"Okay. Why don't you want to ask Gloria or Dan to
help you?"

"You kidding? You said you'd only ask one thing.
That's two things already. They're my *parents*, Uncle
Hutch."

He waited. He let her change the stations on the stereo. She liked how she pressed a sensor and it went searching across the dial, lights flashing, stopping at every strong signal. That was all the explanation, then? Okay, he sort of understood she was a little like him, didn't want a heck of a lot of discussion, long meaningful eye contacts, rehashes, and she knew Hutch would just as soon drop the whole subject, as she also intended to.

"Had to mention it, Trish. Sorry."

"They ask a lot of questions down at the clinic, too. First a skin head guy asks if he can fuck you, doesn't even ask it, and then you get to answer all these questions from about a million other people. All for a few minutes of not that much fun."

"I suppose you're a little upset."

"So are you going to nag at me? Might as well ride with Mom and Dad if you're going to do that."

"Hey, Trish," he said.

The Blaupunkt sensor had found a good station for both of them, a soothing Windham Hill selection. She burrowed her head into his shoulder. With the bucket seats it wasn't a practical gesture. Then she put her head up again and he could see the shiny eyes, the determined child's pretty face. "It's right down this block on Balboa," she said. "Convenient at least. Like a Seven-Eleven."

RICHMOND-SUNSET NEIGHBORHOOD
FAMILY PLANNING
(Ring Bell)

The last vestige of the old-time furtive in this business was ringing the bell and waiting nervously on the street while an eye examined the visitors through a peephole. It had to do with bomb threats and pickets. The word *Murderers* had been spray-painted and scrubbed out with strong chemicals; the shadow of the word still clung in bleached paleness to the door as the lean man in an Italian silk jacket, the girl in a short blue jean skirt, waited to be buzzed in. The man had graying hair, a deeply sun-freckled face; he was holding Trish's hand. He let it go when the door opened.

"Please come in. I'm Debbie."

Hutch was at home with fluid situations. Debbie was a social worker, a nurse, a doctor, a secretary, whatever. He didn't need to say what he was. "Hi," he said.

"You're Trish, right?"

Trish nodded. This show had been on the road awhile and Trish had just asked him along for the last stop. He could relax; Debbie wasn't too bad for an official. With a firm smile, he looked her deep in the eyes, quickly—not too bad—before he looked away. He had less trouble with these darting and probing early stares.

"You're a," and Debbie paused smoothly, "you're a friend."

Hutch grinned. She was on the line of acceptable attractiveness—a little too much weight in the calves and at the shoulders—where he wanted to establish that he was just a good guy, not the father of a fetus. He didn't want to say he was an uncle. He wanted to leave no question of his being the lover, although in some ways that wasn't a totally displeasing misapprehension. "I just thought I might come along with Trish," he said.

"Since he doesn't work regular hours anyway," Trish said.

Debbie shrugged. Probably she didn't give her last name because of the Right to Lifers and general nuttiness in this line of work. But Hutch knew where to find her if he ever needed her.

A Family Planning Clinic looked cleaner than an abortion factory. The people looked friendlier and more official. The shades and protections on windows were in better repair, curtains in a nice shade of green. Hutch didn't mind if things interested him, no harm in that, but he watched Trish carefully to see when she might need his attention. His sitting there, taking in the magazines and the formica, the recessed ceiling lights, the other visitors, seemed to be enough for her. He thought it a considerate touch that they used real light bulbs and not fluorescent strips. More cheerful that way.

This was not assembly-line production, taking in pregnant women at one end and letting them out unpregnant at the other. The lamps looked like floor lamps in the sort of house Hutch never wanted to live in again, an entire lamp display from the Emporium. *Motorland* magazine on the coffee table must have come from some client planning a trip or hoping to buy a new car. Except for one couple, all previous visitors were gone, but the pillows sagged where they had sat. No one here jumped around plumping pillows —other things on their minds.

The nurse striding past glanced at Hutch and Trish, controlling the room with eyes and hips, spending a look on them which prevented their asking any of the nervous questions people ask in waiting rooms. She was not a nurse; she was a doctor—stethoscope dangling from pocket. Or maybe she was a nurse with a stethoscope; everything was possible. Her shoes were puffed up with some kind of foam padding. Hutch wondered if she had cute feet.

On the opposite side of the room, heads together, the other couple seemed to have their due emotions handed out to the wrong concerned parties, the leather-clad boy morose, pale, and depressed, the girl pink and plump and happily chatting away: "There was this gorgeous nurse when I came in for the test and she comes on like this dominatrick, you know, a power trip, and so I go: Hey! you putting me on? and she goes, Just give me a little blood, just give me a little pee. . . ."

"Okay," said the young non-father.

"Hey! I'm just trying to be nice . . . So I go, you a draculette or something?"

Hutch and Trish grinned at each other, sharing the complicity of how voices carry, how everyone hears everything. People engrossed in their own discussion think everyone else is deaf. Everyone else is listening, since draculettes are of interest to all.

"Please come into the private consultation cubicle." The volunteer emitted a radiant smile. She may have wanted to be a paralegal volunteer, but her smile drove her into paramedical, even paragynecological. "There are three chairs—one extra. Yours is the choice, Miss, if you want your, uh."

"Come with me," Trish said. She patted his hand to assure him it wouldn't be too bad.

The doctor who talked to Trish about what was coming was a man, but the doctor who was going to do it was a woman. At this clinic they believed in full preconsultation. Doctor Don—he used his first name, like the honey feller on a kids morning show—made a little vacuum cleaner sound as he entered the private consultation cubicle. "You've given the whole matter a thinkie?" he said, darting a glance at Hutch.

"That a chocolate-covered thought?" Trish asked.

Dr. Don realized the older man was here for company, not as an active participant in the matter. Having shot his older-feller colleague looks at Hutch, he now proceeded to deal with the client. "You've read the papers you signed?"

"I signed," she said. "Let's get this show on the road."

"You're aware of the—"

"I'm aware," Trish said. "I'm not always aware, but

I'm aware this time." She paused and grinned. "What's *aware*? Only kidding, Doctor Don."

"Okay. I think we're mostly set." He made his vacuum-cleaner hum again. "If you'll come in here with me and Doctor Linda . . . It's just a woosh, a juicy suction, and it's gone. Like it was never there. Not much stickiness this advanced equipment, people'd be surprised how little resistance. She can go to school, in seven to nine days she can continue her uh social life, we take care of the wastes. But I always recommend Trish wait minimum seven to nine days before . . . So." He wrinkled into a smile and touched her knee reassuringly. "So you might say it's not on her record."

The shiny tubes and trays were launching quasars into the universe, bright darting rays of know-how.

"It's not on my record," Trish said thoughtfully.

"I guess you mean you'll remember it anyway," Hutch said. "Let's try to make it an experience, not a total loss."

"On-the-job training for life," the doctor said. "Not that you should do this too often. It doesn't really hurt, but there might be a strain there someplace in the hormones, the psychology. The Right to Lifers got a teensie point there. You could count on being a little down, honey. Buy yourself a favorite makeup, treat yourself to something nice. Don't get depressed if you're a little down, okay? And have a nice day."

"I will," said Trish.

"Sir, would you like to leave our little girl here with Dr. Linda? I'll show you back to the waiting room."

Hutch hesitated as the man began to move. Trish said, "Let me talk to him a minute. I'm not going to slow things down."

Dr. Don was used to these huddles. "Take five," he said, "all the time in the world."

She waited until the jabber and shadow of Dr. Don

were gone from the little room. Then she looked at Hutch.

"Sometimes when I, you know, when I'm with someone," Trish said, "I think of you."

"That's nice of you," Hutch said.

"It helps," said Trish. "But with Harry, I couldn't."

"That's complimentary, too."

"So it was really only one time. Maybe two or three. Which is the joke of it, I spose."

"I guess so," said Hutch.

"But I guess it's not very funny."

"I guess not."

Hutch wasn't sure why it helped him to feel it was also his problem. It was his problem because she was his niece, because she was Trish, because she loved him, because she needed him. It was also more their problem together because of what she had just said. He wanted to say he loved her, but that was like looking at someone's eyes, not easy to do. He was whistling to himself and thinking aloud again. "I guess it ain't really very funny, Trish."

Dr. Linda Shelley was standing there with them. They had not heard her enter on her flat, rubber-soled shoes with the funny foam padding. Hutch paid no special attention to the doctor, although he noticed a few things about her. Take off the polyester whites, change the shoes, get some contacts instead of that four-eyes plastic, let the hair down, do a few moves here and there with makeup and she might be the right sort of tired blond. So he paid a little attention to her anyway, while he was saying to Trish, "You're young and you haven't made all the mistakes yet. I'm running out of new mistakes to make. I'm making the old ones over again."

"Uncle Hutch?"

"When you call me that," he said, "I like it and I feel

old. You say my name. I don't know what to do about that."

He felt a dizziness and sweating as he stood there. His face was wet and he wanted to ask Trish if she was okay. He didn't feel this dizziness after a long run, not even a marathon, but his breath was coming hard. Stop! he wanted to say, I'm losing something, I'll take that child, it's mine.

"Is that true?" the doctor asked. "Do you mean this?"

He didn't realize he had spoken. He shook his head.

"If you're just saying that and it's not true," the doctor said, "you better find counselling."

"This is no time to kid around," Trish said.

"I'm her uncle," Hutch said. "I'm crazy."

Dr. Shelley looked at him shrewdly. She spoke in a soft voice, pushing her glasses back up her nose. She shook her head. "Not crazy," she was saying, "Mister, you don't even know what's wrong with you. You're moved."

"There's a little more bleeding than we like," Dr. Shelley said.

"You might want to let her rest here a teensie," Dr. Don added.

Hutch looked at Trish, covered with a sheet, pale, alert, very tired. "You don't have to," she said. "I've got cab fare."

Hutch said nothing, but took her hand. He had heard this telegraph sometimes worked between lovers. After the doctors left them, he sent her a message through the wrists, the fingers, the knuckles, as he rubbed her hands and let her doze and kept the connection.

People want to make me the prisoner of Hutch Montberg. I'm free to be what I want to be, that's what your dad doesn't understand. I'm not the prisoner of myself.

Trish opened her eyes. She looked surprised. "You're still here," she said.

"You're my girl," Hutch said, and winked. "Even if you're not my girl."

12

_____

"I just came from concluding a little deal, give me, how old is the grapefruit juice?" Hutch asked Kenny, his favorite Enrico's waiter.

"Squeezed an hour ago—how about you?"

"Plus or minus?"

"Maybe plus ten minutes."

"Okay, then run with it. Didn't exactly *conclude* the deal, need the vitamin C and the fiber, okay?"

Kenny did his little television host half-leap with index finger extended. "You got it."

Hutch liked to keep on good joking terms with the people who made life comfortable. They oiled the works, they hung the festival decorations, they cleaned up. After his afternoon with Trish at the clinic, he needed lots of fresh pulp from the bottom of the fresh grapefruit juice. Then he would drink water, swishing it unobtrusively to prevent acid damage to tooth enamel.

He had seen an Ivy Leaguer do that once and, always willing to learn, had adopted it into his own repertory of health and attractiveness routines. The Ivy Leaguer was a principal in a major development at China Basin.

Kenny trotted back with a large g.j. on a tray and put it down with a smile, a wink, and a napkin, the wink for no reason but friendly complicity at a time when Hutch needed an interlude of lonely Zen meditation on the crowded terrace. While the Broadway parade eddied around him, Hutch took stock in things and the rest of the evening.

Once Kenny had pinched Hutch's leg and when Hutch socked him on the shoulder—only kidding, both of them—Kenny said, "Hey! If you haven't tried it, don't knock it!" But now he could see that Hutch was tired and he looked for the right amount of distance. "Anything else I can get you, hon?"

"How's about my dream house?" Hutch asked.

"Mountain or seashore?" Kenny said. It was part of the job with the regular clientele at Enrico's, a family establishment for those without families, to giggle them back into good spirits. He could see that Hutch needed both to be alone and to get a little teasing from the good Enrico's maxifamily folks.

"Mountain or beach. Um. A little of both, can you work on it, will you?"

"For your dream come true, you try sending your subscription to the Publishers Clearing House?"

"Thank you, Kenny."

Right there lay the difference between an Enrico's waiter and a practical real estate entrepreneur. Hutch closed his eyes a moment both as a symbol of thinking and to give Kenny his next cue: *Leave the man.*

A black guy at the next table was explaining something to a white guy and kept asking, "You understand what I'm saying?" as he explained away, until the white guy, exasperated, finally said, "Please just tell me, don't keep asking if I understand," and the black guy drew back a little, paused, and said, "I know you're so smart, that's why I'm wasting my time talking to you. Y'understand what I'm saying?"

The nice thing about Enrico's was that there was small-time, medium-time, and big-time, all mixed in together, democratically. Hutch had given up smoking more than ten years ago, but at a moment like this, grapefruit juice didn't entirely do it. While he thought about Trish, thought about his deal with the bankers, he would have liked to have a cigarette and put all that to the side and think, say, about his good Soviet friend Avigdor or some of the terrific girls he'd had in recent years. Or about inviting Dan and Gloria to his vacation dream home up Mendocino way which he didn't need Publishers Clearing House to hand over in a personal awards ceremony.

Still, Enrico's was a home away from home. Hutch liked people seeing him content with his own company, not asking too much more. Enrico Banducci himself presided at the family table inside, his reflection wavery in the glass. His new wife, his two new kids, and his old violin were at the table with him. He wasn't playing the violin. They were watching a ball game on the portable teevee. This was one nuclear family time, where you watch the ball game together, and not the other nuclear family time, where everybody listens to the violin.

Enrico's former wife, normally confined to her side of the room, came up with a sheaf of tabs. Everyone in the nuclear family kept eyes on the backfield play as Enrico took the tabs and said whatever he said and Susie retreated to her place at the bar.

The vibes were okay. Hutch said, "Kenny? You got a cigarette?"

"What? You don't smoke."

"That's why I asked you for a cigarette, doom-kopf.

If I smoked, I'd ask you for a pack. Never mind, you're right, bring me a decaf and no, make it a decaf lattay."

"Ooh, the big spender," said Kenny, flouncing. "You, a cigarette, I like to died of congestion."

This was the place where he came. This was the place where Kenny held him to high standards of behavior. It might all be fun between them, a festival that began over a hundred years ago with the gold rush, continued by Kenny and Hutch and the Enrico's terrace people, all seriously engaged in their fun, but even when Hutch ordered nothing but a grapefruit juice, he left Kenny his tip in folding money. He had taken up his time. Kenny's time counted for Kenny.

Probably Dan and Gloria's time counted for them. Trish spent her time like a teenager, but she would find out, too, that everything counted.

Still alone at his table, soothed by the passing parade of Broadway strollers and his own deep thoughts, Hutch noticed a long-legged blond with the requisite tired eyes sitting at a table across the terrace. He mimed the words, *You're beautiful,* and she blushed and lowered her eyes.

She wasn't alone. The man she was waiting for arrived, bustling and apologizing, and Hutch waved at him. Another real estate entrepreneur, another Enrico's luncher. The man nodded and looked to his lady.

Hutch called Kenny over. He ordered a bottle of white wine—specifically, a Vacheron Chardonnay 1983—sent to the table of his friend and the tired lovely blond. When it arrived, he smiled and waved again. He pushed his chair a little away, waiting to be asked to join them; at least waiting to be introduced.

The waiter uncorked the bottle. The man stopped him from pouring the proper few millimeters to taste. He made sure Hutch was watching; he raised the entire bottle in a beer toast; then he carefully spilled it onto the concrete terrace, very carefully, making sure not to splash anyone nearby.

Kenny grinned. He didn't know what else to do. The slant of the terrace carried a rivulet of Vacheron Chardonnay 1983 past Hutch's feet to the street. For some reason, perhaps confusion, a group of tourists applauded. Perhaps they thought this an old San Francisco custom, like lighting a cigar with a hundred-dollar bill.

Hutch stood up abruptly and crossed Broadway toward his office on Kearny.

The headwaiter said to Kenny, "Get a mop. Put it on his tab."

"You think he'll come back?"

"He'll come back in a day or two. This is home."

Kenny thought about the man who had poured out the wine so carefully and precisely. "I guess they must know each other."

When Hutch called his service, the messages he was waiting for were not there yet. When he punched into the remote-controlled answering machine at home, where he did not expect business calls, he was not surprised to find no business calls. Things were slow. He made a few calls himself. The market was soft and few offers on the property were coming in. None.

As in love, sometimes a person wins and sometimes he loses. The only difference was that in love you just go on to the next opportunity. This time, in business, you just went on to the next opportunity, too. But you owed an explanation to your brother and sister-in-law. Not understanding the complications of venture investment, they needed to have a few things pointed out.

Hutch sat looking at the brown worm of telephone. Very likely Gloria and Dan were getting requests to ante up now. Dan was a big boy and he had signed the paper. Still, Hutch didn't enjoy the prospect of having to talk with him about it.

Sometimes Hutch could make the phone ring by staring at it. Usually he did this when he wanted to make it ring. Today neither the silence nor the ring was a festival.

Hutch didn't usually sit at home among all his glass and aluminum and mirrors, all perfectly reflecting and clean, unless he was guiding some nice tired blond through the display of devices and appliances, Cuisinart and paperweights, knives and sharpeners, tubular lamps and sliding screens, teevee fitted into the bar and bar fitted into the wall, plus a few tastefully framed or mounted great art works by world-famous artists she perhaps hadn't heard of yet, warning her about scraping her shins on sharp edges that didn't seem to be there but were. Usually he preferred to do his sitting and waiting on the cozy terrace at Enrico's. Kenny would call him to the phone if he had a message. Hutch had family telephone privileges at Enrico's.

But today he sat at home, wondering if it would be better to speak with Dan and Gloria before they tried to speak with him, or to wait, or not to speak with them until they cornered him. Call screening was one of the good features of his machine, in addition to the remote punch-in facility, the ability to reprogram the announcement to let folks know he was safe on the Enrico's terrace, but they would find him. It wouldn't do any good for anyone, but they knew his routes. Trying to avoid them would not improve things. Neither the bankers nor the real estate market cared whether life was a festival for Hutch Montberg and his family. Ray Aratunian wore that fat smile, his lips like thumbs, whether or not life was a festival at the conclusion of such and such a deal.

Hutch stared at the phone and waited for it to ring

and it did not ring. A watched telephone doesn't ring. That's true, too. He tried to feel no puzzlement but acceptance. Another run would feel good now, the smell of the bay and the nice breeze cooling his face, but his doctor had warned him about the pounding to his knees. He used a peculiar word, *insult,* an insult to the cartilage. A compressed and floating kneecap— something like that—something that was the doctor's business and not his. Weren't kneecaps supposed to float?

No matter how busy a person kept himself enjoying life, getting fit, getting fitter, getting laid, getting contracts and deals straightened out, enjoying life a whole lot, this person could still find himself a little bit tired. Sitting with a niece while she bled out a baby, an option on a baby. Sitting with a phone, trying to see where the money might still be found to pay the debt with the interest payments going up and up. Waiting and trying to be the big man of the Enrico's terrace.

Wishing the market hadn't suddenly turned sour, due to the goddamn tax laws which were designed to prevent a smart entrepreneur from getting what so many had already gotten without him and they didn't deserve it.

Really wanting something. Maybe really wanting something else, whatever that might be. Not getting what he really wanted and getting tired.

Hutch was on the phone, punching out the numbers without wetting his finger with his tongue or saying Fancy that or fussing any further. "Ray Aratunian," he said.

"Speaking."

"Hey, I didn't recognize your voice."

"Greetings, my friend. Reason you didn't recognize it is you're late."

"Listen, Ray, nothing ever goes exactly cording to plan. We're talking business here, you heard of this

Professor Murphy at Stanford Bee School, he said it's normal in an extended deal, Murphy's Law, no matter how you figure—"

"You're late with the payments, Hutch. People say, my poor late wife used to say, my voice changes when I'm not speaking through the smile of contentment. That's the voice you're hearing."

"Ray—"

"Not late with the payment, just a little installment, Hutch. You're late with the pay-muntz. Pay, *muntz*, Hutch."

"I know, that's why I'm calling—"

"Not necessary, Hutch. Unless you're paying, you don't need to bother. If you're paying, you can just come by with the pay-*muntz*. But if you're not, then we just go to Brother Dan—"

"Hey, listen!"

Ray fell silent a moment. He listened, as requested. What he was listening to was breathing as Hutch tried to figure out what he could supply in the way of words here. But as Ray had already stated, it was not necessary. Nothing occurred to Hutch, no further advice from Professor Murphy of Stanford Business, so he said again, "Listen, Ray. I want to help you with our problem. We're all in this together. I want to help us all."

Ray was silent.

"Listen, Ray."

Ray waited.

After a pause there was a click and Hutch was holding an empty telephone. Ray, who liked a good giggle, didn't laugh even once during the whole conversation. But of course it was a short conversation over the telephone without the benefit of winks, nudges, shrugs, all those pleasant moves between men doing business together.

* * *

Dan came home with an expression of wild enthusiasm on his face. This was easy to misinterpret—the look was rage and despair—and it also made him unable to read the face which his wife was presenting to him. Gloria was speaking to him, he was speaking to her, and they were hurtling past each other.

"He lied! That Aratunian I told you about, he came after me in the garage and said they want money right now."

"Trish was in bed when I got home. She was—"

"He said it was just a matter of guaranteeing a loan while he got the deal in order—"

"She was spotting."

He stopped. "Spotting?"

"Blood," said Gloria. "She was bleeding."

"Trish?"

"She's okay. Hutch took care of her. Hutch took her for an abortion."

Dan smashed his fist against the dish drainer, a plastic-covered nest of metal, and it recoiled like a spring and catapulted itself against the wall, spilling forks and knives. He ran up to Trish's room. Gloria did not follow him. He would find out soon enough how she was and then he would come back to finish his conversation with his wife.

The light hurt her eyes. Trish squinted up at Dan standing by her bed. "Daddy, I just want to sleep."

"What's the matter with you?"

"I already told Mom. I'm okay. The doctor said I just need to sleep and I'm okay. Why are you that way, Dad?"

He didn't need to ask what way. He felt as if he had the flu; he was sweating and breathless.

"Hey Dad, I'm sorry I didn't tell you first, but Mom

was asking. She saw my clothes in the hamper—it's okay, I'm just tired."

She shut her eyes. Dan leaned over her and touched her forehead. She wrinkled her brow and he could feel the corrugations against his hand. She was really sleeping, he decided, or if she was pretending just now, it would soon be true. He put his hand back on her forehead. She looked up and smiled and then closed her eyes again. He stood there a moment and then ran down to the kitchen where Gloria was waiting for him.

"She had a funny way of putting it," Gloria said. "We're just friends. That's what she said about her uncle."

"Did *he*—?"

"Oh come on, Dan. No. It must have been the skinhead, Harry, but he took her to the clinic."

Dan stood there looking at his bleeding hand. He didn't remember how this happened till he saw the silverware on the floor. Gloria had not picked it up. She was waiting for him. She had picked up the dish drainer, but she had left the scatter of silver where it lay.

True friendship in my heart was what Trish had said about her uncle, but Gloria left that part out. She thought it might upset her husband, who suddenly seemed skinny and creepy and jumping around in his taxi-driver's Goodwill clothes, the short khaki army jacket, the twill pants, the construction worker's boots.

He told her that Ray Aratunian had called on him. Ray Aratunian said to just call him Ray but asked for the money and now. Somehow Dan had imagined that one of the meaner boys would come to do the asking and they would save Ray for the better parts, but Ray knew how to do the job. He could be direct enough to suit anyone.

I don't have it, Dan had said.

You signed, nice Ray said. That means you can get it.

"I don't have it."

"Get it."

"That's not what I expected."

"The reason you signed is we wanted to make sure we could be protected in *case* of the unexpected."

"Pardon?" Dan had said.

"I realize that's kind of complicated. It all comes down to get it, mister, or you're in deep shit."

Gloria stared.

"Funny thing," Dan said, "that was the expression Hutch used. I didn't think people used his expressions."

"You didn't think so?" Gloria asked. "You didn't predict this? Didn't think people followed in his footsteps, did you? Fancy that, dear husband."

"You're mad at me, Gloria. I'm mad at myself, angrier than you could ever be."

"Don't count on it," she said. "But I guess it's true that I figure you're only doing what you had to do. What you're programmed to do."

"My brother."

"That's what I'm saying. You're still his kid brother."

"I wish you wouldn't say that, Gloria."

She knew this stranger well. He was the most familiar stranger she knew. "Then what would you wish me to say? How would you wish me to say it?" He had no answer. "I don't think I can even move Trish anymore and she's a daughter. She's on her own way already. What would make me think I can do anything about you?"

"We have to take care of her as best we can."

Gloria wondered if he was saying she also had to take care of a husband who didn't take care of himself.

When Trish was a little girl, she used to hide behind her closed door, having learned the trick of putting a glass between her ear and the door, to hear what her parents were saying about her. Usually they weren't talking about her, but sometimes she fell asleep on the floor in her cuddly flannel pj's and one of them would find her, carry her to bed, never know why she was sleeping at the door to her room with a water glass near her fist.

She learned she could hear them just as well without the glass. Once she thought they were saying her ears were too big. It turned out they knew she was listening; three of them all laughed together, one of them in disgrace. She believed they thought she was as happy and giggling inside as they were. They had forgotten the revenge plans of a kid.

She no longer had to pretend and hide. She could do what she wanted to do, even if she didn't have all her power. Freedom and the promised festival were yet to come.

So now, hearing every word, she remembered the glass for digging secrets out of the wall but came downstairs in one of her father's KorVet Cab T-shirts, nothing else, feeling some sort of blood or seepage between her legs, laughing wildly. "Whatever you say about me, there's someone more important! He's more important to you than you are, too!"

"What are you doing? What are you screaming about?" Gloria shouted.

"What does that mean? What are you saying?" Dan said.

Trish stared at him. She pulled the T-shirt around her, she tucked the ends of it between her legs and blotted. "What do *you* mean?" she asked.

She was planning to leave as soon as she could. She was planning to go someplace interesting. That would be anyplace that was not this house, this mother and father, this neighborhood. Maybe Harry wouldn't take her away on his motorcycle. Of course he wouldn't. It didn't make any difference. Maybe Uncle Hutch would.

"I'm tired, so keep it down, okay? I want to catch some Z's."

"I'll come up and talk to you in a minute," Gloria said.

Trish stared at her mother. "I'll probably be asleep. You two can just have it out, okay?"

"Less than five minutes," Gloria said.

She waited until they heard Trish back in her room and then needed to get it out rapidly, just as well that way. "Okay. About her it happened. We're in that together. That's our deal. But about Hutch, you did it all by your lonesome. You did it about Hutch. You signed us away, Dan. If I don't leave you for that, maybe I'll never leave you."

"Are you going to?"

"I don't know," Gloria said.

"Maybe you should."

"I don't know," she repeated.

"I can't blame you for thinking about it."

She met his intense squint. He needed glasses and he knew she was right. He knew he was wrong and he was just waiting. Instead of answering, she put her arms around him. She felt his heartbeat, the kind of pounding from within that makes a man need to shout and strike out at his enemy, but he said and did nothing, just standing there, letting her arms enclose him. And only then she said, "Dan, I'm thinking about it. Yes."

Sometimes doing nothing was the right thing and he did the right thing. She felt the heat shuddering through his body, the sudden wetness through his shirt. He was doing nothing, he had no answers, he just stood there.

She wasn't sure she was doing the right thing, but she wasn't leaving him today, not yet.

She turned and went to Trish up the short flight of stairs, which creaked under her step like a temporary scaffolding.

When Dan telephoned, he got no answer. Either the telephone rang and rang and no one came on or the machine came on, telling the caller that Hutch might be around and about, might be running, might be elsewhere, try Enrico's Café, and the caller should leave a message.

Dan did not stop telephoning.

At three in the morning the ring must have caught Hutch unawares. The groggy voice said, "Wuh?"

"Hutch, they're coming after me."

"Wuh? What?"

"Hutch, what happened? They want their money now. Why won't they wait for your deal?"

"It's used up. The money's used up. It's over."

"Hutch, I'm coming after you."

Hutch made the effort to awaken. He was breathing deeply, forcing the breath into his alertness. "I'll get dressed," he said. "I'll wait for you, Dan."

13

Normally Hutch had no occasion to wake for his day at three in the morning. But since he had occasion today, he followed his customary routines. Bachelor procedures were a security for a man who lived alone, pending true love. He reset Mr. Coffee and heard the friendly bubbling, smelled the friendly perfume of his own Graffeo blend. Normally he might take a slow hot shower in the sunken tub; the bath facilities were there for company—he preferred the shower. A tad early, he made today normal. He stood there with the water pelting down, surrounded by unlit candles, which were also there for shared bathing; he showered and studied himself in the various mirrors which showed flat belly, knotted rump, a bit too much graying hair on chest and shoulders. All okay. Maybe he could do something about the clump on each buttock, although Linda One said she liked it.

One of the pleasures of arranging things right was that designer plumbing, tub, and drains made a

shower curtain unnecessary. Having checked the mirror, he could begin the day. Everything in order.

He stepped out and whipped the outsize towel
around him, getting the blood going. A good rough
toweling, the threads in the *HM* monogram scratching
a little, gave massage and exercise and got him dry, as
it was supposed to.

All okay.

He picked a thin white porcelain cup for his coffee,
started to pour, and rejected it for a large creamy mug
with a coat of arms and the legend STANFORD on it
in red Latin glaze. He never actually told any of the
tired blonds that he had attended Stanford, but sometimes asked if they had read the works of his good
friend Professor Murphy of the Bee School. He stirred
instant nonfat dry milk, bachelor dust, into the coffee
and it dissolved nicely. He dressed while moving
around and straightening up. All clean clothes, and at
the base of the ensemble, new underwear. Egyptian
long-fiber cotton shirt from Wilkes Bashford. Linen
pants in a soft and clinging design—a star's pants. No
tie or jacket; after all, this was his taxi-driver brother
coming over for a visit at an ungodly hour. Juice and
coffee in various thermoses. A fresh smell of soap,
mixed with steam from the shower, joined coffee,
juice, and an invisible flow of damp night air from the
open window. Not a bad taste among them.

All okay and ready. Hutch liked rich and meaty
smells in the evening, "oil of lady," he called it; in the
morning he liked starting-new smells.

He heard the rattletrap taxi-sale vehicle outside, dis-
turbing the peace of his neighborhood on a leafy slope
of the hill. People around here would go look out their
windows to see what the trouble was. There wasn't
even a hint of dawn yet. Hutch practiced: *Hi, brother-
of-mine.*

He didn't make him ring. He opened the door, grinning. "To what do I owe this early pleasure, brother-of-mine?"

"You didn't answer your phone when I called."

"I been out a lot, hey. But now I answered and there you are. How about some really good coffee stead of that acid you wreck your stomach with?"

"I've got to talk with you."

"I hear you," said Hutch, "else why would you be standing at my vestibule? Listen, health is my ideal, as you know, but Graffeo's is the one vice I can't give up, not quite—the best water-washed brewed decaf doesn't even do it. You remember that Suki, deep personal friend of mine? She served the best decaf, and she put chicory in it, added, and that woman was magic—I thought it was almost *real.*"

"Hutch, can we get past this garbage?"

"Sure thing, brother-of-mine. A deep personal friend'll do that to you sometimes, make the memories flood back. Are you allowed to sit down or does this end-of-the-night powwow have to take place standing in my vestibule, I call it?"

Dan followed him to the heavy blue-gray set of couches. Hutch's condo had been furnished in blues, grays, and white with pink accents; beige, he called it. The several books on the shelves leaned against running trophies, tennis trophies, and ski photographs in aluminum frames—one of them Hutch with Suki of the water-washed brewed decaf, whom Dan now recalled. The glass coffee table had copies of *Connoisseur* fanned out on it. Hutch darted here and there with a last straightening up—*TV Guide* behind the VCR. For easy perusal of commercial television, know what the popular mind thinks. Keep in touch, a person could just ride with whatever came out. Teevee wasn't a major priority in the lifestyle around here. Hutch was pleased with how mirrors strategically enlarged the space, brought the bay and the bridge in, multiplied the presence of this modest throne room at the top of the hill. "Nice," Dan said.

"Suki said it's a fag house but she liked it. Always with the smart put-down, that lady—her major priority was what I learned. She's right but I like it."

"Your money shows, Hutch."

He laughed. "My credit cards show. Hey, y'know, I don't think—is that right?—I don't think you been here before, have you?"

"Not the way you fixed it up."

"Yeah, my last place. You've had one place since the Dark Ages, but I like to improve myself. I've only had this one six-eight months, still working out the kinks. My friend that Russki, Victor, Avigdor, he went bananas when he saw the candles around the tub, candlelit bathing for two—fuckin boorj-wah unreal, he called it. He's a writer like you, Dan, gift of the words. I wanted you to see it when I completed my little condo work of art."

"Unreal," Dan said.

"When I got it perfect, you and family come over for some cheese and wine, juice—you don't know it, Dan, but you deserve the best, if you could only think that way. I know you want to ask me about our deal—"

"One thing."

"—so let's take it one at a time. A snag. In business, there are snags. Ever take a wrong turn up a one-way street with a fare and you had to back up? Life is continuation anyway. Hey, writing your book or books, ever have to throw away a page, hey I don't mean throw away in this context, just revise your outline or whatever, your modus vivendi? That's continuation. I know you think I got it made, but I got my problems, too."

"With me you do, Hutch."

"Hey. Hey. I don't need that tone with me, brother. I brought up the money myself. I'm not an evader with you. I want to get this straight. That tone is exactly just what I don't need together, okay?"

Dan stared into his cup as if to drink from the steaming coffee would be to reduce this to a social occasion. Yet he liked coffee; it was a family trait. He took a rapid little sip. It was his brother, after all. Then he put the cup down. His fists were clenched. Hutch noticed this and wagged his head from side to side. Negativity was exactly what nobody needed around here. All around them mirrors reflected the night sky, the glow of fog, the jagged few lights, the sluggish jewelled traffic on the Bay Bridge. San Francisco was a positive place. There were hills. Even before dawn, in keeping with his philosophy of festival and continuation, Hutch had pulled out all the hospitality stops. The next move was up to Dan.

"My daughter," he said.

For a moment the floors seemed to tilt for Hutch. A thought came across the tape. Why does this guy I like so much, my brother—hell, I love the guy, only want the best for him, think about him every chance I get— why is he mad at me?

That nervous twitch took his shoulders. Hutch preferred to consider it a shrug. Life isn't fair. No one said it's fair. A person only did the best he could and doesn't blame others and doesn't blame himself, either.

Poor Dan.

Nevertheless, Hutch felt a little series of shaking-it-off shrugs taking his shoulders, his upper back, and a twitch of the lean muscles in his legs. Time for a good run: think about the good run ahead. "Your daughter, my niece. Trish. And?"

"I'd like to know what happened."

"You'd like to know what happened?"

"You're not usually my echo. I want to know what she did."

"You know what she did."

"I'm talking about you. How come you were the one took her to that . . ."

Hutch touched his brother's shoulder. "Look a little nervous, Dan. I know this is hard for you. Like to take a pee in my bathroom which is not so much a bathroom as a way of life?" Hutch understood that some words were difficult to pronounce. Perhaps, for Dan, Richmond-Sunset Clinic was one of those words.

Dan followed his brother into the bathroom. He was not planning to void himself, but it was true, he remembered Airplane, the game they played as children, peeing together, one boy's stream making the body of the plane and the other the wings; and he also felt a little queasy in this glass-and-mirrored and entirely neat and childless house with its expensive and meaningless works of kitchenware and furniture and decor, its glass, sleek aluminum, mirrors. Pipes of track lighting lined the walls. In the bathroom, the pink candles stood with their little erect blood-red wicks alongside a bathtub designed for good fun.

Hutch grinned. "Hard to find candles like that. But if she's got a sense of humor, pays off, man."

"Why did you take her there?"

Okay.

"Okay, the kid needed an abortion. I've heard that's a lonely decision. You and I both know about loneliness, don't we, brother? So when it looked like she wanted me . . ." He shrugged. "Show you how this works." Behind the epoxied Bohemia beer can, which held a half-dozen toothbrushes, there was a gleaming aluminum tab. There was a mirror. Hutch slid the mirror and picked a silver lighter from the medicine cabinet. There was a little click and a jet of flame shot forward. "Never fail and failproof," Hutch said. He began to light the oblong of candles surrounding the tub. "A nice long fireplace match might add to the atmosphere, but tends to be messy, ashes drop in the water, goes out, sputter, break the mood in its own way . . ." He showed how, leaning across the tub, he could shoot the flame out to light the candles next to the double pane of glass. "Imagine dusk coming on, lights of the city, skyline, and bay, a boat or two out there, cruise ship, maybe a U.S. government submarine or aircraft carrier, the best kind of music on—wait, let me tell you the whole story about a bachelor's lonely life—and she goes, Hey, people can see in, and I go, Hey, no they can't, we're high on the hill, but isn't it pretty to think maybe they *are* watching? and she laughs, gives one of those kind of nervous giggles, y'know . . . There."

He stood back and admired the pattern of smoothly burning candles. Fine wax and a glow.

"You have to imagine Sunday brunch or night or morning. Two good friends having a soak, steam and bath oil and stuff. Actually, I don't like the bubbles, dries the skin, I prefer a quality scented oil. You have to imagine an attractive young female person for the total effect, brother."

"Why should you be the one?"

"Pardon?"

"Hutch, why were you johnny-on-the-spot? What I'd like to know, Hutch, is why you, who doesn't take responsibility for anything, who learned life is just a festival and never forgot it, why *you* took her to the clinic?"

"Hey, cause I just do what comes natural?" Hutch's eyes began to widen with amazement. It was working up from an even deeper place than his normally surprised *fancy that.* "Are you asking if I . . . ?" He began to laugh, coughing a little, forcing the laugh. He still had a few things to point out to his kid brother before he gave the festival of laughter its run. "Great father," he said. "Great devoted father who runs his life for his family, hey. Don't you know anything about me and your kid?"

Dan seemed to be turning like a top in a small space, although the room was large enough for him to move around and neat enough for him simply to stand still and converse. He could have just spoken with his brother, but instead he seemed to go into this spinning motion, a spinning top all blurred at the edge of a table, waiting to fall off. "How cheap of you to play hero for my daughter when you don't pay your dues— *I'm* her father. It's *cheap,* Hutch."

"What do you mean, cheap?"

"No class, Hutch."

"You're way out of line. I love that kid."

There was an agony in Dan as he stopped moving, stopped turning, and lowered his head. "I know you do. You really do. But you don't care what you do to us."

Hutch just stared. He knew he wanted the best for Trish. He knew he hoped the deal with Dan's investment would work out. He knew no one else understood how he planned for things to be all right but life is full of pitfalls. A person needed to celebrate and understand the pitfalls, both. He knew he couldn't teach Dan by explanation; he had tried all his life; the kid brother was stubborn.

When Hutch knew he was right, as right as a man can be—okay, grant the pitfalls—he also knew he had to just ride on through. He practiced the rare game of silence. He thought it might work this time.

Dan had stopped that spinning, but his head—it wasn't normal—was lowered like an American bison's, a buffalo's. His head down like that, sounds came out of the muzzle, a loud bleating roar. *"Did you get her pregnant?"*

"Are you going nuts? Ow, the echo all these walls,

that was too loud, Danny. Didn't you ever take a good look at her pal Harry? Weren't you interested?"

Dan swung and Hutch was adept and ready. He stepped sideways and blocked the blow with his forearm. "You're not serious," he said. "That wasn't serious because it was telegraphed. I'm not getting angry yet. But don't fuck around, brother."

Dan was panting as if they had already fought. Hutch studied him and wondered about the amount of aerobic exercise his brother found time for. At his age, forty minutes a day, minimum three times a week, would have been a good goal for starters. He watched him warily. He worried about the candles flickering around the tub. A person could get knocked about and seriously bumped in this room. Nozzles and faucets stuck out. A few tabs, a souvenir Bohemia can from Linda One or Two. The candles could be knocked over and broken and they weren't cheap Cost Plus candles. Yet Hutch didn't like the idea of retreating from this arena where he had won so many victories; it was his domain, his place, and he was the elder brother around here.

"You know I resent that even as a remark, Dan. Even a person who is upset shouldn't make stupid dumb-ass remarks to his very own only brother. Even a creep comes around like a crybaby when a deal he went into as a fully aware adult investor—" He shrugged. There were several questions going on here. Hutch was moving too fast and it was a deliberate choice to do so. Winners can sense when to come on strong. He would just like to see his very own kid brother try to knock him through the row of candles and into the creamy marble of this tub in which he had enjoyed so many cleansing good times. This, if it happened, would be a first—no water in the tub.

In a narrow space a few inches made the difference. How seldom one man smells another's breath as it

issues from his nearby mouth, the male pores enlarged, the male bristles on the face reflecting candle-
light. Hutch was ready and it was an interesting experience to feel virtuous and right and it was both
interesting and engrossing. Hutch evoked his mental
bookie. He figured the odds at sixty-forty in favor of his
brother's swinging on him once again. It would be the
second time today, but only the first time since they
were, say, thirteen or fourteen or maybe it was fifteen.

Hutch could increase the odds by what he did next
—laughing or teasing or pointing out the facts. He
could also lessen the odds by just watching and breathing, or maybe not; a person couldn't always predict
how a stupid kid brother might react to daughter
problems, money problems, brother problems. Hutch
wasn't sure about the effects of what he might say.
Probably wife problems were also in there someplace.
Hutch felt a certain itch to offer the truth on highly
selected occasions. This one qualified. He was curious.
It was exhilarating to have the truth so totally on his
side.

"The business between us is not about how I absolutely didn't fuck your daughter, dear brother of
mine."

It was easy to catch the swing which followed Dan's
previous clumsy windup. Dan lurched and knocked
three of the candles into the tub.

"Aw, come on, Danny, don't do damage."

A real man might butt with his head. A real man
might go for the balls. With a real man it might be a
fair fight. Hutch thought: Maybe Dan is a real man and
all I have to do is be patient although generally I'm the
impatient one and have to remind myself—

There was a noise behind them as Hutch was wondering, Coward? is he a coward? and saying, "You
think the whole world—you're just like me, brother—

you think the whole world is just your own personal toy—"

Now it would come. Dan would do it now.

No, he wouldn't.

A bustling young woman hurried into the bathroom. "Hey, you left the door open. Mom said, and I figured —hey, you guys, what is this?"

Lucky Trish, making all the connections. The Muni even got her to Telegraph Hill in time to straighten things out. She moved between them and took to snuffing the candles out one by one, wetting her fingers in her mouth, and then squeezing the wicks, grinning, chattering, as aware as she could be, fully amused because life is a festival, saying, "Hey, but Dad, he helped me. I couldn't have gone through that whole stupid thing without Uncle Hutch, Dad. You think Harry was any good to me? He was about as much fun in this situation as a mother or father, no disrespect to my own mom and dad, but you know? you know? Shit, burned my thumb on that one."

"Young flesh heals quick," Hutch said, and enjoyed stepping out of the way as Dan lurched against him, but this time Dan had learned how his brother twisted; he followed to the left and toppled him into the tub, breaking through the smoking wax sentinels. Trish screamed. "Dad!" as Hutch fell backwards, his body slapping against patterned near-marble. He drew his head up and lay crumpled in the tub, his legs in the air. Helpless and sprawled, he lay there laughing, choking with laughter. "I could hurt myself if I hit my head! You gonna jump in and tromp me now, Dan? Hey, I'm at your mercy now, brother, congratulations, okay?"

Trish let go of her father. She put her fist to her own mouth. She didn't know whether to scream or to stifle the giggles.

Lying there with his legs apart, still shaking with

laughter, not caring if he was hurt, it seemed, Hutch said, "Your dad got a whole list of reasons he's sore at me, Trish, don't be hard on him. Call it his agenda. But don't be hard on me, neither."

Dan stood there fighting for his breath.

Hutch looked from his brother to his niece and saw the truth from this peculiar upsidedown position where he had spilled into an oversize tub, shoes in the air. He had no child of his own. But he recognized the agony of jealousy and need which made his brother pant for life like a heart-attack victim. "Hey, Danny, it's one thing I didn't do, can't you tell that? Hey man, whatever badness you dream up, shouldn't you be a little careful about what you think you know?"

"Daddy," Trish said.

"Listen to your daughter," Hutch said. He twisted on the cold surface; it felt different when a person was fully dressed, lacking hot water, sentinel candles, lacking a nice companion steaming and wriggling and playing with the loofah or the soap and tucking it intimately into creases to make him giggle and play, too.

Dan stared a moment. He turned and ran.

Hutch climbed out of the tub, saying to Trish, "He could be a big success someday, your dad, he keep control of his temper but only let go when he has to."

"Uncle Hutch—"

"You better hurry on outside. What the—you took a bus? He's waiting in his car, give you a ride home. I got things to do, okay honey?"

Hutch stood at the mirror in the empty bathroom. When a person had only one so far, he probably didn't have the right to call it the master bathroom. He pushed his hair back and found a gash on his forehead. He hadn't noticed it before; it was only beginning to ooze a slow whitish fluid stained with red. He stared into the mirror and stuck a piece of toilet paper to the cut. A souvenir, a vacation in Siblingland.

He shook his head in the mirror for that invisible audience which followed him wherever he went. *Fancy that.* He glanced at the spilled towel, the broken candles; he smelled wax and wick; but he did not stop to clean up just now. He made up his mind to take care of first business first.

14
_____

A few donuts for breakfast today as a special treat. After all, when a person has been waked at an ungodly hour, had to deal with a nervous sibling and a nasty little cut on the head, he deserves to slide onto the spoon-shaped orange plastic stool for a little fried grease feast. For the energy. When a person has a runner's metabolism, his body can handle it.

Heading back from Winchell's, Hutch took the scenic route through town. This did not mean the crooked street, the tree-lined streets, or the streets that violated the grid system and snaked like settler trails around the hills, with sudden vistas of bay, bridges, Alcatraz, Angel Island. When Hutch looked for scenes, he looked for scenes inside his head—fun at best, profit in the normal course of events, or solutions in times of troubles. There should have been a song about that: Let the okay times roll.

This time he headed through the Tenderloin, where men or women or in-betweens could be hired at the

best prices for whatever a person had in mind, so long
as he was able to give clear directions. A person could
buy everything from generic, quik-pak sex to the spe-
cialty items—rubber goods, metal, water sports, hurt
or give hurt. Just name it or describe it if you don't
know the name. Folks pulled up to the curb to negoti-
ate their deals through the windows of automobiles
which, on average, were well below the level of the
most stripped-down BMW.

When Avigdor was in town, great little Sovietski
traveller, amazing how good he was at asking for just
what he wanted. They went to the Tenderloin for fun,
because that's where it was, and they went wherever
else fun could be tracked down—Twin Peaks, North
Beach. Efficient tracking and finding was one of
Hutch's talents. When Trish needed help, the doctor
was a good one, probably the best except for her line of
chatter, but here you needed good vacuuming or
scraping—charm wasn't the program. So were the
nurses the best, thanks to the advances in modern
abortion politics and technology. Nowadays you could
get outstanding people for this line of work. Hutch
used to have an ACT acting student for a condo
cleaner—good people, left him notes when the
Windex got low, a little young, bubbly thighs. But no
man can have everything. That's only an ideal.

Same with business. One of the Zen guys Hutch ran
into out at that nice joint in Muir Beach said ride with
the flow. Sometimes you had to look high and low for
the flow. When Hutch needed money and fast to give
him a little breathing time with his investments, the
last resource people had moved north, out of the Tenderloin and into North Beach, keeping only a few interests in Las Vegas factoring or union affairs in the old
location at Turk and Mason. Hutch held them in reserve. The last-resource people were no fun. But
sometimes an entrepreneur who took a few chances

had to go the extra mile to these last-resource folks, Ray Aratunian and his colleagues.

Hutch made a detour onto Turk to pass among the relics of a better time, when the world was filled with hope, herpes was only a cold sore, and AIDS hadn't come to town to scare the public. The six-foot-tall transvestites with their clacking armory of heels and purses still crowded with all their equipment into telephone booths to make their calls, screamed at the news vendor, crossed with stately indifference in front of traffic, turned at the curb to cross again. They were careless and charged-up. You can't kill the life force in folks who have it a hundred percent. This was their outdoor office, an equal opportunity employer. One black personage was wearing white-face stage makeup, a red Brillo wig, and a lace support garment tightly cinched on the outside of his tasteful ballgown. He had gotten dressed inside out, showing off his new corset. It did not make him look like a white woman, Hutch reflected. Too thin. More like the voodoo god of AIDS.

He leaned into Hutch's car. "Hey, I'm a famous dyke-about-town, wanna take me on a run?"

"The light changed," Hutch said. "You don't move your head, you're gonna lose it."

"Oo-ee, you a bad mother, Hutch," said the famous male dyke-about-town, and didn't move, daring Hutch to decapitate him and spatter the inside of his car with schvartze antibody blood. He was counting on Hutch's confusion (a little confused pride in there, too) about how the famous Turk and Mason corner person knew his name. Then he pulled back, out of range of the window frame and the rearview mirror, and showed his really big teeth: "Says Hutch everywhere, briefcase, glove compartment, bet you wear gold crotch chains with Hutch on it, just like me, only I can't see yours, Hutch sweetie."

He was in control on this turf. Maybe he played running forward at Washington High, but decided he was too short for a career as a pro basketball star, too tall for a sex-change operation, but just right for a Tenderloin transvestite. He enjoyed dressing. When he wore his whiteface makeup, he felt as free as a white person, with only the usual human needs. He pursed his lips and blew a kiss. He let Hutch move.

It would have been more fun if Hutch had gotten away with the mystery intact about how he guessed his name—something to ponder in the surprises of being well-known around town.

Among the adult film distributors, the Vietnamese and Cambodian food shops, the Zaire Likker and the competing Rasta Herbs, Tease, Ltd., Trinidad Imports, with its Magic Marker sign: Alcohol—the Man's Slave Whip, plus a death's-head drawing, there was a shop with peeling gilt lettering: Fresh Chickens Open Only on Thursday. Must be something funny about the overhead, Hutch figured, he can amortize on use one day a week, even if he owns the building—what was he really selling? Even here, where the rents were competitive, you couldn't make it on chickens just one day per week, assuming it meant runaway chickens from San Antonio, dropout chickens with acne and speed habits. A rice queen liked Chinese chickens, a dinge queen liked black ones, Avigdor never declared himself, and Hutch always thought the right tenured flight attendant could have as good a case of skin problems as any moronic runaway.

Hutch looked closer. What was this? Sometimes when they said chickens, they actually meant *chickens.* A skinny geezer in a Forty-Niner's cap, visor backwards, was sitting in the window pulling handfuls of feathers off a live bird, which was squawking and shrieking. The chicken-plucker was flinging the feathers into the air and the chicken began to look bald, pitiful, and weary. The door to the shop was open. The chicken's cries were hoarse.

The poultry worker caught sight of Hutch, acknowledged him and his BMW 325is with a bow, tipped his Forty-Niner's cap, then bowed again and snapped off the head of the chicken by biting it.

Hutch didn't have to take this abuse from strangers passing by on the street. For a moment (Hutch was like that) he forgot that he was the passer-by, the driver-by, and the chicken-plucker had a perfect right to bite the heads off chickens in his own chicken-dressing establishment. This was the meaning of private enterprise, although Hutch had standards and tried to deal only with folks climbing as high up on the scale as he was. As much as possible. Allow for feasibilities. Hutch believed in improving achievement as a person went along.

A nostalgic visit to the Tenderloin presented its own problems. Hutch needed to get ready for Ray, prepare himself, but a person shouldn't dwell in the rosy past.

One thing about these bankers: they were always on the premises. They weren't geeks and they didn't bite off heads. Nice guys. A person could find them if he wanted them. Ray was usually awake. He must have slept sometimes, but Hutch had no personal proof of it, on a need-to-know basis. First, waiting was his business, while the money hatched; then cutting the waiting short was his business. Since the banker didn't like detail work, paper, printout stuff, they played a little cards. If they were between hands, they telephoned a wife or a girlfriend. Alongside games and telephone calls and business, they ate takeout. They were ready to deal. For extra fun they crumpled takeout napkins while waiting for people to come to them.

Hutch drove up Kearny and then over to Montgomery and the office across the courtyard from the former Mexican restaurant. The white coat at Elite

Autopark, No Insies Outsies Campers, waved him in—
"Hey Hutch!" The Mexican Mission premises were
still pretty, colored tile, swept clean except for a few
stray piles of paper and takeout cartons in the corners
and a persistent smell of expired tacos. It was your
basic nice North Beach bankrupt real estate, waiting
for an Iranian or Hong Kong investor with hope in his
heart. Hutch felt a little sick, nothing enough to
amend the rule that life must be a festival, but a little
gastric anticipation. This was normal during a hectic
business cycle. For a loyal American entrepreneur,
hope was still valid.

A buzz and a clicking latch. Hutch preferred a human hand, more organic, to open the door. The hefty
secretary with the dark mustache was sitting at her
typewriter. Her fingers lay on the keys. She wasn't
typing, she was just sitting there. The electricity was
turned off. She had brushed the polish onto her nails.
Now she was spackling it, silver on pink. She was sitting at her typewriter and watching the spackles dry,
her pinkies on the A and the colons, the air circulating
among the resting Smith-Corona keys. "They're in
there," she said. "They see you coming."

Ray Aratunian sat at a game with his partners.
"Hutch! I bet you blow in like the wind with good
news."

The old man with the wet pendulous lip was brooding over his cards. "I sit too long, I get sleepy," he said.
"That's the problem, so I should stand up. But I'm
tired. And he don't come with good news, Ray."

Ray gave him a concerned look. Maybe it would be
okay for the senior partner to take a little catnap.

The skinny young bodyguard with the nervousness
and the zits stood up. He was offering to help the old
man to his feet, but he misunderstood. When a person
was that old and tired he didn't necessarily want
to stand, even if it awakened him. The youngster

slouched back down in his chair, moving it slightly so he had a direct beam on Hutch. "What's good news about the wind?" asked the senior partner, and let his eyelids down for a little rest after this mental exertion.

The other bankers stared at Hutch. They were between hands. They expected Hutch sometime between hands. Ray Aratunian stacked and shuffled the cards with a sharp slapping sound, and then set them on the table. "So glad," he said. He was wearing a new tan suit. The seams under the arms were stretched but not yet sprung.

The hefty secretary entered, her fingers still spread to dry. "I'm taking refreshment orders. Who?"

Ray checked around the circle. "We're fine," he said, "unless our friend here . . . ?"

"I'm fine," Hutch said.

"Dieting a tad, like me, though God knows you don't need it, Hutch—slim and lovely as a girl and you move like the wind. Then if the refreshment angle is settled, I may continue. So glad you bring your patronage to Vecchio Investments, Hutch. We may be some veterans around here, but still young at heart in a developing economy. Hey, Hutch, I'll bet you need one of these."

Hutch didn't want a briefcase with Armenian National Home embossed on it, and he already had a briefcase, anyway, but the laugher was pointing past Ray's vinyl folder with the tin lock toward a glass of Bloody Mary mix. Red-stained celery stalks stood there; Ray offered him one, nodding encouragingly and miming the act of biting and chewing with his finger in his mouth.

Hutch didn't move. "Thanks," he said.

"No, really, good this way, Hutch."

"I'm fine."

"No, try it, you'll like it. Two-three calories."

When Hutch still didn't move, Ray pulled a stalk of

celery from the glass, then replaced it, saying, "Maybe you prefer a fuzzier? With all the leaves and shit? Some people enjoy the roughage out here. You sit and stew about things, they tell us you need extra roughage."

The dark old man, emaciated and sleepy, surely diminished by some wasting disease, stirred suddenly and mumbled, "Used to be I gave all the roughage a fucker like that one needed. Roughage treatment he didn't get enough of."

Ray stared a moment before he broke into his jolly laughter. The good old days, what? That's a sure sign of terminal illness. Sometimes, when a partner sat there dying by slow degrees through the fiscal cycle, you couldn't be sure if he really meant a joke. He might be just impatient. Usually when Ray laughed alone, he didn't mind too much, but now he wanted to be helpful. First he cocked his head sympathetically toward his senior partner, then toward the visitor. "So Hutch? You wanted to discuss?"

Hutch was still smiling. He discovered he was smiling, although not particularly happy or entertained, because Ray smiled back. Ray picked it up, he held it, he showed his teeth; he attacked Hutch's smile until he made it disappear. "Feel better now we're straight with each other?" Ray asked. "Okay, you stopped that stupid grin. I do the biting around here, okay? In my offices, y'know—supervised the decoration personally. My daughter does that line of work. Are we discussing yet, Hutch?"

There was a crackle like hard snow underfoot in Ray's voice. There were icy grains and frozen bits. But he was proud of his daughter; maybe that was what the smile was really about, in the way that Hutch was happy with Trish, feeling close, liking her a lot.

Hutch always found it was better to be in control of things than the reverse. Just now the things were in control, so he thought he might try to slow them down. It was hard to do a biofeedback treatment on himself without people noticing. He spoke with exact precision. Sometimes his business voice differed from the social one. "I got a lot going for me at this point in time," he said. "Naturally, there are always little glitches."

Ray began to chuckle again in his nice juicy way. "No more borrow, I trust. Take care of old debts, clean up the interest and charges, the little lateness penalty glitch, then borrow again. That's life in the eighties, Hutch."

"Okay."

"Pyramiding went out, Hutch. Building pyramids just topples over, Hutch. Magic pyramids don't meet the earthquake standards no more, Hutch." Ray was delighted by his gift for telling a tale. "Get my meaning, man? You're an item. A lot going for you could get to be too much—can you track my meaning, Hutch?"

It was not too much to track.

Hutch turned his pale face to Ray, the freckles darkened by his pallor, and said, "I don't know what you're going to do next."

"Neither do we. Probably collect. That's my own best guess."

"I don't know what I can do, Ray."

"That's why we don't know what we'll do, dear friend. That's why you asked your brother in. Because he signed. Because he'll figure out what's expected of him when we spell it out."

"I made an agreement because I expected—"

"You made a deal, not an agreement. An *agreement*, okay, you can play with it, finagle, how you put it. A deal with us . . ." He shrugged. "A deal. You recall that item Hutch, don't you?"

The old guy sleepily shuffled his balls with one long bony hand. Through the thin pants of some sort of

worn polyester the outlines could be seen, elongated
oblong objects, worn by gravity and hanging there in
need of relaxed exercise for the circulation. He woke
himself up. "It ain't no fuckin agreement, man."

"A deal, you heard him," the thin bodyguard said.

Ray smiled happily, as if the wisdom of the child had
spoken through the lips of both these partners with
the dried froth in the corners of their mouths—old
froth in one case, young in the other. "He analyzes
right through to the heart of the question, don't he?"
Ray asked. And the thin young bodyguard was only
learning the business.

Hutch searched for an idea. He made a lunge.
"You're hurrying me," he said—it was a speculative
lunge.

It didn't pay off.

"Lookahere," said Ray, "don't think we're mad at
you. We got ourselves straight with you, got no problems with you, so why talk about hurry? Why act nervous, Hutch? It really don't pay."

"We're not," said his sleepy colleague.

Ray peeked over at him again, respectfully pursing
his lips. With all due respect, he wanted his former
superior to speak up out of his doze.

"Not mad at you slightest," the old guy muttered.

"He's asking what hurry," Ray explained. "Why you
tell us hurry? He wants to know where you get that
idea. I'm of the same opinion. Hutch, you got to calm
down."

"Okay."

"When you're nice and calm, we just want you take
care of this right away. No rush at all. We're just
obliged insisting a little"—smoker laughter and
throat-clearing, a thick sound—"for our own good.
Hey, Hutch. You got the job of being mad at us if you so
choose, if you want to take the time. If you think it's
worthwhile, Hutch—*worthwhile.*" Something went

into the handkerchief from his mouth, he took a quick
peek, nodded at it as if it reminded him of something,
and then went on: "So what I advise is this: you're in a
big floating bunch of caca—shit—you know what that
is? So take some in your hand, work it around, make
yourself an oar, maybe a tiller—you ever go someplace
quiet in a summer, a lake, know what I mean?—take
your shit-oar and row yourself out. That's your best
hope, Hutch. That unimproved undeveloped land
where the real estate boom went bust ain't much
other good for you. You owe us, so we collect. We're
not upset."

Hutch was silent.

"You look a little mind elsewhere. Got those dark
spots on your brain, Hutch? A nice clean tongue on
you when you open your mouth, but I can't see what's
in your head, only guess or what I prefer in these cases.
Not give a fuck."

"What am I going to do?" This was another lunge.

Suddenly, for the first time, the skinny bodyguard
looked away. He had an inner life; he was embar-
rassed.

"You could maybe burn it." Ray Aratunian, a laughing man in an all-tan suit with all-tan skin, was trying
to be helpful. "Got insurance, you could find a torch.
Some people prefer to do it theirself. Hire a black boy,
hire a made guy, hey, you got a chance he'll cop a plea,
go for the insurance reward, hang you up with requests for extra fee, you know, forever—I don't advise
that."

"I'm not going to do it," Hutch said.

"Yeah. That's right." The laughing brown Ray
laughed. Again the juice was building up in his throat
and he got his handkerchief ready. "You're not gonna
do that, Hutch, cause it's unimproved land. Hard to
torch unimproved land, hey?"

The skinny bodyguard was following closely, his

head working like a pingpong spectator's. He didn't like to interrupt. He only had his learner's permit. He thought he noticed an essential point which was being forgotten during this flurry of grownup discussion. "Someways help your brother out," he said.

Ray looked at him with beaming approval. Sometimes the truth speaks from the mouths of baby hoods.

Ray didn't happen to have a toothbrush on him, but his teeth felt coated from all this takeout food plus laughing, coughing, and chatting. He snapped open a little packet and dusted salt on his index finger. He began scrubbing his teeth.

"Pardon?" said Hutch.

"Now I got to rinse my mouth. All that salt's not so good for the cholesterol."

"Pardon?"

Ray got up and lumbered to the sink in the corner, kneeled, put his mouth under the faucet. He gargled a little while he was at it. He came up chuckling. "Better," he said. "That way I get to keep all the teeth I got left, unlike forty-six percent of the population my age. Lungs going, but teeth situation is stable." He licked a grain of salt from his lips and pulled his mouth wide with both hands. "My permanent bridge don't get taken out at night cause it's permanent. Otherwise, person sees that glass there, teeth in it—someone knocked them out when I was a kid, didn't really lose them—it turn off the ladyfriend she see them there when the soft music playing."

Hutch ran his own finger along his perfect teeth. He felt the edge of gum, hardly retreated at all. So far, so good.

"So now, one time or another, I'm gonna take the teeth of a guy who fuck around me, Hutch. With that little comment, you may proceed."

"You couldn't have been talking about me," Hutch said.

"You got the nice teeth I notice, we both noticed,"
Ray said. "So I was more talking about you than anything else I was talking about. I just want to make it
clear, dear friend, I'm a nice guy and all but you are
just, in my personal eyes—make your brother pay
your debt like that—in my personal eyes you are just,
uh . . ." He showed his teeth to the ceiling. He
wanted to find the right word. "You are caca, Hutch."

There was a little isometric jump in Hutch's upper
body. Rudeness was always a surprise—he expected
better.

"For a promoter, Hutch, your public relations needs
work."

"What's the point here, Ray?"

"Your personality. Needs work. Smiles, but it's not
funny. Pathetic, but it's not sad. You're a mess, boy. I'm
trying to clear things up a little, but you don't want to
see it. So now we just find out if you're going to do
anything about your brother's debt."

Hutch had these little shrugs which he used when
people were rude to him. He liked to let the rudeness
slide down off him with greater speed than the law of
gravity provided. Velocity was important in the art of
forgetting insults. It did no good to remember them; it
spoiled the festival. Gently, gravely, almost compas-
sionately, but with rapid shrugs, Hutch forgave the
waster of rudeness. After the series of shrugs he made
a series of sniffs.

Ray watched these waves in a healthy body dealing
with unhealthy ingredients. Ray sort of enjoyed them.
Hutch said softly: "What can I do to persuade you to
leave my brother alone?"

"Oh, easy, Hutch. Live up."

"Pardon?"

"Live up to your agreement. Pay up." Ray liked the
rhythm he had going. "Pay up to your agreement."

"I don't have it, Ray."

There was stillness in the air. The old fellow was snoring. Again the bodyguard looked away. Hutch said: "Mr. Aratunian, I don't have it. What can I do?"

"Get it. This is America."

"I'm temporarily a little short."

"Take your growth hormone."

Hutch decided to try lightening him up with a smile. It came out bleak despite the good teeth. "Ha, can you get water from a dry pipe? What's the good a twisting the faucet?"

Ray leaned forward with a reassuring wink. He didn't want Hutch to fear this near approach. He put out one finger with its sharp ring—just the tiniest of his fingers—and lightly tapped the bruise on Hutch's forehead where he had fallen through his candles and into the tub. "Hey, we didn't do that yet, did we?" He looked at his colleagues, brushing the finger very lightly over the drying scab. "We got no reason to do that, do we?" It didn't hurt. It tickled; it itched. "I know that wasn't us, so what happened?"

"Something about a lady," Hutch said.

"Pretty recent, isn't it? With all you got going in your career, you got time for the ladies? So this deal isn't too hard on you after all."

Shrugging, Hutch again helped gravity slide his burdens off.

"I mean at your age, so sincere all of a sudden about your debts, you're still horny for the ladies? I admire that, Hutch. Personally, I wouldn't be able to get it up without a whole lot of warm tongue. I salute you, Hutch. I almost respect you."

"Thanks."

"I don't believe you."

Hutch would be not incited. It wouldn't help. Even if Ray didn't want to stay with the focus on things, Hutch knew what was important.

"And you said dry pipe, Hutch?"

"Yeah, I just don't have it. That's the bottom line. My brother has a family and no money, his wife teaches school, he drives a cab—"

"He signed. You got him to sign. A plumber cracks a pipe, there's always a few drops inside—I think *that's* the bottom line."

"Ray, I don't have it!" Hutch shouted.

Ray jumped a little. He didn't expect so much volume from Hutch. Sometimes, in his experience, yelling went with emotion, but more often it was quietness. He put up a hand. "We can hear you, man. I'm listening with all my attention. You had your chance to vocalize."

"Ray—"

"Now you listen. A deal is a deal, a paper is a paper, and there's lots of precedent you call it, how things are done, people signing their name, for not coming between us and our deal. You listening now, man? I might kid around, we do so much of our time in business around town might as well have fun with it, but I always come to the point. That's where we are now, Hutch."

Ray had spoken enough. It never tired him, but he was finished. There was pensiveness and gloom in the office. The smells of Tex-Mex food, the floating dust motes, the Frisco way of doing business with a lot of sociability. There was a sudden spurting of masculine cologne smells as sweat broke out on Hutch. Biofeedback let him down. His fingers were working into fists and then the fists were dissolving into mere fingers again. The old guy seemed to be snoozing; the skinny young one had a hand on his pocket, where there was a bulge he preferred (but better safe than sorry) not to use.

Very softly Hutch repeated, "I don't have it."

This hoarse whisper was louder than the shout for Ray Aratunian. He answered gently, mournfully, with no more laughter in him. He preferred for Hutch to find a way out. He said, "I think we just went past the end of the conversation, pal."

The old man had not stood, he remained in his chair; his pendulous lower lip hung ruddy and wet; he was sleeping. Quick naps are a knack old people recover from their babyhood. The skinny bodyguard was bobbing his head; he had switched on his Walkman; he was practicing some of his moves. Ray spread his hands. What could he do with such colleagues? Since there were human limits, he could not do very much. The widow lady had posed her dried fingernails on the typewriter keys to appreciate them more fully.

Hutch just got up and began to walk. Hutch was outside in the deserted North Beach Mexican courtyard when Ray came puffing after him. "Hey! Hey, Hutch!"

Hutch stopped and slowly turned.

"Maybe something'll come up," Ray said. "Pray. You do believe in God's will, don't you? I want to tell you my own prayers go with you, Hutch, since I dearly hate mess and dirt when it happens to patriotic American items like you who just happen to have the normal greed in their hearts."

15

It had been a long day, a visit before dawn from his brother and niece, a business discussion with the folks at Vecchio Investments, both of them difficult occasions, but Hutch noticed that he was different from people who didn't keep fitness uppermost in their minds. Fatigue tended to make him more alert.

So now, as the afternoon faded on the Marina with a wintry ocean glow, and the lights of the thickened commuter traffic blinked on—some people worked these hours—Hutch pulled off Marina Boulevard, parked, slipped his pants down. He was wearing his Ultra-Satin running shorts which did everything from conducting heat to holding cool, everything except answer the telephone and forward calls. There was always a little thrill of kiddish peeking and exhibiting himself for the imaginary others who saw him wriggling out of his pants. No harm done; Hutch allowed himself this pleasure. He flipped his crotch with one finger to tell the small erection, please, go away for now, thanks a lot, come back again some other day.

He got out of the BMW, locked, set the alarm, took a deep breath—smell of bay, winds working, nose working, good—and began his stretches. He neglected no part of the body. The knees were the most important, not much he could do for the shins, but press the arms against the car, repeat the series of knee bends, test the ankles and feet like a ballerina, more knee bends, push with the shoulders against the car, and now it just felt natural to reach. He shivered a little. He reached tall. He even hissed a little wind between his clenched teeth. Good.

Start slowly with jogging before the good part, the running.

He began his round on the Marina path. He had contributed to the mayor's Fitness Day fund which added redwood chips that crunched so nicely, like nonskid snow underfoot. Everywhere in life the best amenities were important.

Now, like an animal that knew its own skills, he began to pick up the pace. Isometrics has a payoff, too. He had stretched with frowning concentration; now he grinned. This smile was for no one else. He knew what he was doing. He felt the salt wind stinging a little on his eyes. Hutch was running.

When thinking didn't do it, or sexing, or concluding a deal, or funning with his buddies on the terrace at Enrico's, Hutch could always count on running. Running was the good way of being alone. When a person was into aerobics, he could let his troubles pass him by, just waving a hand and secure with that shrunken organ backed down in the Ultra-Satin. The problems only receded; they never vanished. That was correct. That was continuation. If he worried about Trish, these were rewards. He had the right to tuck her away among the other priorities—like Ray, like Dan, like himself—when he ran. He would continue forward later.

Hutch felt he was playing rat roulette, a game he had found one night across the bay in Emeryville when he forgot to run, his knee was bad, plus a touch of tendonitis, and he went looking for distraction in the after-hours place supervised by a part-time sheriff who had given him his card, said he was also an "enterprenoor," said to come on over and show the card and he'd be treated real right.

Rat roulette was a game of chance and sport out of Texas, a game with a sense of humor all its own. The wheel spun with a live rat careening and bouncng off the walls. Which hole would it run into? Place your bets, good people. Hutch suspected one of the holes had been flavored with cheese and bet on that one, but the rat ducked elsewhere. Perhaps he wasn't a cheese lover.

Endomorphins, come ease my sorrow. When a person forgets to run, due to a bad knee, rat roulette reminds him. Something had to be done about the bankers, about Trish, about Dan, about the dealings and due dates, the pyramiding compound interest on Hutch's debt which had become Dan's debt. There were too many things to do, none of them easy. Even Gloria was on his case. Just now, a strong run was the way to put things away right, find the proper hole where a person could hide. There didn't even have to be any cheese, just a lack of poisoned confusion.

Running was the place where turmoil stopped. Redwood chips were nice underfoot. It was odd how the whoosh of traffic on Marina Boulevard merged with the slow slopping noise of the bay at the stony breakwater when a person rounded the long green meadow on the running path. The water pulled sucking away; the cars did their Hollywood decelerations at the stop signs, then picked up again. Bums loitered near the litter cans, tried to sleep on the benches despite the handsome new Victorian metal sleeper separations. Divorced fathers entertained their kids with Frisbees and kites on the green. Lovers strolled, holding hands, building the firm foundations of their future divorces. A family of tiny Cambodians foraged in the dumpster; one had found something interesting, edible or salable, and was chirping at the others in tiny Cambodian. Grim runners circled the entire area like border guards.

Hutch fitted himself into the irregular patrol of those working out. Some of them silently moved their lips, counting strides or seconds. Some snorted in a professional breath-seizing maneuver. The stations of the Parcourse, a balanced fitness program installed some years ago, had been abandoned. It was a mere fashion. Running endured; running was what the animal did naturally, pursued by enemies, hunting food, seeking a mate. The counters and the snorters ran; so did the dreamy and abstracted ones, looking for alpha. Hutch ran. There's no *ro*-mance, he sang to himself, without *fi*-nance.

And then Hutch tried to give up thinking in order to busy himself with the body's purer song. When he ran, the little animal biting and nipping in his chest was overtaken by the wolf, Hutch preferred the wolf, it trampled the tiny paws and left them behind; Hutch took long loping strides, he felt a forest ranginess in his stride, he felt happy. Sometimes the deep thumping of his heart became a heavy roar and that felt fine, too. He forgot his other greeds.

Too bad Dan didn't take the time for good aerobics. The kid brother used to be fit and now was thickening around the middle. Skinny and slouching, an unfortunate combo. At his age a person shouldn't sit too much, he should recapture his speed. Hutch always led the way when they used to bike out to Ocean Beach and then back up the slope homeward to the dreary Richmond district. Hutch had escaped the Richmond and the Sunset, he had run all the way out to Russian and Telegraph hills. The magic city of festival was out there when a person reached, continued reaching. Poor Dan thought he was a writer, cabbie, husband, father, and didn't know it all added up to plodder. As a good brother, Hutch hoped to help him never do the arithmetic unless they could come up with something more festive.

When he thought about Gloria and Trish, Hutch felt a disagreeable confusion of indulgence and annoyance with his brother. Dan left himself open to all this. He took a wife, he made a daughter, he didn't get himself organized. Why did it never occur to him to settle life except one day at a time?

Or perhaps it did, and he thought too far ahead, and simply didn't settle matters with Hutch. Brothers should grow up. One brother shouldn't let another one go on kicking him, like kids fighting when the lights are out.

Hutch wasn't entirely clear about these matters, either, and that was okay, but it was another good reason to run. This was one of the times when he was especially not clear about the matter. Stupid Dan just said: Go on, kick me.

Hutch ran. He was older, but fitter. He felt he was growing shorter, men do that, even the voice box hardens and loses resonance, the spine begins to shrink. But Hutch was healthier than he had been as a young guy going places. Running fixed his sinus, it ended his smoking, it cleared the sinus all the way toward its termination in the brain. The brain was the computing part of the sinus, which took care of the breathing and draining of waste products from the head. A person's body was complicated. Hutch needed to know only what he needed to know.

He was scattered in the city sometimes, in the commotion of the city, but he also knew what he wanted about certain matters, money, fucking, respect, and running. He was smarter than some he could name. Thank you, gene pool. Thank you, Lindas One and Two, Sharon, Suki, and a whole lot of others who were listed in a spiral notebook under his bed. Thank you, California. Thank you, more and more careful focus on things.

And Hutch ran for his arteries and looks. The clothes were mere style; his neatly articulated slimness was the substance. Thank you, responsibility to body and soul.

Racquet and team sports were okay in their place, Hutch believed, suitable for kids or grownups who didn't have enough contact with others in the outside world, but running was for the freed animal—loping, sprinting, trotting, nosing the air, letting the endomorphins invisibly sprout. He had heard of aerobic expansion of arteries and lungs. He knew it was good for the body, put off heart attack and stroke indefinitely; maybe paid a small price in the knees, shins, spine. Risks come with the territory; no pain, no gain. Running was for a winner. Sure, there was a chance of excess. Hutch took risks, prudent ones. He was a festival animal. He was a graceful runner.

He ran along the beaches, and liked running barefoot in sand, which cleaned the toes, filed down the protuberances, finessed the calluses, scraped the feet smooth as a cub's paws. A flight attendant with a perfect case of bad skin—nothing oozing, just a little revelation of inner vulnerability—once said his toes tasted sweet. A nice compliment. Maybe he should have married her; it was pleasant to think so, and even better not to have done it. He ran the winding paths of Golden Gate Park. He ran out by the bay under the bridge abutments along the running trails set up by the federal government to give a view of Marin County; *good* taxpayers. When he took a trip, he found a place to run, even if it was on a graveled berm of a highway.

But since he was a city person, a San Francisco city person born and bred, he liked his run around the Marina, preferred the Marina best, where other winners ran in their own varied privacies, in sight of the yacht basin, the yacht club, the Golden Gate Bridge, the breakwater with the fishermen hauling up junkfish and an occasional suicide with the scavenger crabs attached to the juicy parts of losers. He liked the whoosh of the boulevard nearby. He liked to be an object of curiosity for lovers and idlers. *Hey, isn't that somebody? What's-his-name? Hutch Montberg?* The Marina was his best place.

As he warmed into a long run, starting with a marathon deliberation, he thought about the time he really almost got married. Bea was as pretty as a Victorian portrait—one of those soft-focus girls you find in the best mail-order catalogs; a Laura Ashley kind of girl; maybe they have pictures like that in museums, too. (Gloria and Dan would know about such things.) Bea seemed to like Hutch. She smiled at his jokes and teasing. She was a student of art history when he was at Golden Gate Law School. In those days he played tennis; running hadn't come in yet. They played doubles at the Cal Club—her membership. She didn't have all that much money to inherit, but her family was related to people with real money and she lived, sailed, did her tennis with a style of confidence that the bills would be taken care of. That life could be, should be, in fact was a festival struck her as an important insight when Hutch offered it during a moment of tenderness.

She also thought Hutch would take care of her when she got pregnant. She didn't worry about having a baby and was sure he would marry her because she loved him and San Francisco had always been graceful and sweet to her because she was graceful and sweet and she saw no reason why Hutch would not start her off in genuine adult life with a wedding, a child, a condo (the word had just come in).

How stupid could she get?

For one thing, Bea for Beatrice was a name, like Rachel or Fran or Gloria, which did not say electricity to Hutch. It said boring. It said good bones but no muscles.

And everything happened for the best. She lost the fetus without any action on Hutch's part. The last time he saw her she only remarked, "It would have been a girl, Hutch."

She married a curator at the Sacramento Art Something, gallery, museum, institute, one of those, and helped him curate his way through an unfestive career and had nothing in her life but babies. Her skin was milky, not passionate. In those days he wasn't ready to settle for someone who was merely close to real money. There was a richer assortment out there and all the time in the world, maybe ten-fifteen years. Bea was too safe, a mere fallback position who could never make first choice, a lucky miss on the first cut.

Hutch ran. In the rapture of running, the sweetness of a smooth urging of his body through space with no lurches, he remembered how he once picked up a girl at Just Desserts after failing with her twice, both times after a morning run, one morning trying, "Are you a dancer, that how you got those terrific moves despite all the carbo loading you do?" Failed. The next morning trying, "You are a doctor or a librarian or some kind of professional, that why you wear those cute glasses?" Utterly failed, plus a shitpile of silent scorn. She just dumped on him without one fucking word—the cunt had no courtesy.

He stayed away from Just Desserts for a week, giving the matter careful thought. He did four runs in Golden Gate Park, two on Ocean Beach.

Then, at her hour of breakfast, he positioned himself behind her in the coffee and carbo department, so she couldn't duck her responsibility to him, no escape, held prisoner by a bran muffin commitment, and said, "Hey, I been a jerk and I can't think of a single thing'd work. So whyn't we pretend you want to pick *me* up and you try one of *your* lines?"

"Wouldn't work," she said.

"I promise you it'll work," he said.

That night, as he lay beneath her legs, he asked what it was that he had finally done right. "I broke up with my fella," she said. "You were an asshole the first time and you were an asshole today, but you look as if you don't have any physical diseases, only psychological ones. It was a bad day for me."

Sometimes Hutch admired a strong woman.

In the pyramiding high of running, breath and pistons now nicely fitted, Hutch remembered his cleanest real estate deal. How he saw this warehouse and said to himself, "Senior housing! All we need is windows and we got senior housing!"

It's a storage vault, how you get it up to code? the bank asked him, so he went to another bank, crying, "Senior housing! This is a chance to do something for the community!"

And since the market was good and they needed a few minority, equal-opportunity, inner-city loans to fit some state requirement, this new non-gay-owned, non-woman-owned, non-Chinese or Filipino or black-owned bank said, You mean you really got a silent commitment from Redevelopment? For our worthy elderly folks who paid their dues and now need a comfy moderate-priced pre-final resting place? And gave the loan.

And Hutch managed to turn it over to Bekin's, which needed a whole new warehouse to store the Getty and Montandon furs, before the deal even got through escrow on his own account. Clean, that's clean, that's a good deal. And the Montandon pelt was sure a minority item.

Even though running was not the trend anymore, he ran. Running was heading out in the late eighties; people were going back to martinis, snoozing, and beef. But Hutch was not a trend-watcher. He stuck by the old traditions—running, tofu, sushi, and mesquite-grilled fish. The former sushi restaurants were converting back to bait shops. People were hanging their mesquite branches over their fireplaces. But Hutch was still loyal to the ancient ways of the California missionaries.

Even if the trendies pushed toward hamburgers and pork chops, neon-lit Route 66 diners, pastrami, for Christ's sake, Hutch would stick with the grapefruit diet after his donut binges. He noticed that he often fell into these donut episodes at Winchell's after he had a run-in with his brother. Dan and Hutch used to prefer the jelly kind when they spent Saturday afternoons at the nabe. One of those little observations a person likes to make about himself now and then.

Sometimes, due to coffee late in the day or an appointment with the IRS examiner, or maybe no sex for a week or two, a visit from a bill collector, or perhaps even worse, for no reason he could figure out, Hutch had a nightmare. He was standing naked in front of his closet. All his clothes were stolen by a clothesnapper and he was condemned to wear nothing but color-uncoordinated polyester leisure suits in San Francisco. He would sweat, half-awake, as the tape jumped through the sprockets. He was not allowed to run. Working out, even isometric squeezes of the buttocks, was punished by the forced ingestion of Pop-Tarts. He was fed Mars bars and Pop-Tarts for breakfast and fattened up until he looked like the pear-shaped man who was his father. And then he was given a woman with kinky purplish hair, five kids by her previous Hispanic husband, no cheekbones to speak of, and moved by the Federal Protected Witness Program to an unsafe house in Daly City. His lips were treated with barbecue grease. He was no longer what he had carefully made of himself. Oh no. *He was a loser.*

The giddiness of a long run began to take him. There was sweetness in the air and a rhythmic ease in his legs. It was like sliding into drunkenness, the endomorphins doing their work, good feelings flowing. He could imagine Dan and Gloria watching him, and Trish, with familial smiles of pride and approval. His niece was saying, "Yo! Go for it!" He saw Avigdor, his best Russian pal, standing in a plastic ski parka, amazed by his endurance, his steadiness, his legs, his breath; the regular lunch group from Enrico's that liked to laugh, they were there, too. He dreamed he ran past another runner, jostling him a little, and the slow one said, "Hey, lighten up, mister, this isn't rush hour," and dreamed his heel had hit a stone and ached for a second and then was fine, and dreamed he could run forever—knew it for a fact. This was not like not eating. A person has to *stop* eating if he stuffs himself, but a person can't just go on *not* eating forever. A person can pull the trigger, swallow the pill, jump from the Golden Gate Bridge—others could, but Hutch didn't do those things which ruined the fitness forever. He could run and he ran.

His body, like other bodies, had a wonderful talent for pushing protein in the form of hair out of random black spots on his face, arms, forehead. It had to be pruned, his body. He worked at it with tweezers and running, sometimes loping like a happy animal, happy

because he was hungry and sniffing out his prey.
Hutch groomed. Hutch kept healthy.

Hutch had an odd thought: *I'm hurting.*

And then had one which seemed more sensible to
him: *Can't allow that.*

The traffic noises from Marina Boulevard. As he circled the running track, the sounds of tires and trans-
missions on Marina Boulevard. The surge of waves
from the bay along the piled rocks at the breakwater.
As he circled the running track along the bay, he
heard the surge of waves and once felt a slap of salt
spray. The traffic sounds. The surge of waves. He was
running easily and hard, he was settled into it.

Now he began to push. This was too easy. He pushed
until it was no longer so easy; the traffic noises and the
scrape of the blocked tidal bay waves began to blend
in his ears with the rush of blood, the slap of salty blood
in his throat and mouth, the snorts of breath he took as
he went into another gear, gave up the long practiced
deep breathing of skill. He had learned to breathe
easily; he unlearned it. The waves. The traffic. The
running track. He no longer saw Avigdor and Dan
watching him, Gloria and Trish, and those fuckers
from the terrace at Enrico's, laughing at him, and the
bankers, especially Ray; he no longer saw any of them
at the Hutch Show, they were gone, he was running,
and even if he ran round and round in an oval, he had
outdistanced them.

That's better. That's really good.

His breath was coming hard. There was a hoarse
sound in his chest. His body began to separate into its
parts, pain in the chest, acid in the throat, ache in the
knees, stinging at the eyes, and these procedures were
keeping him busy. He felt free. He heard his breath
louder than the traffic noises, louder than the curling
waves; his breath was hoarsely laboring and his heart
was leaping and beating against his chest, and he was

thinking with joyful wonderment: I don't need anybody. Fancy that.

And he fell for a long time, soaring and diving
through space like the endless sky or the deep warm
waters of childhood, thinking through the burning in
his gullet, Better brush the teeth and floss carefully,
better take care of this taste in the mouth—and lay still
across a low railing which divided the running track
from the green.

He fell. He lay there. He didn't die.

He dreamt someone was pissing on him. He opened
his eyes. A girl about Trish's age was spilling from a can
of Sprite onto his lips; she was wiping the flecks from
his mouth; anxiously she was saying, "Drink, drink
some of this, you're okay, aren't you?"

He closed his eyes and seemed to sleep again, and
dreamed someone was standing over him with his fly
open and letting go on him.

The crowd, waiting for the ambulance—"They
called it, they called one already"—watched him
while he threw up, soiled his pants—a jet of vomit, a
stream of liquid brown—and the girl gave up, went off
with her Sprite can to find a litter basket because she
wasn't a litterer. "This guy can do two things at the
same time," someone was saying. "Jesus."

He opened his eyes again. A young woman with
smooth brown skin was watching with a quizzical
squint. He'd have preferred laughter to that look of
puzzlement, as if she had found a giant insect under
her shoe. "There," she said, "he can do three things—"

She didn't tell him the third thing he was doing as he
faded out again.

Hands and a shadow awakened him; a lifting under
his shoulders, the sun out of his eyes; "Hey!" He
twisted away. He was on his hands and knees. His
fingers were spread out, seizing the grass. The seat of
his pants was wet and sticky. His face was wet and

smelled something he remembered from childhood.
He had spit up, that was it. His knees dug into the
grass; so did his fingers.

"You okay, mister? We'll just put you on the
gurney."

"No, no, leave me alone."

"You probably overdid your run, like the idiots do
around here. Whyn't you let us just check you up?"

"I just overdid the run."

"You sure, mister? Don't you need some help?"

He rose to his knees and grinned through his soiled
lips. "Don't need anybody, kid." He hadn't quite settled matters yet. There were still some things on his
mind. "Fuck off with that equipment, thank you,
please."

16

Hutch looked for a safe place for his car. He hated the Imperial Discount Records lot, hated the whole idea that a brother of his lived in such conditions, Trish growing up in an add-on earthquake shack at the end of a discount-records parking lot on Geary, pickup trucks and junkers with flapping mufflers pulling out into traffic from ten in the morning till midnight, the kids inside Imperial spending their money on punk and heavy-metal ear garbage and the trucks piling by on their way out to Daly City or Route One or the feeder onto the Golden Gate Bridge. He didn't like the conversation he was about to have with Dan, either. But because the film of his life moved steadily right along on its sprockets, he ran through the fence and up the narrow illegal walk to the house. There were weeds growing between the crumbling concrete poured by Dan twelve-fourteen years ago, in a fit of house improvement when Trish was just a toddler;

weeds no different from flowers—why do they call them weeds?

As a city person, Hutch didn't have the answer to that question. For a noncommitted concrete-pourer, gravel would have served Dan better.

Still, Hutch preferred to have this business meeting with his brother in Dan's house. If Gloria and Trish were also present, they could clear things up like grown men, mature brothers, and not get into that stupid business of knocking people about, breaking the candles, endangering furniture. Even if Dan was the bad-choice champion of Richmond and the Sunset —look at raising Trish in this shack—he still deserved a say about his little investment that didn't work out.

The door was unlatched. Hutch paused to get himself organized before he pulled at it. The way he sometimes remembered a particular former tired blond when he needed to give himself strength in a particular situation with a new one, he ran through his expert real estate appraisal of his brother's earthquake relic, the roof over their heads. A pipe at the foundation was wrapped in heavy tape and glistening with damp anyway. Why did people live like this? It wouldn't pay to replace the plumbing. If Hutch owned the shack, he could talk to somebody in City Hall, tear down the whole thing, maybe you could do Chinese condos on the real estate back here, they wouldn't mind the record business up front if you came in at a good price. Get a longtime right of way for the parking and walk away with a neat little gain. And then he could put the money into a down payment in condos in a decent neighborhood.

Also, then he would be in a position to work Trish, Gloria, and Dan into something more suitable, a real home—do it in a way that wouldn't embarrass them for taking help from the uncle and big brother.

Positive thoughts always helped Hutch to feel a little better. A run, though he suspected he shouldn't run with a belly full of donuts or indigestible Aratunian remarks, always improved his spirits. The capillaries were nicely flooded; his teeth were brushed. He was easy. He rapped lightly on the door and entered. He heard Trish's music from her room. He heard the plumbing work. Since Dan was sitting at the kitchen table waiting for him—stood up formally, as if this were a business meeting, which he guessed it was—that must have been Gloria nervous in the bathroom and giving out bathroom plumbing sounds. Personally, Hutch preferred romance in a relationship and made better arrangements about noisy plumbing in his careful dealings with the tired blonds.

"Hiya," he said.

"Sit down."

Hutch poured himself his coffee from the cabbie's thermos on the table with DAN MONTBERG printed on adhesive tape stuck to the bottle, just like a kid protecting his belongings at summer camp. Who the hell was going to steal a coffee thermos?

"I'm here. I came like you asked me to. So let's say what you got to say."

Then Hutch stretched out his legs and stretched his body in the chair, arching his back, a little isometric proving that he was defenseless and willing to listen. At the same time, he saw no reason to drag this on. "You want to get right to it, don't you, hey Dan?"

Dragging it on did no good work for anyone, although the way Dan breathed, wheezing a little, a tightness in his chest which good exercise would cure, it seemed that he wanted to take his time. With aerobic exercise, say running, a person can work right through the tendency toward asthma that comes from tension and an unfulfilled life. Through the kitchen window, as he waited for him to get to it, Hutch could see part of the junk tree, weed tree—tree of heaven,

Dan called it—with its dusty fernlike leaves, nothing anyone would want in the alley alongside a house, making a jungly junk look. Might as well also have an old refrigerator on the back stoop. Since it was his only brother's place, Hutch had gotten used to it. He was wondering why people needed to go through conversations which neither did work nor provided fun, but he supposed that was their business. Whatever was right for them didn't concern him. He waited, he wouldn't yawn. He nodded at his brother, crinkled a little in a smile, tried to be helpful. "Okay Dan, thanks for the coffee?"

"Why did I ever trust you?"

"Thanks for getting your feelings right out like that."

"Why?"

"I wondered about that myself." Hutch gave it more thought. "Probably you had your reasons."

"Is that what brothers get? Unlimited trust?"

Hutch shrugged. "Do I know the rules? I didn't make the rules. But maybe you broke them."

Dan stared at him with a puzzled expression, the reverse of a man trying to identify a familiar face. He was trying to see the known face as a stranger.

"Hey, take responsibility, Danny. This is California. This is more than California, this is the 'eighties,' we're trying to grow with the times in San Fr'cisco. You're a grownup orphan now, fella, got a family of your own." And for a moment the old happy smiling ease came over the sun-worn face with its deep freckles and dark eyes. "Unlike ole Hutch here—no family of my own at all, at least I know of, isn't that right?"

Dan also grinned. "I guess that's about right, fella."

Two brothers having a heart-to-heart conversation, just like old times.

"It bothers you I'm your brother, right?" Hutch asked.

"Right."

"But you think I'm not your friend, right?"

Dan's smile was happy and alert now, like Hutch's when he was feeling good. Suffering seemed to work the wrong way with Dan, gave him something to get the blood going.

Gloria, standing, spun around and stuck her finger out. "You don't know where you came from, do you?" Now where the devil did *she* come from. Hutch hadn't heard her enter the kitchen. Talk about paying good attention. He didn't like losing his control of things. "You don't care where you go, do you? You should."

Hutch hadn't paid this visit to let himself be subject to abuse, certainly not from a woman who was only related to him by marriage. "Today is enough for me," he said calmly. "When I look at you, dear sister-in-law, I feel okay about myself."

"You like your life?"

He grinned. "Come see come sah. Sometimes it likes me. I get along."

"Is that good enough for you?"

"Well, into every life a little rain must fall, Gloria. Today we see a little rain."

"Don't you remember anything?" Dan asked. "Do you remember our mother? Do you remember me?"

Hutch was aware of doing thoughtful, his mouth pursing, his eyebrows pinching, the whole shebang. "You, okay, I'm looking at you. There you are. You're pissed. You got your wife and Trish here—" Thoughtful fell away. The smile returned. "—your wife and Trish because you're afraid."

"I'm not afraid of you."

Hutch shrugged. "Of yourself. What you might do if you ever let go. Whatever. But about our mom . . . I don't exactly recall. What did she look like? Blue or brown eyes? Hey, sometimes I wake up, I'm dreaming I saw her, but then I can't remember when I wake up,

I can't see her again." His shoulders were still working. He couldn't help participating in this unpleasant situation. "Dan, let's stipulate I did have a mother, I accept that, cause you guarantee you did and you're my full brother, okay?"

Gloria said, "Hutch, your way is just to nibble us to death. You just talk and talk."

Again Hutch shrugged. He did what was necessary.

"Oh but Uncle Hutch. What Uncle Hutch says is very interesting." The music was still playing upstairs. That was why Hutch didn't hear her footsteps, either. People could come and go and a person, even a wary and observant one, wouldn't notice. "Tell more, okay?" Trish turned to Gloria and explained. "I always remember what you look like, Mom. How could I forget?"

Hutch reached across the space and cupped Trish's head in his hand. "I'm sure I had a mother, just like everybody. But that's how it is. So that's how it's got to be."

Trish liked the pressure of her uncle's fingers on her head. He had a strong and affectionate paw. He was squeezing just enough against her skull.

"Other people forget things too, or they make things up, they have dreams and nightmares and think they're real. That's what a real suspicious person'll do sometimes. A paranoid person, just for one example, would have the real dumb idea an uncle could do something stupid and unnecessary like make his own favorite niece pregnant. I mean how dumb can even a paranoid person get?"

Trish was staring at her father. Her tongue ran across her lips in the sort of habit which, added to the sun on an outdoors man in California, gave Hutch his dry and flaking mouth problem.

"Naw, he didn't do that, Trish. Your dad's the nicest guy. I think I misspoke myself. Let's fast-forward a little. The problem is, and I got to face it, we all got to face it, especially I got to bear the guilt and onus of this deal, is maybe the way things are turning out, I still hope against hope, maybe something I brought to you made you lose a little ground in the war for investment survival. You made your own mind up about this investment, but I brought it to you. Sorry about that."

Gloria's lips were moving. *Sorry about that.*

"Are you off your head!" Dan shouted.

"Not necessary to raise your voice. I got no hearing loss. You put some money into an investment which I described to you was at risk, speculative—"

"Signed a paper for my brother! Because he asked me, begged me—"

Hutch shook his head. "You may be a brilliant cabbie and future writer, but you're not a sensible person, hey."

"And you're crazy, Hutch—begged me, promised, and now he says I was an idiot to help you—"

There was funny talk coming out of Dan's mouth, *you* and *he* all mixed up, first talking to Hutch, then appealing to some judge Hutch couldn't see, and words like *begged.* Hutch saw no beggars around here. Or if there was one, it wasn't Hutch.

He shook his head from side to side. It was important to be sensible and firm, a true older brother. In case Dan could be brought to pay attention—Dan was basically a sweet person, his little brother, lost his temper sometimes when his control slipped—Hutch went on shaking his head an extra moment and then stopped and gazed into Dan's eyes. Into that place just between and above the eyes; the same as the eyes, but a little more comfortable for the gazer. Hutch looked frankly and deeply into the carelessly unplucked eyebrow hairs just above Dan's nose. Stopping movement like this had its own power, a kind of double-reverse momentum of not doing things to regret later. For everybody's sake, the elder brother needed to remind them of who they all were. "Boy, do you know how to pass the blame," he said.

"Is that what happened?" Dan asked.

Hutch looked around. Something might have occurred just now which escaped his notice. "Was what happened?"

"You saw yourself in some trouble, so to postpone it, you just didn't really postpone it at all, you passed it on to me?"

"That a question?"

"Answer, Hutch."

Hutch shrugged. "You think you know already, don't you?"

Involuntarily Dan grinned again. When they were kids and Hutch was accused of something, he developed a trick of saying Fancy That or answering the question with another question. This was grownup trouble and his brother was still playing his games, peeking at the cards, sliding off, tricking.

Hutch noted the smile. He felt proud of his brother for beginning to take things like a man. Even though he was a kid brother and kind of a baby, he could be led along by a firm and steady hand. Things hadn't fully cleared up yet, but Hutch could see the light at the end of the tunnel—Dan's radiant smile was that light.

Hutch moved ahead with another question. "Okay, so we got a little problem here, like Ray says. Anything else we can do about it?"

Mentioning Ray's name was a mistake. Outside matters seemed to upset his brother. Dan was having a relapse and Hutch would need to nurse him through it. "That's the question now, what are we going to do about it?"

Gloria was holding on to Dan's belt, like a rider pulling on a horse so it won't act up. Of course, sometimes you pull like that and the animal bucks, but Gloria wasn't any ordinary rider, she was a wife, and people who have wives often listen to them, especially people like Hutch's kid brother, who was not yet fully formed. At this moment Hutch put confidence in Gloria's ability to keep Dan from bucking. Maybe Trish was contributing something, too. She was paying close attention. She was not jiggling to her music pounding through the junky walls. Her mouth was open and damp in that teenage way of paying close attention. Hutch felt warm, a bit of heat in the air, but not too uncomfortable. He took out his tangerine handkerchief and held it to the itching scab on his forehead. "Hey, we got the whole regular family here, don't we?"

"In your heart of hearts—" Dan began.

Hutch interrupted by wagging a finger. No heart of hearts. Don't believe in heart of hearts. That must be a typical future novelist's dumb idea.

"When we were kids, you remember—"

More of the same. Again Hutch grinned, wagged the warning finger. He was also amused by Gloria's hand on Dan's belt, though she was just touching it now, not holding him. "I stipulate we were kids once. But I don't remember too much about it."

"You can't forget that, Hutch."

Gloria had wrapped her fingers around the belt again. Hutch frowned and tried to be fair. "I remember lots. I remember what I need."

Dan said nothing. Good Gloria, hauling him in.

"Hey Dan." He put his own hand back on Trish's head in that cupping gesture. He suspected Dan would not move on him while he was touching his favorite niece. "Sometimes I need help, Dan, I know that. Sometimes I can't sleep. Get the munchies. Go crazy at Winchell's and eat myself silly with that nefarious crap. Now I got to tell you something. That happens, I can't help myself. I want to throw up."

"I saw you," Gloria said.

Hutch looked at her with his smile bright and happy. "See? And you didn't help. I did and you couldn't. There is no help, is there, Trish? None that we know of."

Dan believed he was going through something wonderful. His brother, his only brother, had ripped him off, taken him badly, and his brother was asking Dan, Gloria, and Trish to appreciate the fact that Hutch found no hope or help for himself, yet managed to see the bright side of everything.

Hutch was also considering a brother with curiosity. He didn't understand Dan; who could ever hope to understand anybody? Dan remembered too much, he was stoop-shouldered with burdens from defaulted times, he didn't run. That was why he couldn't do anything productive, still stuck in ancient history that was gone forever, like the amusement park at Ocean Beach. *Playland*, it was called. Playland-at-the-Beach; now, can't stop progress, it was Condos-at-the-Beach. The Laughing Fat Lady was probably in a Fisherman's Wharf somewhere, some new Cannery Row development, laughing and fat for the K mart tourists. The pair of bicycles was buried deep in the bay landfill in Brisbane.

Hutch fought down the yawn. It wouldn't be courteous when he had an audience of his only three close relatives paying close attention.

"Sometimes brothers kill brothers," Hutch said, "don't they use the word *slay* about that?"

Dan said nothing.

"You just knocked me into my own goddamn bathtub, Dan. You didn't even kill me, did you?"

Dan said nothing.

Hutch hoped to help him finally make his move. He

wanted his brother to get started in real life. "You got a wife and a kid growing up, you got a lot of stuff already, but you don't take care of business, do you?"

Dan said nothing.

"You heard what I said?"

Dan said nothing.

"I guess you did. Fancy that."

Trish raised her hand like a kid answering in class. "Hey Mom and Dad," she was saying. Hutch realized the music throbbing through the walls wasn't hers at all. The discount people at Imperial Records had put up outdoor speakers in the parking lot alongside the board advertising this week's Shave-Off Our Normal Bottom Prices. Even for a daytime permit, those boomers they got away with, they must have had some terrific juice at City Hall. "Hey Mom, hey Dad, listen, I learned a lot from both of you, I'm supposed to, maybe I even learned from school, I sure learned a lot from the street and what I been going through these days, but guess who taught me the most? He ought to get tuition for teaching me."

"Don't say it," Hutch said. "Don't ever be needlessly cruel, Trish, less it helps something."

"Uncle Hutch is like a daddy to me," Trish said. "He's like my best lover so far."

Gloria was struggling with Dan. She saw no point in this. In her reading of history, it had never helped. She would not let him do what he wanted to do to his brother.

She felt as helpless as Dan. She had no room for prayers. She had chosen him, and even if she never forgave him, she still—hard for her to use the word now—still cared for him. The other word could wait. It was a haunted word. *Love.* It was a holy word. Gloria could still imagine prayers, but she wasn't ready to take that word in vain, not at this time.

Watching, certainly not afraid, in no hurry to get

back to his car, Hutch was reminded of something as he watched Gloria wrapping her arms around Dan, holding him down, keeping him from flailing free. Maybe he didn't want to break free. It was almost like some kind of sex that Hutch would never put up with.

He knew what it reminded him of. Why, in addition to everything else, his poor kid brother was pussy-whipped.

17

_____

Hutch sat quietly on the terrace at Enrico's, raising a cigarette to his lips and blowing the smoke out in sharp little gusts. Like bicycle-riding, it was a talent a person never forgot; and if he chose to smoke, polluting the lungs for fun, it would be done as a festival. The Friday lunch club was amazed. This was revolutionary or maybe only a miracle. Who could remember when Hutch had last been seen with a cigarette? Wasn't he running anymore?

It didn't seem to matter. The athletic boyish profile, eaten by sun, was beginning to look distinguished as his hair turned gray. The fine dark eyes retained their eagerness. He still wanted people to say about him, _Tough but fair._ He wanted them to repeat, _People say he's tough but fair._ He sat there, tough, fair, a risk-taker, an entrepreneur, aware that four guys were talking about him because he was a creative business man and they were plodders with nothing better to do.

Larry Klotz was taking a poll. He wanted to know who else had been hit up for a terrific investment in the past month. It turned out only he and Watkins were still on Hutch's list. Frank Curtis wanted to know if six weeks ago counted. Michael Robertson said maybe the favored ones were asked earlier. Larry wondered if anybody in the whole wide world was still willing to go for one of Hutch's terrific deals, reserved only for his friends.

Absent: Ferdinand the Bull, who had telephoned his excuse—a client at the office with a crazy unregistered Ferrari problem. Drove it across the border from Mexico, trying to save diddly, and it only took the license bureau two years to find him. Now smog control was only the beginning of the hassle. Larry said he'd check in with Ferd later.

Hutch concentrated on the art of smoking and watching a cab driver without a fare, sitting in his car in the taxi zone, eating an Oh Henry! bar. They were smaller than they used to be, but probably Oh Henry! technology had improved so they were just as efficient at pulling the fillings out of teeth. The driver finished his lunch, dropped the wrapping on the street. He noticed what he had done. He noticed that others, busy with their crab Louis and petrale and angel-wings pasta, had noticed. He opened the door and reached out to pick it up. The lunchers applauded; Hutch wondered what he would do next.

The cabbie developed an unhealthy purple in his cheeks, leaned over to the passenger side, and opened the window. He dropped his wadded candy wrapper onto the sidewalk and considered it. Then he reached down, pulled out his ashtray, and spilled butts and grit alongside the candy wrapper. He sat there a moment to see if any Enrico's terrace ecologist or antilitter philosopher wanted to make something of it. Then abruptly he started his engine and pulled away, tires squealing.

Hutch watched with eyes alertly taking in the incident, almost as if it interested him. The kind of person his brother chose to associate with. But Dan was family and he couldn't be too hard on him for the bad choices he made.

Hutch put out his own cigarette and stared at the remains in his saucer. It was no worse than a last hunk of jelly donut if you were talking about harm to the body. But then he wasn't a scientist, even if he had ideals about nutrition; there were ideals and laws, yet a relaxed person didn't get paranoid about a little normal human weakness on a fine Friday afternoon in San Francisco.

He was waiting for the friend who was coming to meet him at Enrico's after a night of Frisco fun at Cordelia's house. When he arrived, Hutch stood up and they flung their arms around each other in great hugs, probably the way bears do in the Siberian forest. Their fingers did not dig into friends' flesh because, after all, this was public. This was no Siberian forest. People were watching.

Although Cordelia insisted on thorough bathing, usually with one of the girls in the tub to help, poking around consolingly in all the little crevices, Hutch's friend smelled a little un-California. Probably it wasn't the fault of his rosy body. Probably it was the clothes from a long Moscow winter, where they don't have pick-up-and-deliver dry cleaning, plus an Aeroflot flight that permitted smoking everywhere. Those good Cuban cigars that Avigdor carried with him in a case like a coffin didn't help, either.

"Hutch, my pigeon, my dear, my first guide to the great city of the West! You know Rebecca, Becky? She drain me like a swamp."

Hutch hoped to brief his dear friend on what had

happened to both of them since Avigdor's last American visit. Big things were evolving with some of his deals, some good, some bad, that's free enterprise, and if you read the papers, it was happening in world politics, too. Terrible things in, where was it, the Middle East? But life was not too bad, either. Every day a new tired blond was turning, oh, say, thirty-nine or forty-two. "So tell me about yourself," he asked.

"No no no, your jet lag is powerful, I only listen, pay close attention, feast my eyes on dear friend mine and also to dream liddlebit. That Cordelia she is one individual to turn night into day."

"Kenny!" said Hutch. "Hey, a little service over here."

"Another fresh grapefruit juice, coming dear, and for the cute Commie gentleman?"

Avigdor chuckled. San Francisco and Odessa were two of his favorite towns. He liked the suggestion that life can be a festival; one of the ideas of the West from which his own people, which had suffered so much in the Great Patriotic War, could learn. Even if Hutch did not assure him proof positively that Rebecca, Becky, was a Jewish girl this time, it did no harm to think so. Avigdor lit his Uppman Nativo with the Swiss jet lighter that always gave him such trouble with airport metal detectors.

It was Friday, when the lunch bunch gathered on the terrace at Enrico's—Larry Klotz, the script writer from Mill Valley; sad Watkins, the law prof from Davis, who drove the eighty miles just to eat too much with his buddies, the boys of forty; Frank Curtis, the journalist from Berkeley, who had been dumped by his most recent Significant Other; and Michael Robertson, the token happily married man, who mostly kept his own counsel. But they all enjoyed Hutch, who usually had a tired show blond with him at lunch on Fridays. This time he had the famous Soviet journalist, whom

Frank recognized, saying, "Well, at least he looks tired even if he's not a blond."

Nosy Larry brought some new gossip. "You know what I found in the glove compartment of his car?"

"His BMW 325is?"

"Whatever. I think you got that wrong, Michael. How long you been in California?"

Robertson lapsed into a sulky silence.

"Yeah," said Watkins.

"So what did I find in the glove compartment of his leased BMW numero speciale which we see right there before us in the taxi zone, you ask?"

"Tell, snoop," Frank said.

"In the glove compartment of his leased BMW-according-to-Robertson-325is I found a battery-powered hair dryer and a bottle of Pepto-Bismol. So who says he doesn't have a conscience? He has to blow it dry. And then he has to calm his stomach."

Watkins whispered, "Hey, he can hear us."

"Course he can hear us. He already knows he's a human being, doesn't he? And he sure as shit can hear a guy courtroom whispers like you do, Wat."

Frank Curtis knew about griefs and suspected that Hutch was guilty of them, too. Sleepless nights seemed to have bruised Frank's eyes and the crinkled pouches below them. Hutch's face was also newly marked, and there was an actual bruise, not fatigue, on his forehead. Frank said: "In my opinion, he gets into the hour of should-have-done like everybody else. He wakes up and thinks, Why didn't I? Or maybe, Why did I? I'm sure of it."

"Stipulated! Right on! But then it lasts about a minute and he takes a swig of Pepto-Bismol. Listen, you know what he said to me? 'I like a calm and restive evening—'"

"Restive?"

"That's what he said. '—all alone with a good book

and a girl. . . .' He puts the good book under the girl's
ass to lift it a little higher."

Even gloomy Watkins joined in the laughter. Frank
glanced over at Avigdor, who was paying attention to
them while listening to Hutch, and shrugged. He
couldn't fight a San Francisco tradition. Hutch was
famous in North Beach, the arriviste who was always
on the brink of arriving.

"He sure does love literature, doesn't he?" Larry
demanded. "And the Holy Trinity—Rolaids, Di-Gel,
Pepto-Bismol, and Hot Tongue."

"That's four," said Michael Robertson, who had
been raised by the Jebbies and paid close attention.

Larry shrugged. "Details, Mike. We're talking big
picture here. So I fucked up on big picture, I got an
accountant to do my number-crunching for me."

Michael shrugged. His role was listener, anyway. He
just didn't like to commit himself to the inaccuracy.

"Hot Tongue," Larry continued, "like I was saying
before Michael interrupted the natural flow, is the
service provided by, you know, what they used to call
stewardii. I think he's got a point about the tired ones.
They're more relaxed. They retract the teeth. You
know, guys, he's not wrong about everything. They're
nice."

The boys fell silent. This was an occasion for reverie.
Despite the superfluity of straight men in San Francisco, more or less staight men anyway, these men
with high standards had continuous problems with
women. There was a shortage of the Misses Right. It
sometimes occurred to them that the problem was
that the women also had high standards and they
didn't measure up. Okay, they had problems. But they
still had each other, at least for Friday lunch.

And perhaps they were jealous of Hutch's tireless-
ness. He was an optimist. He never lost the faith. He
ran, he scammed, and he chased. As Larry outlined

the story, using his hands to move from Hutch to the
girl, he grew wistful when he saw still another stewardess with skin problems. They weren't as common
as a person might hope. Diet, Clearasil, and advancing
age tended to finish off this deliciousness. Like his
brother, Hutch remembered things about his boyhood, when the world was full of sexy girls with boiling
hormones, suffering acne. "Zits, I hate it," the tenured
stewardess would say.

"To me you're lovely." Gracious Hutch, it cost him
nothing.

"Only to you?"

"Also to everyone who flies the Friendly Skies, I'm
sure of it."

"Since we became *flight attendants,* yucch, we
don't do what you're thinking about anymore. I never
did, unless it was a powerful overnight attraction."

"You're powerful to the max, Linda."

"I'm Sharon."

Linda was the one with the dreamy look on her face
when she sat in his tub with his Mexican sponge, soap-
ing the cigarette smells off her skin after a long flight.
He jumped into the tub with her and worked the
sponge into all the crevices, making the dreamy look
dreamier with gentleness, then making her jump
("Hey, Hutch!" "Hey, Linda!") when he went hard
into the places where she said, *Don't.* But he did anyway.

"Stay overnight, honey, okay? I'm kind of lonely,
Sharon." . . . The boys listened to Larry's treatment.
Probably he had done research. It was like a pitch
meeting. As a bonus, Larry tossed in the Mile High
Club and Sharon claiming that stuff about going down
on the first class Frequent Fliers in the john was a
fucking myth—no time, with all the food and bever-
age service. Avigdor was telling Hutch those men
were talking about him and Hutch was shrugging and

saying he knew and he waved a tanned and freckled hand at them and said it was all publicity, it helped the image, and Avigdor wasn't sure he understood about still another detail of American life. He asked, Big Picture? and Hutch answered, You got it.

Since Hutch was only a sexier version of the lunching boys, he had no quarrel with them. He had other things on his mind. Avigdor was right. The big picture was the festival.

Larry was now selling his treatment. He hoped his colleagues could see what he saw. He was sharing. He explained how Hutch did not demand perfection in women, but what he wanted was even more rare than perfection. He sought anorexic beauty with a skin defect. What is so rare as a middle-aged flight attendant whose adolescent acne hasn't yet been quite overcome?

Every man needs a goal. And that, along with wealth and recognition by important headwaiters in San Francisco and the outside world, was Hutch's. "Listen, I heard when he goes skiing with a new one, he stops at the snow line near Tahoe, where the sign says Chains Required, gets out of the leased vehicle, goes into the trunk, calls it the boot, and comes out with a set of four gold chains for his neck. And you know what this Linda said? She said, Hey man, I heard you do this."

Even the cabal began to feel depressed. It was sunny, it was sweet and dry, it was such a nice Friday to be so mean. "I hear he likes his brother, his brother's family," Michael said. "I hear he's crazy about his niece."

"Once I was in his brother's cab," Frank said. "His name is Dan, Danny. You see him around here sometimes."

Hutch was grinning in their direction. Despite the Friday afternoon crowd, voices carried, bouncing off

the speckled cement, off the kiosk on the walk, above
the tinkle and clatter and the other voices. Avigdor
couldn't understand it all and Hutch wasn't listening,
but they both knew attention was being paid.

Nevertheless, although Hutch didn't mind, Larry
lowered his voice now that he had gotten to the non-
flight attendant part of his riff. "This is the problem.
This is serioso. You let him see your stomach, he's like a
wolf. Grrr! No, one of those other things, ancestors of
our common house pet, what do they call it?"

"Jackal," said Frank Curtis.

"That's it. He sees your belly, quick quick, he's eating out your guts without even inviting his pals to join
the feast."

The lunchers were enjoying their Friday. Money
and love supplied open-air seminar topics for intelli-
gent achievers. According to their former wives, they
were only semiachievers, but that was a matter of
derogatory opinion. True love and true money lay in
the eye of the beholder; in some cases, the ex-
beholder. For the lunch boys, beholding was something they tried to share with each other. Who said
only women were sensitive and caring? Men could
partake of those commodities just as sweetly.

So it felt good to be concerned with others, not their
own problems. It felt generous. It felt involved in the
outside world. As long as you didn't lend him money,
Hutch was a delight.

A shaven-headed young man in a short leather
jacket and no shirt underneath was heading slowly up
the walk from the intersection of Columbus and
Broadway. He was doing a splay-footed bounce in a
kind of slow motion. He was looking for someone.
People usually know when they are being looked for.
Hutch watched him approach, toes pointed out, trying
to amble and slouch, trying to look cool and stylish, just

as if he wasn't afraid of the Enrico's terrace. "I'm Harry."

"I know," Hutch said.

"You recognize me?"

"I've seen you before."

"When you see me?"

Hutch stared. "What difference does it make? We had a little chat."

"You remember."

"What do you want, kid?"

"Hutch, my friend!" Avigdor said. "You introduce me!"

"This is a skinhead," Hutch said. "I don't know what he wants."

"I'm Harry. Listen. I want you to know—"

"Listen," said Hutch, "I want you to know I want you to get the fuck on down the street right now. I don't want to talk to you."

"I want you to know I never do it to any chick less she wants it. You got no call to be like that."

It may have been that the conversation of the Friday lunch bunch had disturbed Hutch's customary easy temper. Cool was the answer, but cool didn't dispose of all statements, not Ray Aratunian's nor Dan's and not the fragments blowing over from Larry Klotz and his buddies. Still, Hutch had his ways, his little moves. And yet, inside Hutch, there were more than ways and moves today, on this occasion, right now. He stood up and said in a very low voice: "I'll tell you how I am. You don't scamper on, you're gonna be an injured party on the sidewalk here."

"I'm Harry. Listen, I was busy that day. I couldn't take her because I had to get my wheels fixed. I don't have a lot of money like you, I got to go to the right mechanic gives me a deal, I knew Trishie was gonna get taken care of."

"Move," said Hutch.

"Listen, if I had the money, maybe I do something. I got strong sperm, man."

"That's the little chat we already had, Harry." Hutch stood up abruptly. "I want you to get on down the street right now."

"I never do it to any chick less she wants it. You got no call to be like that, mister."

Hutch was speaking very quietly. "You waiting for me to show you what I got the call to do?"

Frank Curtis said softly to the other lunchers, "Who is this guy?" He meant Hutch. "Jesus, looks like he's doing something for someone else," and one of the lunch boys said, "Look at him—he's *indignant*," and somebody else said, "You could put it that way," and Frank Curtis said, "Is this fellow our Hutch?"

Avigdor was beaming. Violent America, and they weren't even drunk. Americans didn't even need vodka or scotch to threaten violence. With luck, the threat would be fulfilled.

Avigdor's luck was not perfect. Harry began to slide away down the sidewalk. He was holding back, but the splayed feet wanted to move, bounce, go fast. Hutch sat down with his hands shaking and his chest heaving. He heard a wheeze in his chest, a buzzing of the alarm. It was his brother's tendency to asthma, the problem Hutch had cured by running, by not smoking, by taking perfect care, by making life a festival.

Down the block, in front of the closed New Joe's restaurant, Harry paused at a silver BMW illegally parked at the curb. He looked back toward Hutch to make sure he was watching. He was taking something out of his jeans. He closed his eyes briefly, happily, and stood in a graceful straddle. He began to pee against the silver BMW with a Mill Valley auto dealer's name on the frame of the license plate. He was grinning at Hutch, shifting his feet to make sure he did no damage to his shoes.

Hutch nodded encouragingly. Dumb kid didn't know one BMW from another. Hutch's chest was clearing. Some people couldn't get anything right; even a coyote, when it pees, knows what territory it's peeing on. Poor Harry was peeing on some Mill Valley psychiatrist's BMW while Hutch's, a different model, a different color, even a different size, stood safe at the curb.

In the future, Trish would surely do better. Hutch planned to take a strong hand in her education.

Avigdor was a close observer of America. He knew when to remain silent, watching Harry, watching Hutch, listening for the lunchers talking in low voices nearby, also observing Hutch. *"Ny koolturny,"* he murmured at last. "Is not even drunk. Is not cultured." A pair of cops strolled past Harry, not wanting to be bothered, but the woman in the see-through net, asking the passersby to come in for the topless show, decided Harry was not up to the standards of Big Al's. She did not invite him.

Harry finished, zipped, and seemed puzzled by Hutch's steady and peaceful regard. He gave up. The splay-footed walk continued around the corner at Columbus.

Avigdor continued to smile. As an investigative reporter for Novosti, he knew some good would come of this. As a true pal to his good friend Hutch, he wanted to share his life. In America everything was a festival, just as his true pal said. "Who is skinny?" he asked.

"Skinhead, that's the word. Friend of mine. Shithead I know. Did a bad thing to a friend of mine."

"Is none of business?"

"That's right, Avigdor. It's none of your business."

His chest was buzzing again. Maybe he should have kicked the kid a little. Hutch always hoped to do the right thing which was right for him. Surely he should have jumped the kid and given the watching lunchers their own goddamn festival attraction.

Considering this, considering Avigdor and the lunchers, then deciding none of them mattered, he asked himself if Ray Aratunian and his banking associates mattered, and yes, they mattered more than the North Beach lunch boys, more than Avigdor, because they made a difference to Gloria, Dan, and Trish. It was important to do something for his brother's family and to do it right now. He stood up. He would go after Harry. It was his rule to act upon his appetites. He hungered to bring the creep down.

Hutch was leaning on the marble tabletop. He felt that bright buzzing ache, like an insistent telephone in his chest, and thought of his Missouri Mutual plan to cover Trish and the family just in case, but of course nothing like that was allowed to happen in San Francisco. The brightness was spreading, hurting. The last notice, the final one, the registered letter in the big envelope with all those jagged red letters on it, came from the Fulfillment Center, Des Moines, some computer yack like that. He wished, just in case, he had paid the premiums.

The buzzing had grown louder, continuing into his head, rolling like the surf at Ocean Beach. He remembered Dan's bicycle, he remembered his own. He wasn't running, but his knees were pumping. In just a second he was going after Harry. He had to settle a few matters, like what he had said to Dan in the park or someplace which was all wrong. It was important to correct it. As Avigdor tried to catch him, and Frank Curtis was knocking over a chair running toward him, Hutch retracted his confession.

"Mama! Mama!"

He saw her at last, and it was odd that a person could be sure, make a positive identification, even without remembering what she looked like. Dan could tell him if this was the one. She was smiling, her arms were opened wide, she had come to take him home. But how strange that she came for him on the terrace at Enrico's—her big boy Hutch, a strict runner who had yet to do his laps today.

Her smile was one of perfect love at last: "Mama!" Fancy that.